# *T*urnip *B*lues

## Helen Campbell

Spinsters Ink
Duluth

Turnip Blues ©1998 by Helen Campbell

First edition published May, 1998 by Spinsters Ink
10-9-8-7-6-5-4

Spinsters Ink
32 E. First St., #330
Duluth, MN 55802-2002 USA

Cover illustration and design by Kathy Kruger, Graven Images

Production:

| | |
|---|---|
| Liz Brissett | Ryan Petersen |
| Helen Dooley | Kim Riordan |
| Joan Drury | Amy Strasheim |
| Emily Gould | Liz Tufte |
| Marian Hunstiger | Nancy Walker |
| Claire Kirch | |

*Library of Congress Cataloging-in-Publication Data*
Campbell, Helen, 1952–
    Turnip Blues / Helen Campbell. — 1st ed.
        p.    cm.
    ISBN 1-883523-23-0 (alk. paper)
    I. Title.
PS3553.A4575T8            1998
813'.54—dc21                                        98–5390
                                                                    CIP

Printed on Recycled Paper with Soy-based Inks

# Acknowledgments

Those who I wish to thank include the living and the dead. Of the former, Roberta Armin-Swords, Des Bovey, Isabel Huggan, John Olsen, Lois Rose, the Pennsylvania Council on the Arts, Joan Drury, the staff of Spinsters Ink, and, above all, Ron Campbell. Of the latter, the remarkable generation of women before me. Their stories ignited my passion to make sense of it all.

# Braddock, Pennsylvania
# Summer

*As* long as I've known her she's listened to Bessie Smith. Dances to that racket, arms akimbo, shaking her loose skin in rhythm. The music makes her dangerous. She knocks down table lamps and drink coasters and Hummel figurines, then warbles along, top volume, as if the voice on the phonograph isn't noise enough. I'll go wait on her porch, even winters, till she's finished, collapsed on the sofa, the needle skipping in the grooves at the end. Then I'll sneak inside and heat canned soup. Slip the record back inside its jacket. And hide it somewhere while she snores.

She plays the very same songs in her car, the Firebird she paid for with cash. Or more accurately, with death benefits, the ones she collected off her two-timing husband, Johnny Lemack. She glued a fancy tape deck to the dash alongside a framed picture of Bessie, right where most people perch their plastic Jesus. Gal beats time slapping her paunch, shakes the whole car as she drives. I've heard "Dixie Flyer Blues," heart in my mouth, as she passes on hairpin curves.

And now she's got this cockamamie idea about visiting Bessie's grave. She read some feature story in the newspaper, a real tear jerker about the old gal's sorry-ass life—a big boozer who ended up crunched in a car wreck, penniless and forgotten. They buried her outside Philadelphia, in a cemetery the story described as *undermaintained*. I guess she didn't sing the blues for nothing.

"How about it?" said my friend over coffee. "It's a straight shot down the turnpike, simple. We could pick up a nice floral arrangement and weed her grave. Pay our respects, as they say."

"Dream on," I said sourly. "At *our* age? That's one trip you can take on your lonesome."

"Being old's no excuse. I've been listening to her music all my life—you too, Mrs. Kuzo. Seems to me you owe her something."

"Her? I don't either," I said, clipping my nails into a napkin. "Anyhow, you're nuts. Just like those old gals in their Airstreams leaving teddy bears and candles on Elvis's grave."

She stood up, all indignant, and pushed me square in the chest with her forefinger. "Pardon me, ma'am, but it's *not* the same. Hasn't never been a weed on that boy's grave or any shortage of nitwit lady visitors. And he was a bum, no class. Remember his wardrobe? Judas Priest! He got just what was coming to him, and now they've put him on a postage stamp!" She was pacing up and down my dining room, all 250 pounds of her, shaking every dish in the china closet. "On the other hand, there's Bessie Smith, a real lady. And an *artist*. And who the hell's window-dressing her grave? Weeding it, even?"

"Seems to me that's something her family should be doing."

She stopped short. "You telling me I'm *not* her family?"

"Well," I laughed, holding up my magnifying glass, "I'd need to use my imagination. Lots."

She wasn't amused. Lowered her voice. "The way I see things, Mrs. Kuzo, family's just a state of mind. The real families are the ones that you pick."

I swept the sugar she'd spilt on the tablecloth into my hand. "You sure got some half-assed ideas, you know that?"

"Do I?" she bristled. "Well, give it some thought, Mama. I sure as hell picked you. So start packing. We've got family business. In Philly."

"You heard me, didn't you? I said no."

"How about I say *please*, then?"

"You deaf, Mrs. Lemack?"

She leaped across the room and grabbed my collar with both hands. "Come on, Old Lady! It's only seven hours down there, a helluva lot less if I do the driving—"

"Lemme go—"

"—and it's been *ages* since the two of us got away!" She was frantic, tightening her grip. "We could have a ball! When's the last time we ate fried clams at HoJo's? Huh? Come on, Mrs. Kuzo, say yes!"

"No, Mrs. Lemack," I stomped on her toe. "Nix. Nein. *Nyet!*"

The woman let go of me, tears in her eyes, skulked off, and headed toward the door. Then something inspired her. She turned around, slid to her knees, wrists flexed downward, tongue lolling out her mouth, begging shameless as a dog. Only thing missing was a string of drool.

I caved in, old fool. Always do, whenever she makes me laugh.

$T$ulevich was my maiden name; Petrunak was Mrs. Lemack's. We're both christened Mary, nicknamed Masha. Always caused confusion, us being best friends, so we've called each other by our last names. First our fathers', then our husbands', to be exact.

I've known Mrs. Lemack since seventh grade. We sat next to each other in homeroom and came down with head lice, both of us, the same day. She had beautiful mahogany-colored hair that the school nurse shaved down to her scalp. I was next in line, took half as long since my hair was short and the bugs less abundant. We walked back to class, heads tingling with disinfectant, her crying in her elbow. The American kids snickered at us. I felt god-awful seeing her, poor thing, bald as well as fat. So I gave her the gumdrop I'd been sucking. We've been friends ever since.

Her old man, Mr. Petrunak, worked at Edgar Thomson—same mill as Dad did before he died—stirring molten iron with a long stick through a hole in the furnace floor. The man made good money, deserved it, standing for hours in the full heat of the furnace. He'd come home scorched and ornery, and beat his ninety-pound wife, a shriveled little lady with eczema. She scratched all day in bed, slaking her thirst with a pint of hooch she kept under the pillow. The woman didn't do a lick of housework, too unsteady on her feet, not only from the booze but from the beatings she got every night. Every morning, too, the year Mr. Petrunak lost all his money in a pyramid scheme. That was when she took in boarders, same as Mum, to make up lost income.

My friend was the fourth of ten sisters. First three of them died from Spanish flu before she'd been born. I'd see her at church, never without a baby on her fleshy hip, wiping snot or dodging sneezes. She stayed home from school every Monday doing the boarders' laundry, her plump hands turning scaly as

4

her mother's. And after school, she scattered sawdust and scrubbed spittoons in an Irish bar to make a few extra pennies. She never complained.

No surprise her grades were bad, worse even than mine. Most of the teachers treated us rotten, especially those bony American ladies with freckles and bad teeth and burnt hair—Miss Williams, Miss Miller, Miss Cole, Miss Sands, Miss Stremple. They had it in for kids with foreign names. Took the attitude we were dumb as dog shit, that we invented body lice and whooping cough and polio, and above all, that our mothers made too many babies. Hunkies, they called us, the nasty name people used for the Slavs.

Masha grew a thick skin. She'd stutter through her readers and count on her fingers, the whole class jeering, and just shrug. But out on the playground, she settled the score. She could lick anyone at any game and wrestle even the biggest bully to the ground, her weight leaving dents in his rib cage.

So she earned some respect. And became my only friend. She didn't care what the other girls said about my family, that Mum was a trollop or Granddaddy'd lost his marbles or Nicky, my brother, was a bad seed. She'd sit with us in church, right next to Mum, and whisper that she'd never seen a woman so beautiful. And Mum *was* an eyeful in her black velvet dress—belted so tightly it raised bruises on her skin—and those tail-biting foxes she draped over her shoulders. All the clothing she'd bought with her unholy money.

We've stayed friends. Lived in Braddock all our married lives, five blocks from each other, in identical brick row houses with striped awnings and box hedges and wet basements. We've buried four husbands between us—three of hers, one of mine. There's not a day goes by we don't speak. Or fight.

⊛

*I*'ve been kicking myself black and blue since she left. All right, the dog routine got her what she wanted. But the fact is, I don't want to go. It doesn't matter she's paying for everything, flowers and gas and motel.

I really blew my gaskets when she told me to call Vicky. Victoria, she calls herself these days. She's my dead sister's daughter. The girl owns a big, old airplane hangar of a house with her doctor husband in West Philadelphia, ten bedrooms and one bath with a rusted claw-foot tub and no shower. No door lock, either. He's Hindu, moved his whole family from Bombay straight into the airplane hangar the day they got married. Last time I counted, there were twelve adults and two dozen kids camped in the kitchen. And Mrs. Lemack thinks we should stay there. I told her I'd as soon pass the night in the Greyhound terminal, propped in front of a quarter-slot TV.

My friend, of course, won't listen. "It's been months since you've seen that girl," she sputtered. "And I can guarantee she'd be glad to have us."

"Then *you* go visit her."

"Mrs. Kuzo"—she was wagging her finger—"I could live to be a thousand, and I'll never understand you. Vicky's a good kid, and you're the only family she's got. You practically raised her!"

It's true she lived with me on and off for years, when Annie, her mother, was sick, poor soul, and her father was hustling new women. But I don't need reminding about all that heartbreak. Makes me want to cry. And I'm already mad at the girl. So I stuck to my guns.

"I'm *warning* you, Mrs. Lemack"—I wagged my finger back at her—"you either get us a motel room, or I park my butt here. Period."

Won that round. She's at the Triple-A office this minute getting maps, a list of cheap hotels, and brochures about road-side attractions and factory outlets. Probably telling the man at the counter exactly where we're headed and asking him along if his buns aren't droopy. She still flirts with men, as old as she is, and even after all her bad luck. And you can be sure there's a line behind her, out the door and around the block, with every lady from my church listening. Old tongue waggers have had something to say about me and Mrs. Lemack for as long as I can remember.

"Pack your gardening tools," she'd called out before she left. "And don't forget that wire brush. We might not need it, but there's no telling what kind of mold's growing on Bessie's marker. This is Philly, after all."

I shuddered as she tore off down the block, emergency brake still on, the Firebird bucking on the pavement. She doesn't know that the last time I drove the turnpike, something awful happened. So awful I swore I'd never head that direction again.

Yeah. Famous last words.

*I* do as she tells me and fetch my rusty tools. I'm not much of a gardener. It's enough work pruning my pussy willows and picking up stray dog poop and weeding the family plot. I lay the rake down on the sidewalk and blast it with the hose. Watch the rust leach into the grass, sitting on my haunches.

"What in Sam Hill you up to, Mrs. Kuzo?" It's my neighbor, Mrs. Kosavitch, standing at the chain-link fence that separates our property. She's got her hair in pink foam curlers and carries a big plastic pocketbook in the crook of her elbow, just like the Queen. I've seen her knock bottles off store shelves and bruise people in wheelchairs, swinging that bag.

"Spring cleaning," I shout back, hoping the dickens she'll scram. She's been my neighbor forty years, and I've never seen her when she wasn't working her jaw muscles or asking favors.

"You ever look at your calendar, ma'am? It's July!" She props her elbows on the fence like she's digging in for the next hour. "You're awful pokey, aren't you?"

"It's my damn arthritis, you know that," I say, rubbing my

spine. "Summer's the only time of year I don't walk in a half-crouch. And better late than never."

"If it's only arthritis bothering you, you're blessed, Mrs. Kuzo. You know what it's like having a spastic colon? And for twenty years?" She's counting on her fingers, frowns, then counts again. "There's days I can't get out of bed, hurts so bad. And I'd lay bets I've seen every doctor in Pittsburgh. Pills, diets, surgery, hypnosis, high colonics . . . I've tried it all. Nothing works."

"Damn shame," I say, closing the spigot.

"Shame? It's the *shits*, believe me. But just take a good look at all this." She sweeps her arm in the direction of her yard. I'll grant it's tidy, roses everywhere, not a single snail or stray dandelion. "And go on, don't be shy, take a good look at me." She plants her thick legs firmly on the grass, lifts her arms skyward, pocketbook banging my fence. "Would anybody guess I'm seventy-five?"

"No, ma'am," I say, drying off the rake with a hand towel, my eyes on the ground.

"It's the gardening that does it. World's best exercise. And the attitude. Don't forget that, Mrs. Kuzo. And I'm probably older than you."

She isn't; we're the same age, and she knows it. But I don't bother arguing. Takes too damn much breath, and I'm distracted anyway.

In the far corner of her yard, I can see her plastic Virgin. Doll stands wrapped in a sky-blue bathrobe, arms outstretched, inside a seashell grotto. Mrs. Kosavitch put it there fifteen years ago, a legend in the neighborhood, with its puckered lips and glass eyes. My high beams bounce off it whenever I pull up at night. Sends a chill down my spine. Right underneath, two feet down, she buried the urn. With the ashes of Stan, her husband.

"*I*'m going down to Philly for a couple days," I tell my daughter Barb. I'd phoned her at work, only place you can catch her. Her office hasn't got an answering machine, meaning she can't dodge my calls like she does at home.

"Philly? What for?" she asks crisply. She works in a travel agency, booking lonely-heart Caribbean cruises. When the work gets slow, she reads self-help books, then mails them to me with no return address. "You're not off to visit *Vicky*, are you?"

"Hell no"—Barb detests the girl—"It's Mrs. Lemack's idea. She always wanted to see the Liberty Bell before she dies, don't ask me why. And she won't go alone." I'm not lying, really. Just don't see much sense supplying all the details. Barb already thinks my friend's a tad wifty.

"I hope it's you who's driving," she says. "Assuming, of course, you value your life." She's referring to my friend's style at the wheel. I can't say Barb hasn't seen it. The three of us headed out mall-crawling one Sunday in Monroeville and got stuck in traffic. Mrs. Lemack lost her patience, drove clear through a police barricade, gas pedal to the floor, cops on our tail. The boys finally gave up the chase—their cruisers no match for the Firebird—and Mrs. Lemack's still boasting about it.

"Naw, we're going Greyhound," I lie again, not wanting to hear any lectures. "Just wanted to set your mind at ease in case you called the house. No sense you worrying yourself sick thinking I was dead in bed. You know, hatching larvae like Mrs. Kraynyak, remember her?"

"For God's sake, Mom!" she explodes. "Why do you always come up with something gross?" She's disgusted with me. Like usual.

"Well, Honey," I huff, "get used to the idea. I'll be seventy-six in November, and you know darn well that one of these days—"

"I know, Mom. I'll be orphaned, right?"

Hurts me to hear her talk snotty. Not that I can tell her.

"Look," she says, five seconds later. "I have to go, there's another call coming in. So have a good trip. And bring me back a postcard from the turnpike, will you?"

"Sure. And Barb?" I've recovered. "Just in case you're wondering—there's a copy of my will in the dining room hutch. Third drawer down. Right under your wedding album."

*I* never take a trip without stopping off at church first. Always light a couple candles, toss my loose change in the collection box, and pray to God and Annie till my knuckles turn white. I start with simple requests, like please no flat tires or state cops on my bumper or roadside attractions Mrs. Lemack hasn't seen, like barn sales or snake farms. Then I move on to more serious matters like blowouts or oil slicks or drunks headed my direction. End up begging just to get home alive.

It's sweltering today, wet heat, not much sense dressing up, even for church. I pull on a pair of Bermudas, a sleeveless cotton turtleneck, and high-heeled sandals. Top it off with a black lace mantilla and slap on some lipstick for color. I almost forget to fish Mum's crystal rosary beads out of my panty hose drawer. She brought them from the old country, all I have left of hers, unless you count the memories. Which aren't much of an inheritance.

I don't forget to holler down to the workmen in the basement that I'll be gone an hour. They're laying new insulation around the foundation, even packing the hot water heater in a fat blanket. It's all free, part of a city program to do good deeds for old folks and save energy. I just wish those boys would quit using the toilet down there. It hasn't got a curtain around it, and whenever I poke my head downstairs to tell them something—like where the fuse box is so they won't get electro-cuted—one of them's parked on the throne, pants at his ankles, thumbing the funny paper.

"Yo, Mrs. Kuzo," he'll say, saluting me.

*S*t. Stepan's is out on the river, not a part of town to take walks, even with a pit bull. It's block after block of empty buildings, stripped cars, and smoking trash cans. The only businesses around are a couple of basement bars flashing Iron City Beer signs and a seedy joint called Mr. Furniture, which sells crushed-velvet couches, mirrored headboards, and lava lights. The sidewalk out front is buckled too badly to walk on, with waist-high weeds growing out of the cracks and bottle caps scattered everywhere. I've never seen a garbage truck go by.

The parish moved here ten years ago. Trustees bought the building at a foreclosure sale for nine thousand dollars. The street had long since gone to seed, but moving was surviving. We'd shrunk to forty parishioners by then, all of us seniors, tithing at most twenty dollars a month—not enough to heat the cathedral where we'd been baptized and married and where we'd wept for our dead. Our kids contribute nothing, of course; they've all left the faith. On Sundays, they go to Episcopal churches or out to the Marriott for champagne brunch. Like Barb.

Nine thousand dollars didn't buy much. The building used to be a nightclub called Zanzibar. Owners had country club taste, covered the walls with palm trees and monkeys and men in grass skirts heaving spears. We took up a paint collection and set to work covering that junk. Nearly ran out of paint halfway through, so we thinned what was left. Bad idea. To this day, there's a monkey grinning through the paint, right over the altar. And a big pot perched on burning wood, three guys in safari suits stuffed inside, a rope around their waists.

*T*he parking lot's empty today. Strange for a Friday afternoon, the time Father Serge hears confessions. Even the door's locked. I check my watch and start to sweat; this is a bad sign. Can't say it didn't bother me in the first place, going on a wild-goose chase to find the grave of an old broad killed in a car wreck. And with the church locked, it all adds up bad. I don't need an astrologer to tell me.

I sit on the steps and wait a couple minutes. Maybe it was last night I should have set my clock back. Which is when I see a car pull up in front of Mr. Furniture, two old gals climb out, disappear inside. Next thing I know, they're back on the sidewalk, huffing and puffing, loading their purchase in the trunk. The ladies start arguing, nastiest language I've heard, till one throws a punch. Cause of the tussle is a black velvet painting of Elvis, hair swirled high, a tight red cumberbund holding in his gut. No way the King can fit in the car.

That's the first time I laugh today. Then I roll up a five-dollar bill, shove it under the church door, and head back to my car. I've done everything I can do. God's going to either bring us home alive or end our lives on the highway. Like Bessie.

*I* hoof it up my sidewalk past the Virgin Mary, keep my eyes on the ground, and cross myself. Always do. I still can't believe Stan's soaking up runoff a foot under Our Lady's plastic feet.

"Hey, Mrs. Kuzo, you mind giving me a hand?" I practi-cally jump out of my skin. It's Mrs. Kosavitch, down on hands and knees on her porch. She's surrounded by grocery bags, running her hands along the splintery planks in the dark.

"Lose your dang key again?" I call out.

"Third time this week. You mind fetching me a flashlight?"

I'm back thirty seconds later, shining a beam on her backside.

"I don't know what the hell happened," she's fretting, still on all fours. "The key's on a rabbit's foot key ring. You'd think I could feel it."

"I'll look. But you're going to have to clear out." She's nearly as big as Mrs. Lemack, grabs both my hands getting up, panting, and I don't know CPR. But I find the dang key ring and open her door.

"Mind giving me a hand with my groceries?" she asks, wiping her forehead with a Kleenex she's pulled out of her brassiere. I do as she asks, know damn well she wants company, and once she's got me in the door, I'm hers for the evening. But it's either that or go answer the phone ringing in my kitchen—Mrs. Lemack for sure. One or another of them's going to yak my ear off tonight.

I help haul in the groceries. I've never known anyone else who ate Mrs. Paul's fish cakes or barbeque Spam. She's rattling on about the new instructor down at Arthur Murray's—says he's a dreamboat—and the dress she's having custom-made for the tango contest. Yellow chiffon with dress shields dyed to match.

"You hungry, Mrs. Kuzo?" she asks, once I've folded the last of the paper bags. "How about some ice cream?"

I shake my head. But she's already rooting around in her freezer, pulls out a half-eaten carton of Neapolitan and sets it down in front of me. It's rock hard and covered with frost.

"Here's the scoop," she says. "How about you just help yourself? And fix me a dish while you're at it. Nature's calling"—she points to the bathroom off the pantry—"but don't go anywhere, I'll be back. Make it two scoops of the strawberry, okay?"

She'll be in there a while, goes potty every time I'm over. I throw the ice cream in the microwave and set it on low for two minutes. Then drift out to the living room and nose around.

She's got one whole wall that's nothing but pictures of herself at dance contests. She wears a different gown in each shot, but her escort's the same. Lenny somebody, a dead ringer for Howard Hughes on his deathbed. He's a retired bus driver, half her width, who's been her dance partner for ages. Nothing romantic; he's got prostate trouble, so she told me the day she brought him by my house for pancakes.

The opposite wall she's reserved for her sons, Buzz and Stevie. There are dozens of photos, from bare-ass babies to bad-ass hooligans, thumbs tucked in their belt loops. Stevie's still doing time for arson, but he hasn't been photographed in years, not with all those facial burns. Buzz neither. She put him on the bus to California the year his daddy died, twenty-five dollars in his pocket along with the address of a county mental health clinic she'd got from his social worker. He's been in a day-treatment program there since.

There's only one photo of Stan. Standing on his head in swim trunks, a beer bottle between his teeth. Just before he drowned in his bathtub.

"You remember to fix me my ice cream?" asks Mrs. Kosavitch, walking into the room, a whiff of air freshener in her wake.

"Sorry, ma'am. It's still in the microwave."

"*Microwave?*" I hear her patter around the kitchen, flip open the microwave door, groan. "Goddam, Mrs. Kuzo, you melted it! And I had my heart set on something cold!"

"You just wait right here," I say, heading out the door. "I've got a half-gallon of Hershey's that's just sitting in my freezer. It's yours."

"Don't bother if it's chocolate chip or butter pecan, Mrs. Kuzo," she calls after me. "I *hate* those flavors."


*T*he phone's ringing no sooner I'm back in the door. "I picked up a couple dozen juice boxes for the trip," says Mrs. Lemack. "Hope you like Hawaiian Punch. And let's see what else I've got here . . ." I can hear the rattle of cellophane, meaning she's breaking into the junk food already. "Barbecue Nachos, potato chips, a tin of butter cookies, Slim Jims, Hershey Kisses, Triscuits, a can of squirt cheese, Oreo cookies, some Planters peanuts, Ex-Lax, and a roll of toilet paper. Did I forget anything?"

"The salt," I say, a little bit nasty.

Water off a duck's back. "Sorry, ma'am, I'm out of room. How about you bring it, then? And don't forget those ham sandwiches. I take mine with butter and mayo, remember?"

"Sure do."

"Good. That should hold us till we hit HoJo's. There's nothing I hate worse than hunger pangs."

Ain't that the truth. The woman keeps a tuna fish sandwich, kosher dills, and a little wheel of cheese on her bedside table, just in case she wakes up with a talking stomach. She has the good sense at least to cover it with Saran Wrap and lay out a couple of roach hotels.

"You get us a hotel room?" I ask.

"Yeah, but I didn't hold it with a credit card. I keep hoping you'll get smart and call Vicky. She loves you, remember?"

I ignore that. "What hotel?"

"The George Washington Motor Lodge. In Valley Forge. Don't worry, I double-checked, and it's Triple-A approved. How about you give them a ring and reconfirm? Got a pen? Here's the number."

But I don't hear a word of it. Mrs. Kosavitch is punching the bell, sounds like Morse code. She thinks I forgot about her ice cream.


*I* knew I wouldn't sleep a wink, up and down all night. Swore I heard scuffling on the porch, like that night thirty years ago when Al snapped on the light and caught those kids going at it on the glider, slaphappy drunk. They took off running, underpants in a pile on the welcome mat, an empty bottle of Southern Comfort rolling down the porch steps.

By two o'clock I don't see much sense staying in bed. Limp downstairs and boil water for Postum. I may as well start making ham sandwiches, too. The doctor's been telling me I need to think more about nutrition, and I can see the ham looks greasy. So I bag up some fruit: bananas so ripe they're spotty and a grapefruit that's been cooling in the fridge door for a month. I keep that stuff on hand for Barb, who just about never stops to visit. And speaking of herself, I double-check just where I left my will. Stuff it inside a padded mailer and scribble her name on it. Not her husband's. Then it's upstairs to stick in my dentures and bag up my blood pressure pills.

I've still got an hour left to kill, and there's not much on TV. I pop open a can of Pepsi and sort through the stack of newspapers on the couch. Thanks to Mrs. Lemack, I've got seven copies of the Thursday paper, the one with the Bessie Smith story, *Nobody Knows You When You're Down and Out*. Gal bought every copy at Rudy's Market, claiming you can't have too much of a good thing. She handed me half the stack and told me I didn't owe a nickel, the treat was on her.

I sigh, turn on the overhead and read Bessie's story one more time. It's true she led a lousy life, grew up poor and orphaned in Chattanooga. Joined a traveling show as a teenager, sang and danced for a pittance in honky-tonks and tent shows and carnivals. It didn't matter the crowds loved her; she never did get rich, even though she made oodles and toured in her own fancy train. Seems the gal had no sense. She spent her money on booze and cards and low-down men. Sang dirty songs. Took girls with her to bed, too. Ballooned big as Mrs. Lemack. And died under the wheels of a truck, in the middle of the night, somewhere in Mississippi.

"She was the greatest," my friend always says. "You name me one fat lady—black, white, or purple—that can sing anywhere *near* as sexy as that! Just one! I dare you!"


*M*rs. Lemack's out front by 6:43, leaning on her horn. I run out, throw open the passenger side door, get blasted by

"Lou'siana Low Down Blues." She practically grabs me by the throat, she's so excited.

"You ready for the time of your life?" There's sweat standing on her face even with the air conditioning blowing her direction.

I'm furious. "You mind getting your damn elbow off the horn? All's we need is Mrs. Kosavitch calling the cops."

"Sorry. Forgot about that old cat." She cuts the engine. "How much luggage you got? Need a hand?"

"Nix. You just keep your fanny in the car. I'll be out in a minute. And keep the music off."

It takes me a few trips. Three sacks of groceries, my gardening tools, twenty pounds of peat moss, a suitcase, beach towels, raincoat, boots, straw hat, crossword puzzles, and Parcheesi. I'm ready for another shower soon's I get it loaded in the trunk. Smell like a dog come in from the rain.

"Hey, Lady, it's 7:03 already!" shouts my friend, all impatient. "We've got a helluva drive ahead of us! You mind hoofing it a little?"

"Just one more trip," I pant. Hope to God she doesn't follow me inside. I've got business to attend to. Head back to the living room and take a seat on the Lazy Boy. It's an old habit I can't shake, learned it from Mum. She never left the house she didn't first sit down and pray a few minutes. Claimed it brought good luck. I've been doing it myself for seventy-five years, and it's true I won the lottery once. But don't get me started on all the bad luck I've had.

I haven't been cooling my heels a minute before she starts tooting her horn again. "Get a move on, Mrs. Kuzo!" she shouts from the street. "You heard me, off your can! Don't worry about a thing! I picked you a four-leaf clover!"

# $\mathcal{M}$onroeville $\mathcal{T}$oll $\mathcal{P}$laza

*I*t was a year ago, almost to the day, when I last drove this direction on the turnpike. Tore out of the same toll plaza shivering in the summer heat, my pulse haywire. I had half a tank of gas, fifteen dollars, and a lottery ticket in the ashtray.

I'd bought the ticket a week before at Rudy's Market. It's thirty years I've shopped there, an easy hike even when my hips pop out of joint. The store reeks of newsprint and chocolate, and a strap of sleigh bells jingles as the door shuts behind you. I always buy a loaf of white bread, a couple pounds of chipped ham, a dozen powdered donuts, and five Super Seven tickets.

That morning was no different from any other. I creaked to the counter, one hand rubbing my hip, and chatted with Rudy about sports and serial killers. He's a stocky little man in a bartender's apron, thumb prints covering his glasses, who throws in a free box of Tic-Tacs whenever my bill is more than twenty dollars. Can't tell whether he's generous or my breath stinks. Then he runs out from behind the counter, holds open the door, and bows, a gentleman. All of which he did that morning.

Three days later, the numbers got drawn. I checked them in the paper—as always—at breakfast. Only this time I spat toast straight out my mouth. There, in boldface, was one of my numbers. With instructions alongside to contact the Gaming Office.

I called them immediately, sweat running out my brassiere and soaking the waistband of my slacks. Rude gal put me on hold with dentist-office music, then picked up and made me repeat my numbers over and over and over.

"Looks like you've won two hundred thousand dollars," she yawned. "You've got a year to come claim it."

I was practically panting. "What'll I need to do?"

"Just bring your ticket to our Harrisburg office. And don't forget appropriate I.D.—driver's license, birth certificate, passport, you get the picture?"

I danced around the table whistling "Zippity Doo Daw." Grinned over tomorrow's headlines, *Steelworker's Widow Hits Jackpot*. At last, I could buy a new Dodge, remodel my kitchen, eat sirloin. Even get that water sucked out of my cellar. I changed into dry clothes, looked at myself in the mirror. Never been a glamour girl, not with my yellow skin and thin hair and sharp features, but what the hell—I was rich.

Ten minutes down the turnpike the bird slammed into my car. I never saw it coming, just heard a thump that scared the bejesus out of me and sent me lurching up on the shoulder. I kicked my door open and limped through a whirlwind of dust to the front of the car. Cursed the air blue. I already knew what had hit me.

The bird—what was left of it—was big, maybe two feet from wingtip to wingtip, spread-eagle on the grill. Wasn't much blood but enough to get me gagging. If Al had been alive, he'd have picked it off with his bare hands, pitched it over the guardrail, told me what a damn fool I was for hitting it in the first place, then finished a sandwich without even wiping his hands on his pants.

But I was alone. And I'd seen that bird before.

So I dropped my head and howled, feathers swirling at my feet. I knew damn well I wasn't getting back in the car. And that I could kiss my winnings goodbye.

🐚

*I've* been queasy about birds since the morning Lily died. Flat on her back in a block of sunlight on Mum's China silk rug.

It was a beautiful rug, handwoven, in fifty shades of red. Mum bought it with bootlegging money and laid it down square in the parlor. She wouldn't let anyone walk on that rug, not even in stocking feet. Which was a silly rule, given that Granddaddy's cats hoisted their legs over it anytime the need arose.

But there were no rules that morning. Just chaos. I'd run to the neighbors for help, then followed Mum's screams back to the parlor. She was down on her knees, wailing and helpless, running her hands over that slack little body, Lily's young blood mixing with the reds in the rug. All of it my fault.

And then a bird flew into the room. Dive-bombed from corner to corner, leaving a trail of wet shit. It beat its wings in our faces, then touch-landed on my head—then Annie's, then Mum's—with needle-sharp claws. Came to rest smack dab on Lily's chest, where it stared me down like a snake. I couldn't move a muscle and went deaf until the neighbors started banging on our door. Then I sprang up and chased that bird with a folded newspaper, got it tangled in the curtains. I would have killed it, but Mum tackled me first, hands of ice, and dragged me to the ground. When she let go, the bird was gone, out whatever way it flew in.

And Lily lay still.

Whenever I'd mention that morning to Annie, she'd tell me the bird had nothing to do with anything. Just a coincidence, was all. That I was sounding like someone off the boat. And this was twentieth-century America.

She was all wrong. Birds are bad luck. And the bird on the Dodge was the same as the bird in the parlor—dead ringer, sent straight from the grave. A warning I should hightail it home. Forget about the money. Tell nobody.

❀

"*H*ave a mint," says Mrs. Lemack, tossing her pocketbook in my lap.

Doggone her. I hate mints, and she knows it. It's just her way of getting me to dig out her Lifesavers, which works every time. I peel open a roll of butter rum and hand her the candies in pairs. They're sticky.

"Crack a smile, will you?" she says, sucking loud on her sweets. "If it weren't for me, you'd be breaking your back right this minute."

She's talking about my hospital work; been volunteering Saturdays the last seven years. Tammy, Mrs. Lemack's daughter, put me up to the idea. She's no stranger to hospitals, been in and out of them since her accident. She promised I'd make dozens of friends, same as she had. I didn't believe her, but Al had just died, and once I've honked through a box of Kleenex, people can talk me into anything.

A week later, I was pushing food carts in a petal-pink uniform and spoon-feeding meals to the patients, as cheerful as Dolly Parton. Most folks would sooner starve than swallow that slop, but it breaks my heart seeing food go to waste, even jiggly green Jell-o. Tammy teases me about it. And I laugh along, a good sport, don't even remind her I'd once stood in breadlines when the mills shut down, the three years Granddaddy didn't work. Even now, I won't throw out leftovers unless they're growing mold.

"To think I gave up my hospital day for *this*," I say as Mrs. Lemack snatches a turnpike ticket out the mouth of the automatic machine.

"What are you bellyaching about?" She rolls up her window. "There isn't a Saturday night you don't call me to say you're quitting. Or did you and your supervisor kiss and make up?"

She's talking about Mr. Blobe, the director of volunteers. He's a beaky little guy, heavy beard, skinny as a strip of licorice, the type that wears dark socks and wing tips to the beach. The man doesn't like me. Or anybody, I suppose, except Karen, his daughter, who shows up for work when she wants. The girl eats every dessert off the food cart, even the butterscotch pudding, then explains to the patients, real sympathetic, that they can't have sweets, doctor's orders. And gets away with it.

Not that I've been so lucky. Last Saturday, the man took me to task for leaving my uniform home. It wasn't my fault, damn bursitis kicked up, and I couldn't work the zipper up my back. I'd spent an hour rummaging through the closet, cursing, never did find that old-lady gadget Barb ordered me from Spencer Gifts, the little fishing pole you throw over your shoulder that'll hook the zipper and pull it up. So I came to work in my green-checkered pantsuit. No go.

"You know the rules, Mrs. Kuzo," he frowned, drawing a line through my name on his clipboard. "Come back next week. Properly dressed."

❀

*M*um was never good with babies, Annie and Lily least of all. It didn't matter they were beautiful. The fact was there were two of them, and she already had Nicky and me. And no husband.

Mum didn't breast-feed. She'd send me to the market for milk and honey, have me lay the babies out in two wicker laundry baskets, and bottle-feed them both. She'd dress in her finery, meanwhile, waltz out the door without kissing any of us goodbye. Then stay away the night.

The twins became my business, the washings and dressings and feedings and lullabies. I'd carry them to Mass, Annie on my back, Lily in my arms, walking ten feet behind Mum, who didn't want her dress wrinkled. When I was at school, she'd leave the babies on a blanket in the kitchen after break-fast—where I'd find them, soiled and crying, when I got home late in the day. She was usually upstairs with her boarders.

Anyone else would have hated her. Not me; that came later. I loved caring for babies, and the twins were wonderful. I never sat down with an empty lap or ate a meal alone. We slept in the same bed, three across, all facing the same direction, hands on one another's hips. I'd stay awake stroking their curls, sniffing their skin, happier than I've ever been. Those babies were mine.

"At least *you'll* make a good mama when you grow up," the ladies at church used to tell me, scowling over their shoulders at Mum. Small wonder they hated her. She'd sampled a few of their husbands—the good-looking ones, at least—any one of whom might have been the twins' father. Mum was beautiful, too, plump and dark and heavy lipped, the envy and nightmare of every woman.

But for all her glamour, she never stopped blaming the twins for her varicose veins, even after Lily died. She kept her hems long and snapped on two pairs of stockings to cover the damage. You'd still see clear through to the purple road map on her calves whenever she crossed her legs.

🈂

"*A*nyhow, tit for tat," says Mrs. Lemack. "You're giving up your hospital day? I'm giving up my bowling game! That even the score?"

My friend's been bowling for years, since her daughter was in diapers. She's awful good. Wins money on a regular basis, but it isn't cash to burn. She needs it for groceries and gas and painkillers for Tammy. That's why she indulged herself the day Johnny Lemack died, tangled up in that machine at work. She took his death benefits and bought herself the Firebird. It's a nice car with white vinyl seats, cruise control, and a cellular phone. She's got a Playboy air freshener dangling from the rearview mirror and vanity plates—"BessieS"—front and back.

She almost lost that car. Turned out Johnny had another

wife—half my friend's age—living four blocks away. The day he died, his blood hadn't cooled to room temperature before both gals were bickering over his death benefits. It was Mrs. Lemack who got them, being the first wife of record. Ticked off the other missus mightily. She filed suit, demanding a two-way split. But the judge held in favor of my friend and let her keep her car.

"I needed the practice, too," she's saying. "The tournament's in another week, and my swing's not what it used to be."

"Isn't true," I say, breaking into the juice boxes. The woman's a legend around the bowling alley. Every teenage boy worships her, the whale of a gal with the Shelley Winters hairdo and swinging udders who can whip their asses blindfold.

She loves the attention. Always jokes about her missed opportunities with those kids in the backseat of the Firebird. And plans to come back in her next life as a wicked old broad, bad as Bessie.

※

Lily was only four when she died, right after Mum and Granddaddy bought the big house in Braddock. It was perched on a hill with the yard sloping sharply toward the street. Granddaddy built a retaining wall above the sidewalk, then attached an iron railing so none of us kids could fall, a dangerous eight-foot drop. Nicky would swing on the rail just to frighten me, his palms turning red from the rust.

One morning—mid-June, cloudless, and hot—Mum was around back trimming her rosebushes. It was the only work she liked—strange, since the thorns tore open her soft skin. I was up on the front porch minding the twins and crocheting a tablecloth. For a year, I'd been selling my doilies at church and getting lots of compliments. Figured a tablecloth might fetch a bundle, four or five bucks, a month's worth of ice cream and tickets to Kennywood Park.

A half hour into my work, I needed a smaller hook. Stood up and spotted the twins rolling a ball back and forth on the lawn. Mum had told me never to leave them, but this would only take a minute. I slipped inside, glancing over my shoulder, counting to ten. I'd left my knitting basket on a table in the foyer. Rummaged around the bottom quick as I could.

Then I heard the scream that still wakes me. Dropped my hook, ran back outside, and saw Annie, alone, at the railing. She was wailing and pointing downward. I couldn't move.

Mum tore up from around back, still wearing her sun hat and gardening gloves. She yanked Annie away from the railing, pushed her my direction, then jumped off the wall onto the sidewalk below. I inched up close and saw Mum lifting Lily off the sidewalk, blood all over her little face, and her neck bent queer. Mum shrieked at me to run next door for help. It wouldn't be easy—a box hedge separated the yards, too high to jump over, too thick to crawl under. I paused a second, then threw the weight of my body against the huge hedge and pushed clear through it, coming out the other side with my dress torn and my bare arms bleeding. I leaped up on our neighbor's porch and kicked the door.

Mr. O'Riordan answered in his bathrobe, red-faced and whiskey-breathed, but still upright.

"Please, for God's sake, help us!" I screamed. "My sister's hurt awful!"

He staggered back inside to find his pants. I didn't wait for him, pushed back through the hedge and leaped up on our porch, following Mum's wails to the parlor where she'd laid Lily on her back in the sunlight. And then the bird came.


*T*hey took Lily to the hospital anyway, wrapped in the tablecloth I'd been crocheting. It was a gut-lurching ride. Mr. O'Riordan either slammed the brakes or floored the gas, his elbow on the horn. Annie and me crouched at Mum's feet, crying and clinging to each other. I could see Lily's tiny foot poking out from the tablecloth, wearing the white cotton sock and little T-strap shoe I'd fastened on her just that morning. I reached up and stroked that foot until we got to the hospital. The last time I touched it.

Mr. O'Riordan carried her inside and laid her across the registration desk, Mum alongside begging for help in broken English. A nurse chased Annie and me out in the hall. I found a folding metal chair and lifted Annie onto my lap, both of us crying noisily. Her underpants felt wet on my bare knees, but no matter. I squeezed her icy hands, my nose in her neck, and prayed out loud. This had to be a dream. God couldn't be so cruel, not to Lily.

But He was. An hour later, Mr. O'Riordan came to tell us that Lily was dead. Said she must have fallen face forward and snapped her spinal cord. Couldn't breathe. But she'd gone straight to heaven, little angel. No doubt about it.

He took us back to his car, all of us shuffling and sobbing. Mum was already sitting in back, red-eyed, watching us approach. She opened the door and called me inside. Grabbed my shoulders and shook hard.

"You were supposed to be watching her!" she screamed, over and over again. "You stupid girl! Do you *know* what you've done?"

I knew. God, I knew.

And when we got home, she had me fetch soap and water and scrub Lily's blood from the parlor rug. I couldn't stop crying. I hated her. And I never did get the rug clean, as many times as she made me start over.

"*H*ope Tammy's alright," says Mrs. Lemack. "I never think I leave enough food."

I can't help frowning. Tammy's as big as her mother, little wonder, bored and bedridden and feeding on Reese's peanut butter cups. She's the same age as Barb, too, but cut from a whole different cloth—no husbands, no kids, no credit-card debt. Up till her accident, she'd been a social worker, took a job in Appalachia teaching teenage moms how to change diapers and file restraining orders. That was where her truck spun off a cliff one night and busted her spine into thirty-six pieces. She'll never walk again.

Mrs. Lemack doesn't let on much, but I know she's heartsick. Tammy's her only kid, the apple of her mother's eye. I don't think it's reciprocal, not that it's any of my business. And I should talk, the way Barb treats me. But the two of them get along well enough, as if Tammy has much choice. She has nowhere else to go.

The first couple years after the accident were rocky. Tammy was in tears all the time, and Mrs. Lemack can't abide misery. She set out to cheer the girl up—by buying her peekaboo nighties with sequins and pasties and feathers. Tammy, of course, wouldn't touch them, but the girl wasn't wasteful. She gave the nighties as gag gifts as each of her friends got married.

Next thing you know, Tammy was getting letters from old college friends. Typewritten. How they'd just heard about her accident, what a crying shame, and was there anything they could do?

"Who's Sally Boyson?" asked Tammy one morning, letters in hand, when I'd stopped by with doughnuts. "She says she was on the same floor in my dorm, but it sure doesn't ring a bell. Or this one. Jill McGarry? From Girl Scout camp?"

"Oh, Tam, you always had so many friends," gushed Mrs. Lemack. "How the heck could you remember them all?"

"Cut it out, Mom. You have something to do with this?"

Of course she had. She'd picked random names from the phone book, typed the letters with two fingers, then mailed them from as far away as Youngstown so's to have an out-of-town postmark.

After that episode, my friend changed her tactics. She started dragging Tammy in her wheelchair to restaurants. And whispering to the waiters it was the girl's birthday, even though it wasn't, just so they'd bring out a cake. I was with them once, all the staff singing "Happy Birthday" off key, Tammy tearing over like a hydrant. I wheeled her straight out to the parking lot, sobbing, her mother still inside blowing out candles.

"Don't mind my daughter," I heard Mrs. Lemack tell the

smarmy maitre d'. "She just doesn't like getting older. Good cake, though. You got a doggie bag?"

Still, things improved. Tammy's got her name up in lights. She volunteers for every telephone hot line in Greater Pittsburgh—suicide, rape, pregnancy, addictions, battered wives. The newspaper even did an article about her, picture too, posed cheek-to-cheek with her mother.

🙊

*W*orst days of my life were the ones after Lily died. Mum wouldn't speak to me, told everyone it was my fault. She locked herself in her room for hours, flat on her back, moaning like a banshee. I'd bring up sandwiches and lemonade, wait outside her door till she'd finished the food, then collect the dirty dishes from her dresser. She was the only one I cooked for those days. Granddaddy took his nourishment from a bottle, and Nicky disappeared. Annie and I weren't hungry.

We didn't sleep, either. The moonlight kept us awake all night, flooding the side of the bed where Lily once slept. We clung to each other, fists in our mouths, choking on sobs and dry heaves. Daytime we avoided the parlor. Lily lay inside, tucked in a glass-covered coffin. I couldn't bear to look at her, poor little baby.

Still, some small good came of it all. Until Lily died, I thought we had no friends. There wasn't a woman in Braddock didn't yak nasty about Mum over backyard fences. Same went for Granddaddy, crazy as a bedbug, the way he'd act in church, chasing kids off his favorite pew and shouting drunken nonsense during Mass. But Lily's dying softened people's hearts. They sent us breads and hams and homemade wines, mowed our lawn, and took up a collection for flowers. It made me feel a little better.

Those feelings, though, didn't last. Ended the day of Lily's funeral. For which I still blame Granddaddy.

That morning, Mr. Kurtyak—Lily and Annie's godfather— came to the house. He'd been Dad's best friend. The two of them crossed the Atlantic together, just before the war, and hopped the train to Pittsburgh. He'd been with Dad the day he got killed in the mill. Brought the news to Mum. And then for years afterward, money. He was a good man.

That morning, he offered to carry Lily's coffin to church. No one objected; it was breezy and dry, high nineties, and too hot to move. We followed behind him for seventeen blocks, Granddaddy reeking of moonshine, Mum fanning herself with a crumpled glove, the back of her dress dark with sweat. I dragged half a block behind in tears, hand-in-hand with Annie.

The parish turnout was huge, two hundred mourners, and most of our American neighbors. The women gathered around us, weeping in hankies and kissing Mum's hands as we passed through the foyer. I started feeling better, even through my tears, but not for long. Mum still wouldn't look at me, even after I squeezed her hand. She was hard that way all her life.

The funeral Mass was too long. Shamed me, watching Granddaddy tippling and talking to himself, people frowning on all sides. Halfway through the offertory, he drained his flask, dropped it clattering on the stone floor, and crawled to the altar on his knees. Mr. Kurtyak stepped forward then, all dignified, and tried leading him back to his seat. But the old man started swinging punches and cursing like the mean old devil he was. Turned heads left and right.

They still talk about that day at kitchen tables in Braddock. About how the mourners chased the crazy old man out to the street. And how his daughter tore after him, left her little daughters standing in tears. And how no one came to the burial, just the priest. The parish had seen enough of that family, thank you very much.

So we were back to where we started, not just Hunkies among Americans but trash among Hunkies. And without Lily. I blamed it partly on Granddaddy, drunken fool. Partly Mum, too, who went back to her wicked ways. But above all, I blamed myself. I'd killed her.

So I was shunned like a leper, which lasted till I met Mrs. Lemack. She charged into my life and stayed till this day. Like it or not.

*I*t was 9:17 in the morning, and the bird was still hanging off my bumper. I knew I couldn't count on the highway patrol for a lift. Just that week, they'd found a body around here, front page news, face down in a gully. I wagered every state cop put in for vacation after that, and the ones who didn't get it were out cruising Canada, claiming they'd forgot how to read a road map.

So I locked up and hoofed back toward Pittsburgh. Found a phone at the next exit ramp, then wondered just who I should call. There are only four other numbers besides my own I know from memory: Barb, Mrs. Lemack, Mrs. Kosavitch, and Tom, my son.

Slender pickings that day. Barb was off in the Caribbean, got herself a cheap cruise, free bikini waxing thrown in. And Mrs. Kosavitch wouldn't drive anywhere the speed limit's over thirty miles an hour, said it cranked up her blood pressure. Worst possibility was Mrs. Lemack. She was home, sure, watching "Hulk Hogan" with Tammy. But she'd beat me with a bowling pin until I'd admit where I'd been headed, and after that bird episode, I just wanted to tear up the ticket. Which left me with Tom.

I started to tremble. He's my son alright, but he frightens me. Mum always said he was God's punishment for the things Al and I'd done in her hammock before we were married. I didn't believe her, but it's true he's raised hell. They know him real good at the jail.

His personal life's in shambles, too. Last count, he's been married four times. I can't keep up with my grandchildren— there are so many by now, and each wife brought along a few of her own from earlier arrangements, none of them marriages. Last gal left with everything except her credit-card bill. He's been licking his wounds since and moved into a trailer. Found himself a new woman—Tracey, the best of the lot. She has the sense not to marry him.

I'll grant Tom's got business-smarts. He owns an auto body shop, probably a chop shop, and turns a nice profit. But it's in the worst part of Rankin, gang territory, a stone's throw from a housing project where the dumpsters are about the safest place to hang out.

"Stop piss-moaning about the neighborhood," he snapped, first time I came by his shop and wouldn't get out of my car. "Punks around here don't mess with us. Know why? 'Cause we can match their firepower easy. And then some." He pointed to his shoulder holsters and steel-tipped boots, a regular Johnny Rambo. "And these are just the *toys*."

It wasn't a week later, though, a thief broke in, stole all his tools, and redecorated the joint with spray paint. Tom drove his truck to the city pound and picked out a couple of the meanest mongrels he could find, then chased them up on the roof of the shop with a baseball bat. They've been up there since, howling like coyotes and lunging at airplanes overhead. I never saw animals so ugly, all torn ears and missing tails. The meanest one, Brian, he'd let loose inside the shop at night. Mongrel always swallowed the keys that Tom's early bird customers dropped in the door slot, so he'd have to wait for his pet to poop before he could work on the car.

*I* reached the shop third try. He wasn't thrilled with my news.

"What d'ya mean, some bird ran into your car?"

"Sweetie, don't ask me how it happened." I know from experience it pays to be patient. "The damn thing rammed into me out of nowhere, and I think it broke the engine block."

"The engine block? Oh, for crying out loud, a *bird?*"

I started to sweat. "Alright, maybe I'm wrong. But all's I know's that I can't drive the damn thing. How about you come get me? Please?"

"Jeez, Ma, it's Friday morning! I've got more customers than I've had all week, and you expect me to close shop over some bird blood?"

"Look, I'll *wait*."

I heard him spit. "Well, don't hold your breath. It's gonna be a while."

"I've got the time."

"Yeah, yeah. Now go find yourself a comfortable chair, and someone to yak at," he barked and hung up.

I ground my teeth. I'm the first one he calls, of course, whenever he's behind the eight ball. Like the Thursday a week before, when some guy opened his car door into Tom's truck, and Tom rammed his knuckles down the poor sucker's throat in full view of a plainclothes cop. Kid called me from the station that night, asking for bail money. I had to head out the door, hair still in curlers, and go beg at the Moose Club. I can always find Al's old drinking buddies there; boys front me money whenever my Social Security's late or Tom's in trouble. Once I got what I needed, I scuttled down to the bail bondsman's. Got the kid sprung.

The cops had impounded his truck, so I had to drive him home. He didn't even ask me in for coffee, just kept belly-aching. And he still hasn't paid back what he owes. Figures he has no obligations, I suppose. At least not to me.

*T*om pulled up in his tow truck three and a half hours later. Not a sight for sore eyes, with his hair in braids and half his teeth chipped. He's as skinny as a whippet, dowel rods for legs, wearing a sleeveless denim jacket, shoulder holster, and leather head scarf.

He kicked open his passenger door and waved me inside. "So where's your car?"

I climbed in, shrugged. "Shoot if I know, back the road a mile or two. Just drive." He smelled like a brewery, so I knew he hadn't come straight from work.

"You lost your marbles, Ma? What's this crap about a dead bird?"

"Just drive, you'll see. It'll make you sick."

He pulled up behind the Dodge while I sat in the truck. I heard him kick up the gravel as he circled around the front of my car. Closed my eyes for what seemed like minutes, then jumped out of my skin when he rapped on my window and threw open the door.

"Jesus, Ma, you crazy?"

"What you talking about?"

"Just get out of the car. Come on, come on, have a look for yourself."

I reached for the door handle. "I swear to *God* I'm not going near that durn thing!"

But he was dragging me out of the truck by the soft skin of my upper arm, his grip as tight as a blood pressure cuff.

"There!" he shouted, once we got to the grill. "Not a damn thing the matter with it!"

I blinked twice and tried to focus. It was my car alright, same Dodge I'd bought secondhand the year Al died, had a hundred thousand miles back then. Only there was nothing on the grill, not a spot of blood, not a single feather teasing up from the ground. The bird was gone without a trace. Just like the bird in the parlor.

*H*e drove me home without saying a word. Didn't bother coming around to open my door. Lit a cigarette instead, tossed the match out the window, and turned, facing me.

"Listen, Ma, next time you want someone playing rescue, you get yourself a cab, alright?"

I wasn't about to fight. "Yeah, yeah."

"Good girl," he smirked, all satisfied. "Now how about you fix me a meal while I unhitch your car, huh?"

The fridge was practically empty, a quart of orange juice, Velveeta cheese, and Senior Citizens' butter. I'd forgot to take the ground beef out of the freezer that morning. Rock solid. Thought about banging it with a hammer, then had another idea. Tom was standing behind me by then, reaching for the last bottle of Rolling Rock Beer.

"When's the last time you hit the market?" he said, opening the beer with unwashed hands. "Day I left home?"

"You just sit your can down in front of the set," I said,

pointing toward the living room. "The remote's on the mantel-piece. I'll whip up something."

Which I did as he watched "Combat" reruns. A pot of buttered turnips on top of Uncle Ben rice, just like Mum would cook up for herself and take to bed anytime a boyfriend left her.

"What the hell's that?" he sniffed when I brought out the meal on a TV tray.

"Guess."

He brought his nose close, wrinkled it like a walnut. "You didn't go fix me some *turnips* now, did you?"

"Yeah, so? *I* eat them."

"Figures. Last person on earth." He stood up, ground out his cigarette, kissed me on the forehead. "I'm outa here, Ma. Food's all yours. But thanks for the beer."

I stood dumbfounded, the plate still steaming in my hands as the screen door slammed behind him. Cursed the air till I was hoarse.

Then I did as Mum would have done. Sat down and ate his turnips, every one, wiping away my tears. He'd hurt me bad, like always. But food shouldn't be wasted.


$\mathcal{N}$ext morning I headed to Rudy's looking for roach spray. I noticed a handwritten sign scotch-taped to his door, little smiley faces scribbled in each corner. It said something about a winning ticket that'd been bought there the week before, would the lucky sucker please fetch their reward.

I thought about heading back home, but I'd had it with roaches. And I wasn't exactly stumbling around with the ticket pinned to my forehead. I'd hid it in my panty hose drawer after Tom left, right under Mum's rosary beads.

That's when I nearly collided with Mrs. Kosavitch. Gal was on her way out, lugging three jars of kosher dill pickles, dressed in a hip-length overblouse and mule slippers. Judy Garland minus the mike.

"Good morning to you, Mrs. Kuzo," she said, pointing at the sign with her chin. "You see that?"

"Hard to miss. You the winner?"

She blew air out her mouth, fluttering her lips like a mare. "Ha! When's the last time anything good happened to *me*? Shoot, I'd be happy if my damn air conditioner just worked." She lifted her arm and sniffed underneath, making a sour face.

"Rudy have any idea who it is?" I asked, holding my breath and trying to slide past her.

"He's narrowed it down to about thirty-odd customers. And you're one of them, Lady. You check your numbers?"

"Yeah. Zilch."

"Well, it kills me there's some lucky sonovabitch out there running around, head in the clouds, with a winning ticket. I'd *kill* for it . . . say, you want to stop by for some coffee? You bring the doughnuts?"

# &xit 9 — Donegal

"Listen, girl," says Mrs. Lemack. "You're going to need to do *something* to keep me awake. How come you been so quiet?"

"Just thinking, is all."

"Thinking?" she says. "I'm practically *unconscious!* You want us to end up wrapped around a guardrail? Imagine that in your obituary!"

I've weathered this before. The woman needs amusement when she drives, and it's risky to ignore her. Left on her own, she drags you to roadside attractions, like miniature frontier towns or petting zoos. She even picks up hitchhikers. Last week we drove home from Foodland with one of her playthings, seven feet tall and a sloping forehead. I thought for sure we'd end up famous on "Unsolved Mysteries."

"I'm still waiting," says my friend, glancing at her watch. "Where's your imagination, Mrs. Kuzo?"

I sigh, do what I hadn't intended to do for another couple hours, and then only as a last resort. I pull out my well-thumbed copy of *Information Please, Almanac,* the one off the back of my toilet. Flip through a few pages and clear my throat.

"Let's see how smart you are, Mrs. Lemack. How about you tell me—page 568—the date and location of the worst U.S. railroad disaster since 1900? And no cheating!"

🐚

*S*peaking of disasters.

It was in March of this year, nine months after I'd won the lottery, that my phone rang all morning. I was wrapped in an afghan watching "Wheel of Fortune." Don't care for interruptions, not during that show, but forty rings later I started to sweat. I figured the caller was family with news that someone had died—or worse, a phone masturbator. So I picked up slowly, without saying hello.

"Hey, Mom? That you? It's Barb." She always identifies herself, as if I wouldn't recognize my own daughter's voice. Today she sounded worried. But it was good hearing from her, even bad news, as little as she calls.

"What's up, Sweetie?" I asked, snapping off the set.

"Well, for starters, we're back."

"Back?"

"From Barbados. Remember?"

She must have forgot to tell me she was taking a trip. Hurt my feelings, but I didn't let on. "Well, how was it?"

"Fabulous—you wouldn't *believe* the beaches. We're gung ho to move there"—she lowered her voice— "when *I* win the lottery."

I winced. Any mention of that word, from her especially, got me crawling. She was furious how I'd spent the money and wouldn't speak to me for months afterward.

"Well," I said breezily, "I hope you took lots of pretty pictures."

"Hundreds. Videos, too," she said, brightening. "You'll have to see them. And my tan, of course."

"Sure. Want to stop by here for lunch this week?"

"I'd love to, Mom, but I'm overbooked." Same old story. "But I've got an idea. How about you come over here for a change? For dinner tonight?"

I was downright delighted, see her so seldom, which isn't my choice. Breaks my heart we aren't better friends. Or even friends at all. And it's been like this as long as I can remember, not just since she got married.

"And Mom? There's something else I need to talk to you about. Important."

I was flattered. "Sure, Sweetie. I'm listening."

"Not now. Tonight."


$\mathcal{B}$arb was living in "The Hills of Provence" back then, a hoity-toity subdivision built around a golf course. Each house was identical, with Greek columns and circular driveways and white-faced jockey boys swinging lanterns out front. You had to pass through a little gate with guards and cameras, state your name and business, then sign a roster just to get inside, like "Mission Impossible."

My son-in-law, George Priakos, opened the door. His freshly shaved face was patched with toilet paper.

"Well, if it isn't my favorite babe!" he boomed. He's a dentist, always slaphappy and stinking of aftershave. The man can't keep his hands to himself and puts them in places that could get him arrested.

"When you going to put a decent bulb in your porch light?" I asked, dodging around him and untying my babushka. "It took me durn near twenty minutes finding this place."

He pulled me toward him, puckering his lips. "Hey lady, where's your manners? No kiss?"

I pushed him away. "Hands off. And I *don't* mean maybe."

"In that case, Mama"—he scooped me up, slung me over his shoulder, my fanny hanging lumpy as a feed bag—"you and me are going for a walk."

"*Barb!*" I screamed, slapping his back as he headed for the living room. But he's well padded and didn't flinch.

"Put on a few pounds, Mama?" He shifted me to his other shoulder. "This didn't use to be so hard. I could pop out a hernia, for Chrissakes. Don't you want more grandsons?"

"Put her down, George." It was my daughter in the doorway, a blur of red— sweater, lipstick, and nail polish.

"Bug off, Barb," he panted. "We're just having ourselves some fun, aren't we, Mama?"

"*Now!*" she screeched.

He eased me down on the sofa, no apologies, and saluted his wife. Turned to me and grinned.

"Rest assured, ladies, I *shall* return."

"Get out," she said, closing the door behind him.

❀

"*I*sn't he a stitch?" Barb giggled the first time—Easter ten years ago—she'd brought him to my house. He'd just juggled my hand-painted Easter eggs three at a time, dropped my favorite, then kicked the shell under the china cabinet.

"What rock did he crawl out from under?" grumbled Al back in the kitchen. "Can't she do better than that?"

"*Ssshhh.*" I shut the kitchen door. "She says he's a dentist. He makes lots of money."

"What of it? He's a jerk, is all. Hope to hell you didn't ask him for dinner."

"Barb *asked* me to! You think I'd say no?"

The meal was a nightmare. George handpicked the tomatoes out of the salad and swatted the Tiffany lamp back and forth. Then he pushed away his plate, pulled on my raccoon coat, and chased Barb on hands and knees, barking. He caught her skirt in his teeth and wouldn't let go.

"Georgie Porgie, pudding and pie," she squealed, playing right along. "Kissed the girls and made them cry."

By then, Al was out the door and headed to the Moose. He didn't come back for hours. And when he did, it was on his knees.

🐚

*A*l had good reason to drink that day. Barb's choice of men up till then ran to losers. And George fit the pattern, dentist or not.

He wasn't her first husband. She'd married fresh out of high school, to a Vietnam vet named Dickie Hamm. The boy was missing an earlobe, bragged it got chewed off by the Vietcong. Truth was, he lost it in the barracks after calling a Green Beret queer.

It made me sick, her marrying so young and without any skills, just like me. I'd been working in a factory, saving every penny to put her through secretarial school. But she spent all that money on her wedding—a fancy affair with five hundred sit-down dinner guests in the Moose, a polka band, an open bar, and a diamond the size of a doorknob.

Dickie was no catch, either. He drifted from job to job with his half-ear pressed to a transistor radio, listening to everything, even static. But Barb didn't care, what with all the money he spent on her. He even gift-wrapped a little Mustang for her birthday, with zebra-print seat covers and a box of pink Kleenex in the rear window.

They weren't married a month, she was bored—at first with her husband and later with motherhood. She'd go out with her girlfriends, dressed to the nines, hair ratted high, and head for the clubs. Finally stayed away for good. She found herself a new husband at a New Year's party, an insurance adjuster twice her age. She'd brag how he'd win at the racetrack and take her for steak and champagne. I've still got the honeymoon postcard Barb sent from the Poconos. A big circular bed with a mirrored headboard, just like they sell at Mr. Furniture.

That marriage lasted a year. She moved back home with me and Al and took a job selling G.E.D. courses to high school dropouts. It was one of those outfits advertised inside match-book covers that I used to wonder whether I should call.

❀

"Sorry about George, Mom," said Barb, crossing her living room. "I'll make him apologize. Promise." She planted a noisy kiss on my cheek, then rubbed off the lipstick with her thumb. "What can I get you to drink?"

"You got any pop?"

"Pop?" She shuddered. "Mom, when are you going to grow up? How about Chablis?"

"Pop or nothing, okay?" I was irritated. We always have this conversation in her living room.

She shrugged, opened the little refrigerator in the bar, and banged around. Went through this ceremony of crushing ice, filling a tall glass, and garnishing it with lime. She plunked my Coke down on a lacquered drink coaster, making a sourpuss face. "You never wanted me to see you tipsy, did you?"

That much we agree on. I never touch alcohol, not after living with Granddaddy. Same doesn't go for my daughter, who drinks more than she eats. I watched her fill a tumbler and nestle barefoot on the loveseat across from me.

"Well, why don't I get it over with," she sighed, "and tell you my bad news. I mean, what are mothers for?"

That surprised me. She'd never been the type to share confidences, one of my biggest frustrations. I tried reading her diary once, picking the lock with my fingernail while she soaked in the bath. The pages were blank.

❦

*B*arb had been an ugly baby, small and saddle-nosed and misshapen. We christened her Eva, after Mum, but she changed her name the first day of kindergarten. She didn't look a bit like me or Al, not with her aquamarine eyes. Ladies at church swore she'd been switched in the nursery—the nice ladies, at least. The rest had their own version, which worked its way around to Al.

I was nursing her in the kitchen one Saturday morning, Tom at my elbow, balking at oatmeal. None of us had slept well. Al was out drinking the night before, stumbled home coatless, and passed out on the sidewalk. I'd gone outside in my nightgown, mad as a she-bear, hooked his big feet under my arms and pulled him up the stairs, thumping his head on every step. I couldn't get back to sleep, both kids stirring and him heaving so loud in the bathroom.

So I ignored him that morning. Ticked him off enough he started staring.

"You got something to say?" I asked at last, laying Barb down in the wicker laundry basket I used for a crib.

"Yeah. You got someone on the side?"

"What the *hell* you talking about?"

He stood up, still unsteady, pointed at the baby. "Take a look at that kid, Masha. Blue eyes? That's no Kuzo!"

I couldn't believe it. He was the only man I'd ever had in my bed, and mostly his idea. I turned toward him, whispering, a catch in my throat. "You . . . calling me a *whore?*"

His face got ugly. "I ain't calling you no names, Mama, not *yet*. But don't take me for a fool. Ain't a guy in Braddock doesn't know about your mum."

So that was what it came down to. Like mother, like daughter. I smacked him in the face hard as I could.

"Jesus, woman"—his nose was bleeding—"what the hell you trying to do?"

I snatched the baby from the basket and shook her under his nose. "She's your daughter, you hear me? *Yours!* And that's the *last* time you ever talk trashy like that! Ever!" I kicked his foot. "You got anything more to say?"

Then I marched out in the rain, all the way to Mrs. Lemack's house, clutching Barb with my good hand. My friend was in poor temper, too, just had a fight with *her* husband for pawning the silverware to pay off a gambling debt. The louse had tossed hot coffee on her housecoat, then took off running round the neighborhood, her puffing barefoot in the rear, till he hopped a truck and got away. I met her in the street, her hair in tangles, crying. Gal forgot about her silverware seeing me. She helped me to her house, packed my hand on ice, and called the doctor. The fractures were bad, took two hours for the cast to dry, which Mrs. Lemack couldn't wait to autograph. Then she took me for a milk shake and back home to my husband.

I found him alone in the kitchen laying shelf paper. The place was whistle-clean—linens changed, floors scrubbed, laundry dripping over the bathtub. Even the walls had been washed. I smelt pot roast and potatoes simmering on the stove, which made my stomach talk.

"Ya hungry?" That was all he said.

"Starving."

He pulled out my chair, piled a plate high, and took Barb from my lap. "Dig in, Lady."

We never talked about it. But he nicknamed me Sluggo after that, teased me about the time I'd flattened his ass, and warned his drinking buddies to watch their manners when I was around.

And funny thing, Barb grew up to look just like her father, same black hair and big feet and bad temper. I couldn't tell her anything. Pure Kuzo. And, like her father, she never cared much for my company.

"*There's* really not much to tell," said Barb, stirring the ice in her second drink with a little plastic pirate sword. "And it doesn't even make a good story. The fact is, we're broke."

"Broke?" I glanced around her living room, all silk rugs and Ethan Allen furniture and original oil paintings she'd bought at the mall—French country scenes, each one worth hundreds of dollars.

"Unbelievable, isn't it?" she said, following my gaze. "There was a time when I couldn't spend money fast enough, remember?"

"So what the hell happened?"

She sighed, drifted to the French doors, and ran a hand along the velvet draperies. "It's complicated, Mom. For starters, being a dentist doesn't pay what it used to. George lost tons of business to those damn HMOs. He made some bad investments, too. And he could never budget. He can't even use a calculator! He's always had someone else handle his accounts at work."

I propped a cushion behind my back, damn sciatica acting up. "Well, just how bad is it?"

She pressed her drink to her cheek. "About as bad as it can get, to be honest. I've drawn up to my limit on all my credit cards. We couldn't use a single one in Barbados."

"Then maybe it's a blessing in disguise," I said, letting my breath out slowly and wondering why they took the trip in the first place. "You know I never trusted those things. The only card I ever had was Exxon. And I cut *that* into a hundred pieces the day Mrs. Lemack got hers stolen."

She threw herself next to me on the sofa, picking lint off her cashmere sweater. "Believe me, Mom, the cards aren't the problem. It's the lawsuit."

"*Lawsuit?*" The hair tingled on the back of my neck.

"Yeah, for debt collection." She put down her drink and

started to cry. "One of the banks served me this morning, right before I called you."

"What the hell are you kids going to do?" I whispered, frightened.

"I don't know . . . but maybe *you* can help us."

"Me? How?" My lottery money was already gone. Damn.

She wiped her eyes, then spoke low and clear as if she'd practiced it beforehand. "Call Vicky. I know she'll float *you* a loan."

Every muscle in my body tightened.

"Mom?" She grabbed my shoulder, her face in mine. "Please? Won't you do that for me?"

"I don't know," I mumbled, pulling away. "You're putting me between a rock and a hard place. I know how you feel about Vicky."

"Jeez, Mom, I'll pay her back. You know that!"

"Then how about you call her yourself? She'd loan me money, but she'd want to know *why*. And how could I lie?"

"For love, maybe?"

"Love?"

"Good God, Mom!" She threw down a cushion, all petulance. "I'm your daughter! Doesn't that count for something?"

҉

$\mathcal{V}$icky isn't Rockefeller, but she's comfortable. Her husband, Siddhartha, works hard and with good reason; he's got phone bills and food bills I shudder to imagine. His live-in aunties call Bombay every day, and he's feeding a nation, not a family. Thirty-odd people, once you count Vicky's guests and the street folks she feeds on their porch.

They've been married a few years, met at a folk dance in West Philly. She moved in with him a week later, her usual habit with men. Sent me a postcard of the Taj Mahal and a scribbled message that she'd finally found love. And she brought him to Braddock that Christmas.

I wasn't surprised he was Hindu. Girl always preferred her men dark and speaking broken English. I'd met boyfriends from Saudi and Bahrain and Jordan, graduate students in business and finance. She'd show them a good time before they flew back to Daddy for good. Full of tales of easy American girls.

Sidd, at least, was different. He wanted to marry the girl. And I was tickled pink any man, even a Hindu, would make an honest woman of her. Since adolescence, she'd been easy, lost her cherry in her parent's driveway the summer after eighth grade. Annie caught her, pants down, in the rear of a Mr. Softee ice cream truck. Under Mr. Softee.

Still, it's a marriage with problems. Sidd's family comes first, not his wife. Vicky isn't thrilled but keeps the peace, a weakness she gets from her mother. She's even gone native to please him. She patters around in bare feet and a sari, her hair in a messy braid, her breath as garlicky as the rest of them.

But Sidd's a good man. He noticed her efforts and bought her a Jaguar. She parks it out front my house whenever she visits, doors unlocked, windows cracked. Gives me the jitters, with all these car thefts. I cover it with a couple bedspreads when she stays the night, just so I can sleep.

And she's here every couple months for a weekend, brings me gifts and takes me to dinner. She likes "imaginative dining," her words. Drags me to places with non-English menus where you squat on fat cushions. I'll order anything just to get rid of the waiter. Hasn't happened yet he didn't return with something from an autopsy.

She always gives me something to talk about—more than my own kids—which still doesn't make us friends. But she's all of my sister that's left, so I try to ignore her shortcomings. Isn't easy. Especially her habit of bringing up the past, twisting my heart with her stories of Annie. I already know too much about my sister.

"*You're* really doing good, Mrs. Lemack," I say. "Too bad none of our teachers knew just how smart you are." The woman's a whiz. She just named President McKinley's assassin, a Mr. Leon Czolgosz, the three highest dams in the world, the latitude and longitude of Chicago, and the seven warning signs of cancer.

"Them's easy questions," she laughs. "How about you *really* try busting my chops? Go ahead, I dare you!"

"Alright, then." I flip through sections I normally don't read. Find something that should trip her up. "What are the colors of the Bulgarian flag?"

"Red, white and . . . *green*."

"Okay, smarty pants, game's not over. What's the Recommended Daily Allowance for Vitamin C in women over fifty?"

"Sixty milligrams, am I right?"

"Yeah, yeah, Here's one. What's the stage name of Harold Lloyd Jenkins?"

"Why, Conway Twitty, of course! Mrs. Kuzo, you're going to have to do a lot better than this! It's child's play!"

*The* Greek was eight years younger than Barb, still in dental school when they met. She'd gone to the university clinic for a root canal, which was half the asking price anywhere in town. Cash was a problem. She was managing apartment buildings and getting death threats from people she tried to evict. The salary wasn't enough to pay her bills.

The Greek made his move once she opened her mouth. He told her she had the deepest throat he'd ever seen except for Linda Lovelace. Barb giggled so much she bit his finger and gave him her phone number even before he asked.

They married six weeks later and moved straight to The Hills of Provence. Lived like a country club couple, easy to do with every Greek around here bringing him business. He bought her whatever she wanted, even breast implants, so she could sashay around in a ribbed-knit dress.

But rich as George got, he couldn't buy hair. What little he had traveled south from his head and reattached in the wrong places—neck, arms, back. He's embarrassed being bald. Bought himself a rug, Barb's insistence, that blew off his head on the golf course. The loss put them back a couple thousand dollars, but in those days it was nothing. They owned a time-share condo in Maui, imported cars, a sailboat, even a tanning bed to keep their skin looking like cooked meat in February.

⚇

"*I* asked you to dinner, so let's eat," said Barb, once I promised I'd call Vicky. "And you're in for a treat."

I cringed at the thought of her cooking. Last time I was over—a party for her jazzercize class—she served snails in their shells. I didn't want to hurt her feelings, not in front of her bony friends, so I ate every one. Then spent the night chugging Kaopectate.

"You didn't fix anything fancy, did you?" I asked evenly. "Like that French food?"

Her shoulders bunched. "Mom, I cook the way I cook. Okay, so it's French. *Canard à l'orange,* duckling with orange sauce. That sound okay to you?"

"Just fine," I lied. "I'm only hoping you didn't go to any bother, that's all."

"Relax. And don't worry about George, either—he's not joining us. I fed him a steak before you got here."

Good girl, I thought, hid a smile. Lost it when I saw what she was piling on my plate. I always hated duck, and she was cutting me the whole bird, less a sliver for herself. Dieting again, probably. She'd do better to cut back the booze.

"That's all you're going to eat?" she asked after I jimmied

off a leg and carried the rest to the counter. She was pouring another drink, fourth or fifth, I'd lost count.

"It's those damn blood pressure pills," I lied for the second time, covering the bird with Saran Wrap. "They've been killing my appetite."

"Well, I hope you can handle dessert. It's chocolate-pecan-praline pie. I told George to keep his grubby hands off it till you were done."

She cut the pie in four pieces, buried one in Reddi Wip—for George—and called him to join us. The whole house trembled as he broad-jumped down the stairs and bounced into the kitchen, grinning.

"You girls been talking about me again?" He ran his cold hand down my back.

"Cut it *out*," I snapped, changing seats.

"Mama, you love me and you know it." He kissed the top of my head and flattened my hairdo—for which, just the day before, I'd paid my beautician twenty-five dollars.

"George!" cried Barb. "Look what you've done!"

"Sorry about that, Mama," he said, mock-apologetic. "But at least you've *got* hair." He ran a hand over his bald head. "How about we kiss and make up?"

"No more rough stuff, Hon," said Barb, her hand on his arm. "And I *mean* it, George."

"Hot Lips, you've got my word of honor," he grinned, then turned toward me and bowed from the waist. "My apologies, Mama. But with you in the room, my hormones go haywire, honest to God. Probably has something to do with Barb and her headaches every night of the week."

I could have cried, watching Barb wince. She was not just a Kuzo, my daughter, she was a Tulevich, too. With Mum's bad taste in men. And my bad luck in everything else.

*I* called Vicky as soon as I got home. Told her I needed some money to reroof my house. Fifty thousand dollars.

"Look," she said, "I know you're hiding something. It doesn't cost that much. We had ours done for under five."

"It's not just the reroofing—" My voice was starting to shake. "The man says I'll need to have the walls replastered and the kitchen tiles replaced and—"

"Why now? You're not planning on moving to the Sun Belt, are you?"

"No, but I want the house in good shape, so when I die—"

"—Barb and George can move in?" She snorted in disbelief.

"I never said—"

"Jeez, Masha, what's really going on? Who put you up to this? Is Tom opening another shop? He in over his head?"

I didn't answer. Ten seconds passed.

"Look," she said quietly. "I don't have a problem loaning money. I just want to know—and it's a reasonable request— who the real debtor is. Tom's a big boy. Tell him he can call me."

"I never said it was Tom."

"Well, *whoever* it is, you've got my number. Pass it along. And I'm home all day tomorrow."

I gnashed my teeth. Maybe Barb was right about the girl. That she's lived a charmed life on other people's nickels. That she's cheek to jowl with forty, never worked a full-time job in her life. And still a student, of psychology no less.

I've been mad at her since.

※

*A* week after my visit to Barb's, the phone rang again, swear to God, during "Wheel of Fortune." This time it was Tracey, Tom's girlfriend. She was calling from the hospital.

"It's Tom," she said in her smoker's voice. "He's been hurt."

"Hurt?" I sat down. Almost couldn't breathe, remembering Lily.

"Yeah, beat up bad. Some punks walked into his shop last night right after closing and wacked him with a steel pipe. For sixty-seven fucking dollars, you believe it? He's in sad shape, Lady. I'd suggest you get yourself down here. *Now.*"

"It's really that . . . serious?"

"I'll let you be the judge. He ain't dead, if that's what you mean. But he's got a skull fracture front to back, and the doctor's told me that's nothing to sneeze at. They stuck him in the ICU. He's unconscious."

I struggled for words. "You call . . . a priest?"

"For Tom? That old devil? *You* do it. But don't go burying him already, okay?"

I called Father Serge, who said he'd come in an hour, then slipped on my skid-proof boots. I took the bus to the hospital since I didn't trust myself in the underground parking garage, no power steering in the Dodge and concrete supports everywhere.

Tracey met me in reception and dragged me down the hall. There's nothing about her you can say with certainty: her age, her weight, her hair color, whether she likes you or loathes you. She's a scrawny little thing, maybe mid-thirties, with two grown sons. She doesn't own an outfit you can't see her belly button.

"You're sure you're up to this?" she asked, pulling open the ICU door, bright and noisy as Foodland inside. "This isn't for sissies, you know."

"I'll manage, okay?" Maybe not.

"Well, then, have a look at your son." She pointed to a bed in the corner. "And don't say I didn't warn you."

I walked pigeon-toed to Tom's bed. Poor boy looked god-awful, his face a purple plum, his nose flattened, his hands cracked and bruised. I didn't dare touch him; there wasn't an inch of him wasn't swollen. I stumbled back out to the hall, face in my hands, all tears. He'd grown up to disappoint me, sure. But I'd once sung him lullabies, fed him my milk.

Tracey was waiting for me. She's not the physical sort, didn't even squeeze my hand or pat a shoulder. Just offered me my choice of coffee, tea, or bouillon out of the corner machine. On her.

"I'm really sorry, Honey," I whispered, still in tears, blowing the steam off my coffee.

"Why?" She lit a cigarette, shook out the match, dropped it on the floor. "Isn't your fault. Tom let his guard down. He didn't have a piece on him when it happened, you know that? He left his goddamn .44 out in the truck. In his *lunch* box, of all places."

I sighed. "Look, Honey, you want to come stay at my place for a while?" Figured it was the least I could do, cut down on her commute from the trailer park.

She exhaled against the wall. "Why would I want to do that?"

Took me aback. "Well . . . at least . . . till we know . . ."

"Whether Tom's gonna make it, that it? Naw. He will. But if it's a good deed you want to do, fine. How about bringing me some aspirin?" She peeled off a fifty-dollar bill from a half-inch stack and handed it to me.

"That all you want?"

"Yeah. But not cheap stuff that turns to powder in the bottle. Get a brand name, like Anacin. And keep the change."

☙❧

*H*e was unconscious four days. Mrs. Lemack moved in and took charge: polishing my silverware, hanging new wallpaper, and answering the phone. The staff wouldn't let her in the ICU—family members only—which triggered a tantrum. I might have laughed in a different situation, as little as she likes Tom.

It was Mrs. Lemack who answered the phone the fourth day, eight in the morning, Tracey calling to say Tom was awake. The woman thundered upstairs to wake me, whooping like Geronimo.

"It looks like he'll make it," she panted. "Tracey says he was ragging at the nurses first thing to get rid of the IVs and his catheter. They blew him off—it was during their change in shift—so he yanked every one of those doohickeys out by himself."

"That boy *nuts?*" I reached for my crotch, like any person would do who'd ever been catheterized.

"Nuts I don't know about," she chuckled. "But it'll be a coon's age before he'll feel like making water—or whatever he does with his thing."

I was pulling on stirrup pants over my pajamas and asked her to call Barb with the news. It turned out my daughter had customers. She couldn't talk but a minute.

"Mom?" Her voice dropped low once she heard the news. "You talk to Vicky yet?"

I knew it was coming. Sighed. "I did, Sweetie."

"Well?"

"I wish I had good news."

"You're kidding! She won't float you a loan?"

"It's not she *won't* lend the money—" God, I hated defending that girl to my daughter. "It's just she won't do it unless, as she says, I 'reveal the true party.' She didn't buy the story I fed her, that I needed work done on the house."

"You didn't say it was *me* needing the money, did you?"

"Hell, no. She thinks it's Tom. And I don't think she'd lend him a red cent. She says his politics are embarrassing."

"Oh, for God's sake, I thought you and her were supposed to be so tight!"

I stiffened. "Look, Barb, why don't you give her a call?"

"Are you kidding? Her? Not on your *life!*"

"*K*uzo?" asked the lady at reception when I asked for an ICU pass. "Let's see . . ." She clicked away on the keyboard. "Why, he was discharged just an hour ago."

"Discharged?" I cried. "You've got to be mistaken. That boy was in the ICU just this morning."

"You're free to see for yourself," she said, twisting the terminal toward me and tapping at Tom's name with her fingernail.

"Look, I'm his mother. I've *got* to talk to the doctor."

"Have a seat, ma'am, I'll page him."

The doctor answered fifteen minutes later, then kept me waiting another forty-five outside his office door. Man was no spring chicken, big gnarled hands and a wispy goatee.

"Ah, Mrs. Kuzo," he said, pointing to a seat. "Your son. An unfortunate situation."

"Look, I don't know what's happened," I said, sitting ramrod straight. "But you can't tell me that boy was well enough to walk out of here. He looked ready for the undertaker."

"Mrs. Kuzo, I understand perfectly why you're upset." He sat across from me, his forearms resting on his knees. "And in my clinical opinion, your son wasn't suitable for discharge. But I had no other choice. His behavior toward staff was wildly inappropriate—*abusive,* in fact. He actually assaulted one of the nurse's aides. He's had significant frontal lobe trauma, of course, which could explain his behavior, and for which he'll require extensive follow-up, but I would be putting our staff at risk keeping him here. Do you understand?"

I nodded. Goddamn kid was always a troublemaker, whacked on the head or not.

He stood up and opened his door. "Now, if you would be so kind, please stop by the Accounting Office on your way out, would you? They need Mr. Kuzo's address."

That was where I saw the bill. Four days in the ICU, twenty thousand dollars. And my son didn't carry a penny of insurance.

# Allegheny Tunnel

"*W*hy you worked yourself up over that is beyond me," says Mrs. Lemack, both hands in a bag of Nachos. "Alright, your money was gone and you couldn't help them. But your kids shot themselves in the foot. *You* didn't do it."

Criminy. Woman doesn't miss an opportunity to point out the errors in my thinking. Only this time she's wrong. Barb could have kept her house, Tom could have paid the hospital, if only I'd kept my winnings.

"Don't tell me your money would have helped them." She's reading my thoughts, another of her habits. "Even if you'd handed over every cent, you think Barb would've paid off MasterCard? Pshaw! Bought herself a sailboat is more like it. And Tom would've spent it on guns. Tell me I'm wrong."

"I'm not saying you're wrong," I bristle. "Only how come you're always so sure of yourself?"

"I know your kids. Period."

"Mrs. Lemack," I suck in my breath, "you don't know from shit."

"Maybe," she laughs. "But haven't you noticed Barb and Tom survived? And *without* your help?"

I roll my eyes. "Well, I'm so glad *you've* got everything figured out. Really I am."

"Now, now, Mrs. Kuzo, why start fighting?" She crumples the Nacho bag, then lets out a puppy yelp. "Hey, Girl, see that sign? One more mile to the tunnel, hot dog! You mind holding my sunglasses?"

I take them from her—red-and-white-striped frames—and hunker down in my seat. I hate tunnels. Figure the ceiling's about to collapse, or I'll choke on exhaust. Same doesn't go for my friend. She's tooting her horn as we enter and tailgating so close I can read the time on the digital clock in the car dead ahead. At least she's stopped talking.

⊕

*O*nce we're back in the sunlight, I throw a hanky over my face and hold it in place with my sunglasses. Pretend to be dozing, one way of shutting her out. I still can't help chewing on what she just said. That Tom and Barb are grown-ups now. That I'm not to blame for their problems.

Vicky, on the other hand, wouldn't agree. Her head is bulging with ideas she's learned in psychology courses or between the sheets with professors. She repeats every one in my kitchen like Gospel.

"*Surely* you agree parents are responsible for what their children become, don't you, Masha?" The girl was crowding up against me while I fried onions for stew. She'd just finished her first term in graduate school and had all the answers at last. Her and Mrs. Lemack. Two experts.

"Think about it, Masha," she was saying, even after I switched on the radio. "Parents teach us values—love, loyalty, honesty, to name a few—and adaptive behaviors, like how to listen, how to express anger, how to deal with frustration, and so on and so forth. If they're good parents, that is. Not that there's any abundance of *them*."

"Seems you turned out good enough," I grunted as the oil started smoking. She was rubbing my nerves raw, given that Tom was due in court next day. He'd assaulted a deadbeat customer.

"Wrong. I'm *not* okay," she said. "I've got this recurring nightmare that if people really knew what I was like, they'd run the other direction. That's why I've gotten pretty skillful—" she smiled— "with putting up façades."

"Putting up *what?*"

"Façades. You know, acting in ways that are pleasing to others. That aren't necessarily pleasing to the actor."

I felt like asking her to put on one of those façades right then. And start talking about something else, like the Super Bowl or Princess Di.

"Annie was the same way," she said, rearranging the magnets on my fridge. "She had the lowest self-esteem I've ever seen." I knew she'd get round to her mom. Always does. And I still can't abide the girl using her mother's first name. "Of course, part of her problem was generational. I mean, women from that era weren't supposed to speak up. That's why you're so amazing."

"Your mom was a good person," I said, turning the onions in the pan, my blood as hot as the oil. "And a good mother."

"Look, I'm not passing judgment," she bristled. "I'm only *saying* she modeled certain behaviors. And that you modeled others. More adaptive ones, actually."

I grit my teeth. "I never 'modeled' nothing for no one, and

anybody who'd follow my example needs their head examined. Who do you think I am? Mother Teresa?"

❀

$\mathcal{S}$o parents teach us everything, she says. Or should, if they're any good. It's true, I learned a lot from Mum. But it wasn't the usual instruction.

"Don't trust anybody," she'd lecture. "People'll just kick you in the teeth. And kick you again once you're down."

Still, Mum had her loyalties. Her best friend was her father, my Granddaddy. A scoundrel, she called him—not how I describe people I admire—but Mum had her own point of view. She never got tired of telling his story. How back in the old country he'd gambled and drank and dueled, knocked up a half-dozen girls, and stole money to pay passage to America.

I thought the old man was crazy. He loved cats, hated people. Stuffed strays in his pockets, whistling, on his way home from the mill. I grew up with cats everywhere, hissing from windowsills and the backs of toilets. He fed them fresh chicken while the rest of us ate borscht.

"That fucking bastard," whispered Nicky the morning Granddaddy boxed his ears for stepping on a cat's tail, which sent it shooting up a lace curtain. "Someone oughta whip his ass."

Not Mum. So Nicky gave in kind. Nighttimes he started stuffing cats in a pillowcase, then crushing them in the street with rocks. The screeching woke Granddaddy one night. Old man hoofed downstairs, buttoning his nightshirt, and caught Nicky in the act. He beat the kid unconscious and left him lying face down between two parked cars, his nose smashed so flat it sat cockeyed the rest of his life. Mum didn't say a word.

Of course, back then, no one knew Nicky never left a score unsettled.

*I*t's true I'm not Mother Teresa. Or even a good mother. Ask my children, they'll give you an earful. We've never been friends, not for want of me trying. They left me standing in my kitchen a long, long time ago.

It was Barb who broke my heart. I loved that girl the same as I'd loved Lily. She slept in our bed until she was seven, me kissing each damp little ringlet, and praying to God not to harm her—as He'd harmed my little sister.

I guess He heard my prayers; it's true she's never been hurt. Still, I lost the girl in other ways. She grew up quiet. Sullen. Cold. I didn't understand the thousand nasty names I read in her face. There were times I wished she'd just say them.

"It's not her way," said Mrs. Lemack. "That kid would rather sulk. And she's missing one of life's bonuses—prize-fights—ain't that a pity? Why don't you pick her apart and clear the air?"

Worst advice I ever took. I cut her down next morning over her appearance. She'd ruined it with war paint.

"What's the matter with you, Honey?" I said as she dressed for school. "A girl as pretty as you doesn't need all that crap on her face. Don't you know you're beautiful already?"

She wouldn't answer, kept painting her eyelashes blue.

"I'm *trying* to talk to you!"

She shrugged, blotted her lipstick, shaved her eyebrow with a razor. I counted to ten.

"Look, Barb, let me get a washcloth, okay?"

She scowled at me in the mirror without turning around. "This is my face, and I'll do with it what *I* want."

I couldn't help thinking of Mum. Said the one thing I'd vowed never to say to my daughter. "*Tramps* is what they call girls done up like that. You want people calling you names?"

She slapped on some orange blossom cologne, straightened her falsies, and stood up to leave. "Yeah. Better a tramp than a Kuzo."

*I*'ll grant Mum had her tragedies. She lost Dad when she was twenty-one—mill explosion—which threw her in a tailspin. She had me and Nicky to feed, an empty bed, and bills to pay.

Back then, widows didn't sue the mill. They waited for the company accident relief check—eighteen months of a man's wages, plus an extra ten percent if he'd left children—and budgeted best they could. Mr. Kurtyak, Dad's friend, offered to help her manage the money. But Mum cashed the check and bought herself pearls, silk stockings, and furs, then traipsed into church in her finery. Hussy, the ladies sneered. Not that Mum cared.

But the rest of us did, for different reasons. With the money gone, there was only Granddaddy's income—most of which went to feeding his cats—and whatever Mr. Kurtyak gave us. Those were a lean few years. We moved to a basement flat near the mill, no toilet, no sink, no privacy. Shared a courtyard privy with twenty-four people, handkerchiefs to our noses, and pumped water from an outdoor hydrant. Mum sold her bedroom set so we could eat, the one Dad had bought before they married, beautiful bird's-eye maple. She sent us to school in patched clothes without undershirts or socks. And took in boarders to help pay the rent, two Slovaks who slept in shifts on a little cot near the stove.

"I know how to economize, believe me," she'd boast. "We lived in that hellhole three years, and I never pawned my wardrobe. You think you could do so well?"

<hr/>

"*Of* course you're not Mother Teresa," said Vicky, as I tossed a pound of ground chuck in with the onions. "No one's that goody-goody. She's a media creation."

I never gave Mother Teresa much thought, not half as much as Vicky, who was routing through a drawer for a bottle opener. "What makes you *you*, Masha," she said, pushing the hair out of her eyes, "is that you wear your warts and don't apologize. You're real. You're . . . *ballsy*." I watched her pop the cap off the beer, drink it straight from the bottle, like a man. Ballsy.

"Huh-uh," I said. "Not compared to your Grandmother. Now there was a lady who didn't take jackshit off anybody, not even—"

"Yeah, I've heard about that," she interrupted. "Family legend. Why's it always someone dead that seems to have the answers?"

"Lordy, what you don't know," I said angrily. "She *didn't* have the answers. And she made plenty of mistakes."

"Well," she said, kicking the drawer shut with her foot. "It sounds like she had chutzpah at least. Too bad Annie didn't get any."

"Look, Kiddo." I touched her elbow. "Do me a favor? Lay off your mom? The dead can't defend themselves."

She took a long, hard pull on her beer and stared straight at me. "Neither," she sniffed, "can the living."

I shuddered and salted the meat. And wondered if she knew I'd killed Lily.

🍥

*I*t was really Prohibition that saved us, not Mum's budgeting skills. She formed a partnership with Granddaddy that got her name up in lights.

She'd always made hooch for the old man, and not from the goodness of her heart. It was strictly economics. Her moonshine was strong enough to keep him out of the taverns and keep his money in her pockets. But once the town went dry, she built a clientele. And got Granddaddy to deliver the juice in pockets she sewed inside his coat.

The business made Mum rich. After Annie and Lily were born, she bought the brick house in Braddock, three stories, indoor plumbing, leaded-glass windows hung with flower boxes. Our neighbors were English and Irish and German— prosperous families who'd been in America for years, and who owned small businesses. They'd hire Hunkies to run their machines and muck up their messes.

It made me uneasy, moving next door to Americans. I preferred living with our people, no matter what they thought of us. Said so to Mum.

"Go ahead, stay here!" She was forcing the latches on an overstuffed suitcase. "But if you think I'm going to spend my whole life in this alley, you're crazy. I won't have nobody calling me bumpkin anymore!"

She was mistaken. The new neighbors called her that and worse. They'd drive by in fancy cars, look the other way as if she was covered with boils. This ruffled Mum's feathers. She dressed up one Sunday and dragged me door to door, ringing bells and banging knockers and introducing herself in her choppy English. The ladies stood behind their screens, hands on their children's shoulders, lips pursed, wouldn't ask us in. After that, whenever they'd see me or Nicky playing tag with their kids, one by one they'd call Susy or Margaret or Chuckie indoors.

$\mathcal{E}$xcept for Mrs. Sonnenschein, three doors down. She talked to us plenty, at least for a while. Truth was the Sonnen-scheins—like us—weren't really American. Difference was, they were Jews.

I knew their daughter Ida from school. The girl was shaped like a spider, her big round midsection attached to skinny little arms and legs that were always in motion. She'd pass gas right in class, eyes on the ceiling, whistling. Everyone laughed, but nobody liked her. It didn't matter her family owned the biggest clothing store in Braddock.

After Lily died, she invited me to her house once. She

showed off her dolls, dozens of them, each with a miniature steamer trunk full of clothes. Her mother called us to the kitchen for cookies, pulled up a chair, and asked me about my family. I knew to keep quiet about Mum's line of business— which wasn't easy, as nosy as Mrs. Sonnenschein seemed.

Next day, the lady knocked on our door and asked Mum point-blank if I'd like to earn money. She needed kitchen help Friday evenings and half-day Saturdays, Jewish Sabbath. In her opinion, I'd be perfect for the job. "A well-brought-up young lady," she called me, patting my head.

"Let me think about it, Mrs. Sonnenschein," Mum said, crossing her arms on her chest. "Masha's only eleven."

"You do that," said the woman, pushing aside cats on her way out the door. "I can pay her thirty cents a week, but the offer's only open till tomorrow. Good day, Mrs. Tulevich."

Mum turned to me frowning, first time I saw her hesitate where there was money to be made. She told me straight out she didn't like Jews. That they'd work me to death, call me names, rob me blind.

This was all new to me. "I don't care," I said. "I want the money. Please, Mum!"

She looked me up and down half a minute, rolled her eyes and smirked. "I guess now you're getting a shape you want money for clothes, that it?"

I blushed.

"Well, you *do* want the boys looking at you, don't you?"

"Mum . . ." Mothers weren't supposed to talk like that.

"Well, suit yourself," she yawned. "You can start Friday if you want. Go out, buy yourself a brassiere. But don't tell me I didn't warn you about those people."

She was right that they worked me hard. I'd cook the meals and serve the family, even Ida, who'd slouch in her seat while I'd ladle her soup. That's when she'd fart on purpose and get her little brothers snickering. After the meal, I'd wash dishes, polish crystal, scrub floors. Then head to the bathroom with a fresh roll of toilet paper, cut it into twelve-inch strips and leave them in a bag next to the hopper, just as I'd been instructed. Seems the family wouldn't tear paper on those days.

But as hard as I worked, I liked going there, and mostly on account of Uncle Max. He was Mrs. Sonnenschein's uncle, twice her age, and stuck in a wheelchair in the kitchen. He'd strum a guitar while I polished the silver, croaking along like a frog in a tree, or read me the comics, changing his voice with each character until I'd laugh. I'd heard about his illnesses from Ida, how he'd lost two chambers of his heart and a leg to diabetes. Surprised me that he never complained. Like me, he didn't care for beets or peas or cats or Mrs. Sonnenschein. Whenever she'd march through the kitchen, all haughty, he'd wink my direction, then make sourpuss faces behind her back, hands on his hips. Saturday evenings, just before I'd leave, he'd slip me a quarter, pat my head, and make me promise I'd come back next week. *Bubula*, he called me. I wished to God he was my granddaddy.

*M*um's operation kept growing. She'd moved her still from the basement flat to the Braddock house and kept the fires burning. She never missed a mortgage payment, bought her China silk rug, and repurchased her bedroom set. By then, the business had grown so big she needed full-time help. She hired Nicky to run bottles on his bicycle, just like a paper route, only better, with a whopping 10 percent commission.

"Where'd you get all that money?" I whispered, watching him count quarters on the kitchen table.

"None of your damn business," he said, scooping his coins into a handkerchief and pushing me aside.

I made it my business. Trailed him for weeks as he peddled his wares, hiding behind billboards and fire hydrants and parked cars. I was fifty feet to his rear the day the cops chased him down a ditch. Must have been five on his tail, swinging billy clubs. I didn't stay to watch. Scrambled home fast as I could.

"Cops've grabbed Nicky!" I screamed to Mum as she shucked corn on the porch. She didn't ask questions, just called Granddaddy, then rushed down to the basement taking three steps at a time. I watched her bust up the still with a sledgehammer, then pass the parts through a window to Granddaddy outside. He loaded it all on a wheelbarrow, then took off running down the alley. By the time the cops knocked on our door, the basement was whistle-clean, Mum perfumed and powdered, Granddaddy reading an English newspaper, right side up. I'd been instructed to serve our company lemonade and keep my mouth shut.

Of course, they couldn't bust her. It was Nicky who took the heat. Kid never ratted on Mum, which would have made things easier for him. The juvenile judge played hardball, too, sentenced him to eighteen months in reform school. That's where he learned to throw punches as nasty as Granddaddy's. And a helluva lot more.

Mum lost her nerve after that, cut back her business by half, and invested her cash. She took in some boarders again, young fellows, who'd stare at me dirty during dinner.

And she never thanked me, not once, for saving her.


*T*he Sonnenscheins finally fired me, but it had nothing to do with my work. It had to do, like so many things, with Mum. The axe fell the week of Annie's first communion. The kid needed a pretty white dress.

"Let's go over to Sonnenschein's store," Mum said to me brightly. "Maybe I'll get a good price since you work for them."

"I wouldn't count on it," I mumbled.

"We'll see about *that*. Now go get your coat."

I took my time. I hated shopping with Mum. She haggled hard, pitching scenes so embarrassing the clerk would give her whatever price she wanted just to get her fanny out the door. Afterward, she'd strut around in her purchases, boasting of her skills to whoever would listen. Shamed me to death.

That afternoon, Mrs. Sonnenschein was working the store. She was smartly dressed, in purple silk and patent-leather pumps. "Why, good afternoon, Mrs. Tulevich," she said, all fakey, in perfect English. "How may I help you?"

"Good afternoon yourself," said Mum, pulling off her gloves. "How about showing me your communion dresses? And nothing too fancy. She's only going to wear it once." She nodded Annie's direction.

"Of course." Mrs. Sonnenschein rustled in the back and returned with a dozen starched white dresses, laid them out, side by side, on a glass display case of handbags. They were beautiful, all of them, yards of lace and tulle and satin. She beckoned Annie to the counter and smiled.

"This all you got?" asked Mum, shaking out the plainest of the lot and holding it up. It was still pretty, with a big round collar and perfect puffed sleeves.

"Oh, Mum," breathed Annie, reaching up to touch it with hands that were still dimpled. "Can I hold it up against me in the mirror? Can I? Please?"

"Of course you can, Honey," said Mrs. Sonnenschein, coming out from behind the display case and leading Annie by the hand. "The mirror's right over here."

"Not so fast," said Mum, touching Mrs. Sonnenschein's elbow. I started to tremble. "First, before she gets all excited—" nodding again at Annie—"how *much?*"

"Let's see," said Mrs. Sonnenschein, feeling the edge of the hem for a price tag. "This one's seven fifty."

"What?" boomed Mum. "Seven fifty? Too much!"

"Look, Mum, we can go somewhere else," I said, stepping between her and my boss. But Mum pushed me aside and walked up to the woman.

"I'll give you a buck seventy-five, Mrs. Sonnenschein. That's my best price."

"Sorry," said Mrs. Sonnenschein, folding the dress in half over her stomach. "That's not how we do business. But mark my words, Mrs. Tulevich, you're getting a steal at seven fifty."

"A steal?" Mum snatched the dress and did what I'd seen her do a hundred times before, search for some real or imagined defect. As usual, she found one.

"Seven fifty for a dress with crooked seams? And look how it bunches up around the . . . the . . ." Mum couldn't think of the English word, nudged me for assistance.

"*Armhole?*" Mrs. Sonnenschein sneered.

"*Yeah,* armhole. This dress ain't no steal. You should be ashamed of yourself."

Mrs. Sonnenschein didn't answer, just piled the dresses over her arm and headed for the back. I could see she'd had experience with ladies of Mum's type.

"I'm not leaving until you give me the price it's worth," Mum hollered after her. Then she threw her handbag on the counter and leaned against it. Stood there an hour making evil eyes at my boss.

"Excuse me, Mrs. Tulevich," Mrs. Sonnenschein said when it got to be closing time. "But I'm going to have to ask you to leave."

"You deaf? I told you I'd *leave* when you give me the dress. Buck seventy-five."

A few customers tittered. I made eye contact with my boss. The woman was furious, and I knew High Noon had come.

"Get out!" Mrs. Sonnenschein shrieked. "And don't come here again, you hear me? And I don't want *her*"—pointing at me—"in my house again. *Ever.*"

Mum picked up her handbag, real deliberate, pulled on her gloves, and grabbed our hands. She pushed us ahead of her out the front door, but not before she'd lifted her foot and kicked down a rack of women's hats.

I hated her for that. She'd had the last word, but she'd lost me my job. I apologized at school next day to Ida, begged her to tell Uncle Max that I missed him and hoped I could visit him sometime. Of course, I never did. And till this day I don't know if he ever got the message.

*A*nnie took her communion in a pale blue dress that had been a hand-me-down from a cousin. I'd been wearing it to church for a year, and even on me the fit was lousy. The bodice was fitted with pointy darts that made me blush. I'd cover them the best I could with a gray cardigan sweater that was missing half its buttons and unraveling at the wrists.

"We'll cut the dress down, that's all," said Mum, sharpening scissors on a flat stone. I shuddered. Mum was no seamstress. Took her five minutes just threading a needle, let alone altering a whole garment.

"But it's not white!" cried Annie. "I'm supposed to have a *white* dress. The deacon said so."

Mum stopped midstream as she snipped at the hem. Glared at Annie, then returned to her work. "This is what you're going to wear. You don't like it? Then stay home! This dress has been enough of a nuisance."

Annie struggled not to cry. "But Mum, everyone'll laugh at me. All the other girls have white dresses."

"Thumb your nose at them," shrugged Mum. "What do they know?"

"Maybe we could bleach it white," I said hopefully.

"Damn!" Mum shouted. She'd just pricked her finger, then thrown the dress down on the bed. "Well, Kids, you do it yourselves. I'm not sticking *my* hands in Clorox."

So Annie and I stood shoulder to shoulder at the kitchen sink, soaking the dress in bleach. We ruined the fabric. Turned it steel gray.

"I can't wear that!" wailed Annie. "It looks even worse!"

"Just wear my sweater over it, like I do," I said miserably. "Nobody'll notice."

She did. Marched down the aisle of the church in those tatters, carrying a long white candle, a wreath of daisies in her hair, tears skipping down her face.

"Poor thing," I heard a woman whispering, motioning toward Annie. "Who'd stick a kid in rags like that?"

❀

"*D*on't you think the stew will be enough?" asked Vicky as I breaded half a dozen pork chops. "It's just for you and me, right?"

"You can take home whatever we don't eat," I said stiffly, dumping oil in my electric fry pan.

"Look, Masha, I think we need to talk. You're mad at me, aren't you?"

"You want ice tea with your meal?"

"It's what I said about Annie that's bugging you!" she cried. "Why's it anytime I breathe a word about her, you get upset?"

I opened the silverware drawer. "How about you set the table?"

"Alright, have it your way, then—my mother *was* a good person. Too good, maybe." Her face was so close I could smell her beer breath. "She put everyone else in front of her. Don't you remember how she wouldn't even buy herself new clothes?"

Of course I remembered. Her closet was full of limp dresses, worn jeans, and scruffed shoes she'd bought at yard sales and thrift shops. She never asked her husband for a nickel.

"She even bought her underwear secondhand, did you know that?" whispered Vicky. "She had nightgowns and panties she'd got at a peddler's fair for a quarter a piece. And then I wonder where *I* got my low self-esteem!"

*M*um, in addition to being well-built and well-to-do, was now well-respected—at least in certain circles. She owned a big house, a fashionable wardrobe, and tasteful furniture. For the first time since Dad died, men came to our house talking marriage.

I remember them, dozens, shaven and spit-shined and stuffed in a suit. They always showed up carrying flowers or chocolates.

"They were nothing but cons," Mum scoffed, years later, when I asked why she bounced all those boys. "You think I couldn't see the dollar signs in their eyes? They'd sit in my parlor, salivating over my furniture and my China silk rug. Love? They wanted my *money*, was all. You think I was going to let them in the same bed I shared with your Daddy? Tell me what to do? Hell, no. I was my own boss!"

She didn't remarry for years. Not that her bed was ever empty. Her boyfriends came and went, men from church, neighbors, shopkeepers. And most of all, her boarders.

Her longest romance was with Vlado, a Serb who came to live with us the year I turned fourteen. He spoke pidgin English and held a hand-rolled cigarette between his sticky lips. Daytime he worked as a puddler at the mill; evenings he sat on our porch whittling wood figurines. The man had green eyes like a tomcat and a tangle of hair at his throat. He frightened me.

Not Mum. Afternoons, I'd hear them shaking the house while I sat on my bed doing homework. I wasn't a good student and couldn't even make it through *Ivanhoe*. Poor concentration, said my teachers, who knew nothing about the distractions at home. In the room above mine, to be exact.

There were times at dinner I'd look up and lock eyes with him. I'd just got my period and wasn't altogether sure how babies were made. But something about his smile had to do with babies, at least how they got in your belly. He'd run his hand along my thigh, licking his lips as I'd clear away the dishes. I started avoiding him. Which only seemed to perk up his interest.

One afternoon I was carrying a basket of laundry upstairs. Ran into the man halfway. Smelled his damp skin next to mine.

"You want help?" he smiled, laying his hand on the bannister, so I couldn't get past.

I wouldn't look at him, just shook my head and pushed against his arm with the basket. He laughed and snatched it from my hands, then pulled me toward him. But I was wiry, thank God; I rotated right out of his grasp, bounded down the steps like a deer, two at a time, and headed straight to Mum's room. She'd just had her bath. Stood in a cloud of talcum powder, wearing only her wedding ring.

"Mum . . ."

"What?" She shook out her garter belt irritably and struggled getting into it.

"Vlado . . .Vlado just tried to . . . kiss me. I *think*."

She stopped what she was doing. "Kiss you? Where?"

I blushed. "On the steps, I was going upstairs with the laundry—"

"On the mouth?"

"Well, not really, but I think he would have . . . if I'd let him."

Her voice turned icy. "Don't come running to *me* with your stupid stories."

I was speechless, then indignant. "Mum . . . I'm telling the truth!"

"So?" She hooked the garter belt over her hips and snapped on silk stockings. "When you live in *my* house, you look out for yourself. Now leave me alone."

But he wouldn't leave *me* alone. He knocked softly at my door every night, whispering through the keyhole. *Masha. Masha. Masha.* Sometimes it lasted for hours. I kept him out with a chair propped under the doorknob and told Annie it was only Nicky trying to scare us. Meanwhile, Mum and him rocked and groaned and grunted upstairs every afternoon.

I couldn't tell anyone, not even Mrs. Lemack, shamed as I was. So I stayed outdoors for hours walking the streets of Braddock. The same streets Mum and Dad had strolled while they courted, her head on his shoulder, planning their future.

❀

"Do you remember Vlado?" Annie asked, flat on her back in a shapeless hospital gown. It was February, the middle of a blizzard, the last winter of her life. The building was deserted, the staff home calling in sick.

"Of course I remember him," I frowned, taking her chilly hands between my warm ones. "Why?"

"No good reason. I had a dream about him last night. He was sitting on the edge of my bed."

I stiffened and crossed myself. Dreams are bad luck.

"You know," she said, "after you and Al got married, maybe even for a while before, he'd been following me around and touching me and saying filthy things."

"That bastard!" I thumped her bedside table and rattled a can of Coke. "He did the *same* damn thing to me."

She slid up on her elbows, stared me dead straight in the eyes. "Really? The *exact* same thing?"

"God, yes. I'll bet you forgot how I'd stick the chair under the doorknob when we'd go to bed. I told you it was to keep Nicky out, remember? You'd want to get out to go potty, but I'd make you hold it till morning. And you were such a good kid! You'd go back to sleep with your knees tucked up under your chin, and you never wet the bed, not once."

"That's why the chair was there? On account of Vlado?"

"Of course."

"And that kept him out? Just the chair?"

"Yes. How did *you* manage?"

She slid back down on the bed, staring at the ceiling. "I didn't."

⚈

"*Y*ou know we're nearly halfway there?" says Mrs. Lemack, glancing at her watch. "How's the food holding out?"

"Just fine," I grumble without checking.

"Speaking of food . . . look, Mrs. Kuzo, I've got a favor to ask. How about we at least stop at Vicky's for dinner?"

I'm fit to be tied. "We've *been* through that already, ma'am. The answer's *no.*"

"We don't need to eat there," she says hurriedly. "I know you hate the swill those Hindus cook. So why not let's just ask her out, okay? Denny's or somewhere? I'll pay, promise."

I ignore the woman. Peel myself a spotty banana, the one I was saving for Barb in my fridge.

"You haven't got me fooled, Mrs. Kuzo," she says. "You're just sulking because Vicky wouldn't loan you the money. And you're blaming *her* about what happened to Barb, that it?"

I peel Barb's grapefruit next. It's moldy. Toss it inside the bag we're using for trash.

"Haven't you learned to forgive anybody?" she asks.

# Breezewood

*An* hour down the road, she takes the Breezewood exit. It's been years since I've stopped here. Nothing's changed: same billboards in your face for the hundred-odd motels and smorgasbords and breakfasts with bottomless coffee cups. But none of the ads interest Mrs. Lemack, who's only looking for a full-service station. She flat refuses to pump her own gas and won't hear any arguments.

"If you think I'm going to stand out there, bent over, with my fat old fanny hanging out, you're wrong, Girl," she says. "It's worth it to spend a little extra money to keep my dignity."

I don't have much patience with this. "You'd think you were the only wide bottom up and down this road! Here, just pull in the next self-service, and *I'll* do the honors."

"You sit tight, Mrs. Kuzo. You're my guest, remember?"

Maybe I'm too critical. Her habits could be worse. Like Barb's, who keeps her air conditioner running even the two weeks she spends at the shore. Says she hates coming home to a hot house, can't stand sticky armpits, and she'll spend her money as she pleases. So I hang loose and pull out a crossword puzzle.

It doesn't take my friend long to find what she's looking for, an empty Gulf station with a kid out front sudsing over oil slicks. He couldn't be more than eighteen, black eyebrows, bronze skin, and big hands. Good-looking.

"Fill her up, ma'am?" he asks, as she lowers her push-button window.

"*Any*time!" she giggles, one hand to her mouth like a teen-ager covering braces.

"Check the oil?"

"I've still got plenty," she leers. "But go ahead, Kiddo, poke around a little. I dare you."

I shake my head without looking at her. "Damn, if you're not making a fool of yourself."

"Well, who can blame me? That kid's a hunk! Go on, don't be shy, take a look. I swear, he's a dead ringer for Nicky, no?"

I shrug, wrack my brains for a five-letter word for serendipitous and hope she'll take the hint I'm not fixed for conversation.

She doesn't. "Did you know I dreamt about that very man last night?"

"You did?" I'm not interested. Or surprised, either. Sure wish I owned a dictionary.

"Yes'm. Of course, not about the way he was after the war—like he was in high school. You remember. Cute kid."

Nicky never seemed cute to me. Rotten is more like it, all the things he did to Annie. But Mrs. Lemack never lets an opportunity slip to flap her trap about him.

"He was the very first boy to ever heat up my pants, years

before the Italians. You know that?" The Italians, of course, were her first two husbands. Hoodlums.

"Yeah," I sigh. "You've told me. A few times."

"Well, *Nicky* never knew. He didn't take the least notice of me no matter how tight I sewed my clothes. And all he'd have had to do was crook his little finger, and I'd have come crawling. The hell with that bullshit they told us in Sunday school about keeping your knees together."

I groan. "You were that lovesick?"

"Yes, indeedy. That's why it shocked the living daylights out of me when I saw who—*what*—he ended up marrying," she says, shuddering. "A movie star like him? Even with that broken nose? Lordy! I swear that broad was older than your mum. You ever hear from her?"

I hadn't, not since he died. She'd written to tell me how much she liked the silk flowers I'd sent to his funeral, that she'd decided to keep the arrangement sitting on top of her TV, in front of the rabbit ears.

"I'll bet you dollars for doughnuts she didn't last a day longer than him," says Mrs. Lemack, pushing up her sleeves. "She already had her foot on a banana peel the day they got married. What was her name, anyhow?"

"Phyllis."

"*Phyllis*. Of course." She lifts the tip of her nose with an index finger and rolls her eyes. "Not one of our people, if I recall."

No. Phyllis was American through and through, Scottish ancestry, had her house hung with plaid drapes and matching plaid slipcovers on her loveseat. She'd traced her family back to the War of 1812, the year they'd come to America tooting bagpipes. When I visited her and Nicky in Florida, she showed me a brass plaque to prove her pedigree and spit-polished it before my very eyes. Her china cabinets bulged with heirloom silver, beautiful stuff. Nothing like that silverplate tea service

I'd got with S&H green stamps for Barb and George's wedding gift, the one they tried to unload at a yard sale.

"Well, there are marriages, and then there are marriages," says Mrs. Lemack, fluttering her eyelids at the kid as he washes the windshield. "But I'll never figure that one out."

It wasn't a mystery to me. My brother was a snob. He even changed his name—at Phyllis's suggestion—to John McAllister. That had been her Granddad's name, some general who'd fought in the Civil War, Confederate side, shot through the hip, so the story went. Like Nicky, he'd limped his way through the rest of his unshaven life with a fifth in hand, cursing everybody.

Phyllis was a good fifteen years older than Nicky, probably mid-forties at the time they were married. She'd been widowed twice, divorced twice. After their honeymoon, Nicky brought her to Braddock for a few days, parading her up and down the streets like she was some kind of high-stakes racehorse. They didn't visit me. But Mum passed on that the bride had crimped hair, a broad back porch, and a triple chin that covered her collar. Phyllis blamed it, giggling, on her Georgia peach pies, which must have been damn delicious. Mum said even Nicky was growing a gut, his shirt buttons working overtime.

"That old gal wasn't in my dream, you can be sure of that," Mrs. Lemack says, coating her lips with cherry-flavored Chapstick. "Just him and me. I swear we were crossing a creek together, holding hands."

Pretty corny. Brings to mind the cover of one of those Harlequin romances I keep on my bedside table, right next to the Vicks inhaler and my can of mace. Barb laughs at me for reading them—says they're for dopey teenagers or people who read with their finger. A lot she knows. Last time I visited her, she sat me in front of the TV so she could finish some book and kept putting up her hand anytime I'd try to say something. She answered the doorbell, though—thought it was UPS with lingerie. Got her ears chewed off by Jehovah's Witnesses instead, three of them in pleated skirts and Peter Pan collars, all total fifteen minutes. I wasn't going to rescue her, but I did take the opportunity to peek through her book. Turned out to be some hokum about a photographer bedding this horny farm wife, then the two of them pining away for each other another hundred years, dry humping their pillows. Judas Priest.

"I was holding my high heels in one hand, hanging on to your brother with the other," my friend giggles, paying the kid for the gas. "Gives me a thrill just thinking about it."

"Yeah, yeah. Now are you ready to hit the road?"

"Sure, Doll." She counts the change. "Unless this young man invites me over *there.*"

She's talking about a little motor court across the street. The Snow White Cottages, with life-size ceramic figures out front of Dopey and Sneezey and Drooley and Dumbass.

$\mathcal{N}$icky was Mum's first live birth. She'd had three miscarriages and a stillborn girl before him, and had long since given up on babies. Nicky was born hog-healthy. She kept him in her bed a full year, turning in her sleep to nurse him. There was never enough milk.

He grew up in the streets. Mum turned him out the day he was four years old—a note pinned to his jacket with his name and address—and threatened to bust his butt if he came back before sundown. She had me and Granddaddy and her boarders to take care of and didn't want a toddler running underfoot, sticking hairpins in sockets.

He started school, like most Hunkies, without a lick of English. Kid learned a few words on the playground that he'd shout to get the teacher's attention. *Shit. Piss. Suck.* Teachers soaped your mouth for bad words back then, so he'd come home still popping bubbles out his nose. He'd play hooky with his ragamuffin friends and climb huge slag piles alongside the mill or pinch candy from drugstores. The truant officer visited us regularly, shouting Mum down in English she'd pretend not to understand. The very same night, she'd have Granddaddy punish him, using a fat wire scrub brush. But twenty to one, Nicky would play hooky again next day, limping along the alleys, his pants soaked with blood, smoking cigarette butts he found scattered in the leaves.

He and I should have been friends. We weren't. He stole from me what little I had—pennies, rubber balls, jacks—and amused himself with mean pranks. He chased me with dead animals, baby birds he'd snatched from nests or rats he'd caught in traps. Kid even left a live snake inside my dresser drawer, crawling in a stack of folded underpants.

Mum turned her head. Still sets my blood on fire. Nicky would cuff me during dinner, right under her nose, but she never refereed, just picked at her food and read the American newspaper, mouthing each word. There were times, granted, she'd tap his shoulder and ask him to pronounce a word she didn't know. This gave me a few minutes' respite. But then he'd go back to bruising my shins under the table.

Over the years, Nicky backed off. He'd found himself fresh prey—poor Annie—which made me feel even worse. She was seven years younger, just a kid, no defenses, and he treated her a helluva lot worse than me.

And my starry-eyed friend dreams about this guy.

🐚

*O*f course, Mrs. Lemack's always been fool-headed when it comes to men. Freshman year of high school, she started keeping company with her first Italian, Frank Marlucci, a neighborhood tough who worked for a loan shark. Kid's only business expenses were his brass knuckles, a six-inch hunting knife, and a length of thin rope.

Mrs. Lemack's grandmother—old world Russky you'd never see without a hand-strung broom—got wind of the court-ship and locked the girl out of the house. That mean old babushka meant business. She flung my friend's clothes from a second-story window, called her a tramp, and told her to beat it. Italians, back then, were the worst group you could mix with, lower on the ladder than Hunkies.

Mrs. Lemack didn't see things that way. She picked up her clothes, headed for Pittsburgh, and rented a basement room—no windows, no door lock, just arm's length from a privy. She never went back to school. Found a job in a cigar factory stripping stems from tobacco leaves, then left it for a nut-and-bolt factory where the pay was better but the conditions worse. She'd stand on her feet ten hours a day, hands wrapped in rags, screwing nuts under a nonstop drip of stinky fish oil. She couldn't wash it off her skin.

A year later, she left work and married Frank. Catholic ceremony, every one of his kid sisters a flower girl, guests drinking and dancing and backslapping. Next morning, Frank's mama tumbled the newlyweds out of bed, snatched their sheet, and hoofed across the yard to show the bloodstains to the neighbors. My friend charged after her, pleading, then shouting, and wrestled the sheet away. She tore it up for dust cloths.

The marriage lasted a year to the day. The night of their first anniversary, Frank got shot into Swiss cheese by the hoods he worked for. She wailed mighty pitiful at the funeral, dressed in the widow's weeds her mother-in-law sewed for her, which she'd altered to show her cleavage. She swore at the grave she was through with Italians.

I didn't believe her. And sure enough, she took up with another one before she did her next laundry. Sal Tagliatello. A distant cousin of the deceased.

❧

*W*hoever Annie's father was, he'd been a looker. She didn't resemble Mum at all, not that Mum wasn't beautiful. But Annie was a knockout, even by American standards, with blue eyes and creamy skin, not at all like Nicky and me, who were dark as Sicilians. She stood a full head taller than either of us, six feet when she was grown, and topped me by twenty-five pounds. Smart, too, a straight-A student. And back in the days when a Hunky was rare in school choir, she was singing the solos.

Annie never knew she was gorgeous. Boys teased her about her height till she started walking stoop-shouldered, knees bent, knuckles practically dragging on the ground. Things changed when she went off to college, of course. She couldn't stroll across campus without a clump of boys behind her, playing pocket pool or pestering her for dates. She made top of the Dean's List, could have become whatever she wanted. It broke my heart when she threw herself away on Ted.

She never asked about her real father, even though everybody else was interested, seeing how beautiful she was. She'd stand between Mum and Granddaddy in church, towering over them, with every eye on her, every finger pointed her direction. She moved in and out of rooms all her life to the sound of whispering.

$\mathcal{S}$ophomore year in high school, Annie got picked to sing the National Anthem for a school board luncheon. Mum danced a jig in the parlor, arms overhead. She handed my sister a ten-dollar bill with instructions to buy herself shoes.

"And get heels, you hear me?" said Mum. "I don't care *how* tall you are! I want my daughter looking like a lady in front of those big shots."

That afternoon, Annie and I took the trolley to Pittsburgh. We combed every shoe store before we found them, pearl gray, perfect to set off her shapely legs. Size ten and a half.

She kept her new shoes wrapped in tissue and took them out at night, sniffing the leather and sliding them on her bare feet. The girl couldn't hide her excitement. The following

Saturday, she invited three of her choir friends, American girls, to lunch. She wanted to show off her footwear.

That morning, I helped her bake gingerbread, lay the table with Mum's best lace tablecloth, and chase the cats down the cellar. She dressed in a freshly ironed shirtwaist, a hand-me-down from Mum, and the new shoes. She met her friends at the door, lifted her feet for their approval, then invited them into the parlor.

"Where'd you get those big shoes?" Nicky sneered from behind a newspaper. The room got dead quiet. "Never thought they made 'em that big."

"Nicky," I pleaded, "*not* today."

"Must have got them specially made," he scoffed. "Annie'd bust up even the biggest pair in the men's store stuffing those big old duck feet inside!"

I glared at him evil and waved the girls into the dining room.

"Come to think of it, ain't nobody around here with feet that big," he called after us. "I seen them that size on the Swedes. Hey Mash, remember that big lunk that rented the spare room back before she was born?" He'd followed us into the dining room, jingling the change in his pocket. "I'll be damned but his feet weren't the same size! Same yellow hair, too!"

$\mathcal{H}$e lived to humiliate her. I couldn't stop him; Mum wouldn't. So I stood by and watched it all, heart in my mouth.

One day when Annie was home by herself, a punk named Roy Smedwig phoned, looking for Nicky. Annie couldn't get him off the line. He started in with twenty questions—her age, whether or not she had a boyfriend, whether or not she'd meet him in an hour. Got her flustered and stuttering, as young as she was. She told him she had homework and couldn't talk, but she'd be happy to take a message for her brother.

"Sure, Sweetheart," said Roy. "Want to write it down?"

"No, I can remember."

"You sure about that? It's really important."

"Positive."

"Suit yourself." So he gave her his message and hung up.

She delivered it, all innocence, over dinner next day. It was Sunday, everyone eating in the dining room, Mum and Grand-daddy and Vlado and the rest of the boarders. We'd always speak English during that meal. Mum insisted on it; the boarders needed practice. And the discussion was lively, about a murder in Homestead, some German lady who'd strangled her husband. Not that I saw anything funny about it.

"Nicky?" Annie whispered during a lull in the laughter.

He ignored her, washed down his potatoes with beer, and let out a loud belch that got the boarders chuckling.

She tried a little louder. "Nicky . . . I've got a message. Roy called."

"Yeah? So?" he sneered, mouth full of food.

"He wanted me to tell you something . . . *important*." I was starting to sweat.

Nicky swiveled in his chair, lips curled. "And just what the hell could that be?"

She looked down at her plate. "He said . . . he'd like you to—"

"Can't hear!" shouted Vlado, eyeing her breasts.

She raised her voice, cheeks aflame. "He'd *like* you to give him a blow job. When you have a chance."

The room went dead a full thirty seconds. And then all was bedlam, the boarders choking on food and thumping the table and laughing at Nicky. Kid's face turned as red as a beefsteak tomato.

"What's so funny?" Mum shouted over the noise. The men ignored her, then burst into fresh guffaws as Nicky fled the room. She tapped my shoulder and repeated her question. I covered my face in shame.

"Hey there, Mrs. Tulevich," shouted Vlado. "You don't know what's a blow job? *You?* Here, just watch."

He stood up grinning, raised his middle finger and passed it in and out of his mouth, running his tongue over the tip. Mum got the idea fast enough. She tossed a glass of lemonade in his face and chased all the men from the table with a closed fist.

Annie, like Nicky, was long gone. She walked the streets for hours, no coat, weeping. It was midnight when I heard her knock on the bedroom door. I held her under the blankets for a long time, hours maybe, until her skin grew warm and rosy. We didn't talk, never mentioned it to each other, not for years.

Nicky stayed away a couple days, licking his wounds. But when he returned, it was all-out war against Annie.

❀

*H*ard to say which of Mrs. Lemack's first two husbands was worse, Frank or Sal. Sal, of course, had the disadvantage of living longer, which allowed him to kick up more mischief. On the other hand, he fathered Tammy, the light of my friend's life. And Tammy *is* a good kid.

Sal was a plumber. He ran a little basement shop with his brother Tony that turned a nice profit. Tony would take the phone calls—usually hysterical housewives with overflowing toilets—and send over Sal in less than an hour, who'd pretend he didn't understand English. The ladies would throw up their hands, point to the broken fixture, and go back to their kitchens. That's when he'd bust up the plumbing even worse, then fix everything. A few days later the housewife would get a three-digit bill, prepared by Tony, with a careful accounting of all the work done, just to make it seem legit.

The boys got rich. By the time Sal went down on bended knee in front of my friend, he could promise her a honeymoon in Cleveland, her own little row home, and two thousand dollars in the bank. She didn't hesitate. Even offered to help with the business and balance the books, which Tony wouldn't allow.

They were married twenty-five years. He was a crook alright, but I'll grant he didn't beat her or trail other skirts. Problem was the man gambled, without a shred of skill. My friend started following him to card games and dragging him out by the ear whenever his luck took a dive. But they'd no sooner be home in bed, her snoring loud enough to shatter glass, than he'd pull on his pants and head back to lose more.

It was Tammy that changed him. Tamara Angelica Tagliatello, her christening name. Sal swore off his habits the day she came home from the hospital, only happy story ending that I know. By the time she'd cut her first tooth, he'd managed to get his own radio show—"Ask Mr. Plumber"—followed by a live TV show, same name.

I watched his show whenever I was home from work. It was always the same. He'd sit in one chair, this floozy interviewer in the other, her struggling with her bra straps and asking dumb plumbing questions. He'd answer by drawing diagrams on an easel and pulling tools out of a briefcase he kept at his feet. This always involved him getting up and bending over, his backside smack in the camera, blacking out the screen.

❦

*J*ust as Mum predicted, Nicky went to work at the mill as unskilled labor. He never finished high school, and Mum didn't argue. He'd been held back twice, then lost another eighteen months in reform school. And he was nineteen now and itching for money, to add to the greenbacks he'd already stolen.

They put him to work at the blast furnace, same job Dad had when he first came to America. The work paid well, but Nicky didn't last long on account of the heat. He left to drive a milk truck, then bus tables, then sell shoes. He was drinking heavy and spending every cent. One night, he hot-wired a car and drove it nose down off a pier into the Monongahela. The cops brought him home sloshed and shivering, and tossed him on the porch.

The next day, he enlisted in the army. Not that he wanted to be a hero. It was just part of the deal he'd cut with the law, so they wouldn't file charges against him for auto theft.

❧

"*I* damn near cried my eyes out after what happened to him in the War," says Mrs. Lemack, heading back to the turnpike. "One helluva thing to happen to a beautiful boy like that."

He'd stepped on a land mine in Anzio and lost his left leg. Then spent a year in a VA hospital where they fitted him with a wooden leg and a pair of dark glasses to cover his charred eyebrows. He wouldn't see any visitors, not even Mum, who took the train all the way to New York and then stood three days outside his hospital room. Only to find out that Private Tulevich had vanished.

Every time I'd visit Mum after that, she'd start wailing about Nicky, running those big hands through her thin hair and tugging at her pearls. She loved to get herself worked up, not just over him. It embarrassed the daylights out of me watching her at funerals. She'd get handed more hankies than the widow.

But this time Mum wasn't just hysterics; she truly made up her mind to find him. She telephoned his old buddies and visited beer joints, looking for leads. It wasn't hard. Most of his trashy friends were still in Braddock working the mills, got out of the draft same as Al on account of doing defense work. She met up with Roy in an East Pittsburgh speakeasy, lit his cigarette, and explained her problem. It was him who finally slipped her a scrap of paper with Nicky's address on it, but only after she'd bought him a couple rounds of scotch straight up and written him a check for a hundred dollars.

She called me all breathless from a phone booth and told me to meet her at the train station. She and I were going to Chicago. To find Nicky.

"*Chicago?*" I cried.

"That's where he's at. Someplace called Hotel Anaconda."

"Mum, you know I can't just pick up and leave. What about Al and Tom?" Tom was only a toddler.

"Look, I can't do this alone. It's a day out there, a day with Nicky, a day back home. Three days at most. This is your *brother* we're talking about."

She was always so bossy. "Mum, I've got my own responsibilities—"

"Then bring Tom along! And don't worry about Al. Just lay out a couple day's worth of clean underwear. He'll know what to do with them."

An hour later, I was down at the station, Tom at the rear. He'd been sick that day, belching up a foul smell and soiling his pants no sooner than I'd change them. He bawled at the ticket window and wouldn't shush till I'd bought him a globe of pink cotton candy. Which he rubbed straight into his hair.

It was still wartime, and the train was packed with smoking soldiers. I let Mum lead the way down the narrow aisles, cutting a path with her hips and suede handbag. We got to the sleeping car and spread out our luggage on the dirty bedding, leaving a space free for Tom to stretch out and sleep. He wouldn't, little bugger. Kept asking to go to the john.

And the john was where we spent the night, between his flu bug and my bladder, swollen every ten minutes from the cold coffee I kept drinking out of Dixie cups. Mum, meanwhile, kicked off her heels and slept under her beaver-skin coat. She didn't stir till morning. I watched her powder her nose and wink at a soldier struggling with his duffel bag, his Adam's apple bouncing up and down yo-yo style. He found an extra arm to carry her luggage to the curb.

We took a cab to the Hotel Anaconda: a gray brick box, five stories tall, with newspapers stuffed in every broken window, and barely a working lightbulb. There was no furniture in the lobby, just an ash can and a rusted umbrella stand. The floor was linoleum, scruffed and sticky, and you'd trip on the seams as you walked. It was noisy, too, old soldiers everywhere—smoking and quarreling and shooting chipped dice. They all stared when we walked in.

"Ain't anyone working reception today, ladies," snorted an old chinless geezer. "Who's it ya looking for?"

"Any of yuns know Nicky Tulevich?" I shouted.

"Hell, no," answered a voice in the corner. "Ain't nobody here with that kind of Polack name."

This got a few snickers, which Mum ignored. She opened her handbag and took out a picture of Nicky. He was four years younger, posed in dress uniform, and cocky as General MacArthur. I took it from her and held it high above my head. "Anybody recognize this boy?"

They all crowded around us, passed the snapshot from one to the next and back again, covering it with fingerprints. Still, no response.

"You might not recognize him," I said, quieter. "He's missing his left leg now. And maybe he's using another name."

There was some murmuring.

"Look," said Mum, extending her hands, her voice breaking. "Can't you boys help me? I'm his mother. You want me to go to my grave without ever seeing my boy again?"

She got the result she wanted, even before she honked on her hanky. "Yup, he's here alright," said a voice slowly to my left, a southern drawl. "Third floor, end of the hall. But he ain't in right now. Doesn't ever git in before dark."

"You know where we can find him?" I asked.

"Naw, don't nobody knows where he goes. You gals may

as well take a seat. You've got yourself a wait. Let me fetch a couple chairs."

So we sat. Seven hours, passing Tom back and forth, except for the time we spent at the corner luncheonette slurping cold chili. It rained for awhile, then changed to sleet, then snow. We trudged through it all in high heels and bare legs. You couldn't get nylons back then.

But Nicky, as predicted, came back. I knew him immediately, not that he looked anything like I remembered. He resembled the men we'd just talked to—gaunt, unshaven, smelling of body odor and alcohol. But unlike the rest, he walked with a cane.

Mum jumped off her chair, clattered across the linoleum with her arms outstretched, calling his name.

"What the hell? . . ." he blurted, took a few steps backward and collided with the door. By then she had her arms around him, a death grip, wailing, her head burrowed in his chicken chest. That was when he noticed me behind her, Tom on my hip. His glare could burn flesh.

"What the *hell* are you doing here? Huh?"

"We thought . . ." I swallowed. "I mean . . . Mum wanted . . ."

"When I want my goddam family for a visit, *I'll* do the inviting! Who the hell do you think you are, just showing up like this?" He finally pushed Mum off and headed past us toward the staircase. And waved us away with a sweep of his cane as we tried to follow him.


*W*e didn't hear from Nicky another four years. He shocked the living daylights out of Mum one summer afternoon, grinning in her doorway. Hugged her as if there'd never been a nasty word between them, then led her down the steps to the curb, and opened the door of a brand new Ford. Sitting at the wheel was Phyllis, all corkscrew curls and coral lipstick and grins.

"Why Honey," she squealed at Mum. "I'm plumb amazed! John always said his momma was gorgeous, but he didn't do you near justice!"

"John?" said Mum. "Who's John?"

"Honey," laughed Phyllis, "have we got a lot to talk about!" She slipped her arm through Mum's and led her back to the house while Nicky smoked a cigarette, leaning against the hood.

He never came to see me that day, just visited with Mum those few hours and then took his bride for a walk around Braddock. Mum told me he was a new man, that he'd finished high school at night, weaned himself off the bottle, and managed a shoe store in Ft. Lauderdale. Maybe his new wife was nothing to look at, for sure no spring chicken, so there'd never be grandchildren. But what the hell, Phyllis had done the impossible, straightened that rotten kid out. And she had a good job herself; she was a loan officer at a bank.

After that, I started getting Christmas cards with *Mr. and Mrs. John McAllister* engraved on the bottom. Sometimes Phyllis would write a short note, purple ink, in big, loopy letters. Or enclose a snapshot of their dog, a teacup poodle named Bonnie Prince Charlie.

*T*he next time I saw him was in Florida, ten years later, when Al and I drove down on vacation. We were headed for Miami. I asked Al whether he'd mind stopping off and seeing my brother.

"Him? You're *crazy*, Mash. What the hell you want to go sniffing his pant leg for?"

"I'm curious, okay?"

That wasn't good enough for him. "That bastard never did much but kick you in the teeth."

"Yeah, yeah, but Phyllis is nice. She sends me a card every Christmas, don't you remember?"

He shrugged. "Okeydoke. But don't come crying to me when he calls you bad names."

I tried phoning him from a gas station. No answer, which bothered me. I decided to stop by his place anyhow and drop a note in the mail slot—real cheerful and with plenty of exclamation marks—and leave it at that.

He lived on a treeless street in the bottom of a duplex. Out back I spotted an in-ground pool with dead insects afloat in the water. The neighborhood was noisy, thanks to the hum of air conditioners, drippy ones that poked out of every blessed window on the block. That was when I noticed Nicky's units running, too. Maybe he'd got so rich he ran them all the time, same as Barb, liked his place frosty whenever he'd come home from selling shoes.

Then it struck me that maybe he was home, only hadn't heard the phone over the noise. So I rang the doorbell. Once. Twice. Third time he answered.

I saw at once he'd changed, even with the screen door between us. He stood unshaven in a terry cloth bathrobe with his legs—one hairy, one wooden—peeking out underneath. There were little purple veins in his cheeks, just like the ones Mum got on her calves. His boozy breath was the worst part. It stung me he didn't recognize me, but Annie always said alcohol turns your brain to bread dough. She'd spill it down the sink, even the couple drops of Manischewitz I'd serve with the Easter ham.

"Yeah?" he said, rude as a New Yorker.

"It's me, Nicky. Mash." My voice was shaking.

"Mash?" He squinted his bloodshot eyes.

"I'm down here on vacation with Al"—I pointed toward the car—"and I just thought I'd stop by, see how yuns're doing."

He moved closer to me, opened the screen door halfway. I noticed he'd lost most of his hair. "Well *I'll* be damned."

"I was just going to leave a note—see, here it is." I pressed it into his palm. "I didn't expect you'd answer the door."

He unfolded the note and read it. Handed it back, then straightened the cloth belt around his wide waist and glanced at his Timex. "Sorry, but I can't have you come inside right now—the place needs picking up, and Phyllis won't be home for another hour. How about you come back later, huh?"

"Well—sure—I mean, if it's all right."

"Yeah, yeah, it's all right. We can't put you up, though, and Phyllis doesn't do any cooking, so eat before you come, okay?"

"What time?" I asked awkwardly.

"Oh, anytime's fine after seven. She'll be home from work by then."

So back we drove that evening, Al cursing in my ear. It was Phyllis who greeted us this time, dressed in a paisley caftan and gold sandals. Three inches of wrinkled cleavage. And a Polaroid camera in hand.

"Well, come on in!" she gushed. "I'm so excited y'all are here! Heavens, to think for all the years me and John've been married, we've never met! But they say it's never too late to start new friendships. What would you two like to drink?"

"Ice water's fine," I said, nudging Al to ask for the same. "But please, don't go to any trouble."

"No trouble at all," she sang from the built-in bar.

Al and I took a seat on a wide plaid loveseat. It amazed me how much junk was crammed inside the room, boxes and end tables and china cabinets. Stacks of drink coasters anywhere you looked. A roller rink organ against one wall with sheet music, "I Did It My Way," on the music rack.

"Where's . . . John?" I asked.

"John? Didn't he tell you?" She set down our water. "Thursdays are boys' night out around here. Him and his chums always hit a couple clubs on the boardwalk. I can't believe he didn't tell you he'd be gone!"

So that's when I got the tour of her china cabinets and heard all about Clan McAllister. She even took me out back, along the swimming pool, where she'd buried the poodle in a safe-deposit box.

❀

*I*'ve talked Mrs. Lemack into setting the cruise control now we're out of Breezewood and back on the turnpike. Won't admit I'm scared of that gadget. Given my luck, it'll get stuck the minute a slowpoke pulls out ahead of us. But with Mrs. Lemack, you've got to weigh the alternatives. And this way she avoids a speeding ticket, no small change on this road.

She's muttering something about the cows along the road. How she's read cattle breeding is strictly artificial insemination these days, which means someone's got to jerk off the bull. Cool Hand Luke maybe.

I don't laugh, not with Nicky on my mind. I shudder to think all the things about him she doesn't know—things I'll keep to myself, thank you kindly, at least till I make it to purgatory. Which might be soon, given how she tailgates.

# The Tunnels:
# Tuscarora
# Kittatiny
# Blue Mountain

*T*his crossword puzzle's wicked, and it doesn't matter I'm using a pen. So far, there's nothing for me to erase. I get my first break at fifty-seven across: a seven-letter word for *turkey draw*. Know that one cold. The answer's lottery.

Lottery. Not a day goes by I don't think of that word. For hours. Twists my guts into figure eights, all the heartbreak I caused with that money. No undoing it, either. The money's long gone and my kids along with it.

On the other hand, *lottery* has a place of honor in Vicky's vocabulary. She says life's a lottery, called me collect with that nugget the day of her wedding in India. The line was so crackly, I had her repeat it.

"You heard me," she shouted. "I'm gambling as much on this marriage succeeding as most people do on the Super Bowl."

Took my breath away, as flip as she sounded. Her thinking's always been fuzzy, of course, for all the degrees on her wall. Since eighth grade she's charted her horoscope and played with a Ouija board. I don't believe in that foolishness. But Vicky's got more of Mum in her than she'll ever know. She likes to shock people, too. And college can't undo those bad habits.

The girl never knew I won the lottery. That's not the only thing I haven't told her, either. I wouldn't spill the story of her mother's life for all the tea in China. It's hard enough just thinking about it—and Vicky wouldn't buy my story anyhow. She's got her own one-sided version, short on love and truth and pity. And then Mrs. Lemack wonders why I don't like her.

❀

*I* didn't lay bets with myself the day I got married. Of course, my situation was different from Vicky's. I was seventeen years old, three months along, and flat broke. I never owned a hope chest or a wedding ring. And couldn't lay bets even if I'd wanted.

I'd met Al in church the year before. He'd pressed a wrinkled stick of wintergreen gum in my hand at the end of Mass, then winked, and ran off through the parking lot. I saved the wrapper and ran it up and down the dark hairs on my forearm all week. It gave me goose bumps.

I'd known about him for years. Everybody did. He'd made a reputation in the Braddock bars as a champion arm wrestler. A kick-ass, too. The boy could deck anyone, not that he looked for fights. But they had a funny way of finding him.

The only place he behaved himself was church. He came every Sunday with his lame little sister, who he carried up the church steps. She couldn't fit in the pews with her crutches, so he'd fetch a metal chair, then help her to her feet at the end of Mass.

The Sunday after the gum episode, he asked if I wouldn't mind some company. It puzzled me he would take any interest in a plain-faced, skinny girl like myself; a girl without breasts, just two fried eggs; a girl who'd never had a boyfriend, not even an admirer, unless you counted Vlado. And Al was twenty-three years old, sturdy and dark, and good-looking in only the way our people can be. Women smiled at him in the street.

It flattered me he looked my direction. I doubted it would last. But for the time being, I didn't think about it. I was important.

❀

*I*n spite of his fame as a fighter, Al was a good kid. He quit school, eventually to work in the mill, and turned over his meager paycheck—most of it—to his mum. The poor woman had seven younger children and a good-for-nothing husband who never worked a day. She needed every penny.

People yakked about the Kuzos. How the old man disgraced our people, sitting on the porch in his underwear, belching beer, and shaking fists at passing cars. How he never gave his wife a moment's rest, at her like a crazy mink. Poor woman had her last baby the year after Tom was born, when she was forty-five and missing all her teeth. I never saw her when she wasn't elbow deep in soapsuds. She took in all the neighbors' laundry, for pennies.

Al ran away from home when he was eleven, the same day his old man knocked out his two front teeth. He joined a traveling circus, a caravan of horse-drawn wagons with gingham curtains in the windows. Stayed with that outfit three years, raising and lowering the tent, down and back to Florida twice. He learned a few things they don't teach you in school, like drinking and poker and rolling a reefer—and things more peculiar than that. He kept me awake the first year of our marriage with his stories.

His favorite was about Debby the dog lady, a knock-kneed old gal with a wrinkled turkey neck and wooden teeth. She took a shine to Al, reason being her old man had fixed *her* face the same way a century before. So Deb let Al sleep on a cot in her wagon rather than under the stars, which worked to her advantage. He had to fix her breakfast, tidy the trailer, and brush all the dogs. Nasty little ankle-snappers bit him up and down his arms.

One night, he woke up in her wagon smelling smoke. Turned out to be a cigarette burning between Deb's wooden teeth. The ashes burned bright enough he could see the whole room, Deb in particular, down on all fours getting pumped from the rear by a sheepdog.

"Go on!" I choked, first time he told me, under the sheets. "With a *sheepdog?*"

"You heard me. And I ain't lying."

"Baloney." I set the alarm clock. "You were dreaming, is what."

"Yeah? Same dream for three years?"

I pulled up on my elbows. "You *watched* it that long?"

"You bet," he chuckled. "That was back before radio."

I didn't smell booze on his breath, so I guessed he was telling the truth. But he'd left out the one thing I wanted to know.

"You ever . . . knock a piece off that old gal?" I asked.

He grinned at the ceiling. "I get to keep a few secrets, don't I?"

"Not from *me!*" I straddled his stomach, mock-angry, and tickled his armpits. We wrestled and landed in a heap on the floor, bruised and laughing. Went at it right on the carpet, the floorboards creaking, the wind whipping the curtains in the window.

But I never did get him to talk.

*F*our Sundays in a row Al walked me home from church. We never talked much. He'd nudge a rock along the sidewalk with his toe and whistle off-key.

"Next week?" he asked that fourth Sunday, shaking my hand at the door.

I was always surprised he wanted to see me again. Scared, too, he might try to kiss me. I hated the thought of his tongue in my mouth, the way grown-ups did it.

"There any chance"—he laid a hand on my arm—"you'll ever ask me inside? Like today, maybe?"

I knew saying no might cause me to lose him. So I showed him into the parlor. As usual, cats were everywhere, tumbling off furniture, stretched in windowsills, hunkered on the China silk rug. The sight of them ruined his mood.

"What in the hell kind of place is this?" he said, chasing a tom off the sofa so he could sit down. "You got a rat problem here?"

"Kind of," I swallowed, pulling up a high-backed chair. I didn't care to explain Granddaddy's craziness.

"Well, I hate cats. Next time I'll bring you some traps."

And he did, his very first gift, a dozen of them neatly packaged and tied with string, along with a hunk of smelly cheese. He set the traps up throughout the house, me on my knees alongside, cutting the cheese into triangles. That was when he first kissed me, our noses bumping.

And so he became my steady. Over Mum's objections.

"Why, he's a grown man already," she grumbled, picking ladybugs off her rosebushes and crushing them between her fingers. "He's probably been shaving since before you were born! Can't you find someone your own age?"

I shook my head. I wanted *him* for my steady, not any of those fair-haired American boys throwing spitballs in homeroom. They didn't interest me at all.

"Go ahead then, amuse yourself," she shrugged. "But I

don't see much good can come of it. That boy won't amount to anything. God forgot to give him brains."

Burned me up to hear that speech. But it was nothing compared to the dirt out of Nicky's mouth.

"So Masha's in *love?*" he sneered, so wide I could see the decay on his teeth. "You put out for that boy yet? Or he still prefer the sporting life, huh?  I know all about *him.* Isn't a cat house in Braddock he hasn't spent his paycheck. Go on, Mash, save him from the clap before he gives it to you!"

I didn't repeat this to Al. No reason. Conversation was just a distraction, and we were too busy passing hours in the parlor mouth to mouth. He stopped only to kick the cats out from underfoot or swat them with newspapers. Then we'd be at it again, him pressed against me, begging for sex, almost till I couldn't breathe.

I finally gave him what he wanted on the Fourth of July, only night of the year we had the run of the house. Everyone else, even Granddaddy, was off watching fireworks and wouldn't be home before midnight.

"You sure you want to do this?" he whispered as I closed my bedroom door behind us.

I frowned. "I . . . guess. Don't tell me you're getting cold feet."

"Like *hell* I am!" he grunted. "Like *hell!*"

He started out kissing me hard and dirty, then unbuttoning my dress and helping me work my arms out the sleeves. He held me against his scratchy shirt, kissing my hair, my neck, my breasts. Then he reached inside my underpants and pulled them to my ankles.

"Here, let me have a good look at you," he whispered, stepping backward, his arms folded on his chest. He let out a long whistle as I backed up and sat on the bed, embarrassed, my legs crossed, trying to hide my pubic hair. He unbuttoned his shirt, dropped his trousers, peeled off his socks. Then he helped me stretch out, kissed the tops of my knees, and threw them up around his shoulders. It hurt like the devil as he worked his way inside me. He was whispering my name, his tongue in my ear, pumping fast, moaning. Startled me when he screamed—thought *I* was supposed to be doing that—but I'd heard even guys get noisy when the sex's really good. And when he bounced across the room, his balls in his hands, I figured it was downright sensational. He'd probably want to go at it again.

"You ready for some more?" I asked, pulling up on my elbows.

"Jesus fucking Christ, Masha! *More?* Take a look at this! *Shit!*"

He showed me a long, ragged scratch on his balls. Only a cat could have done it—slunk up from the rear as Al pumped in and out. Sure enough, I spotted a tom on my wardrobe, rear leg raised, licking its butt. We couldn't reach it even with the mop handle, Al crying out for revenge.

Poor guy walked around in a half-crouch for a week after that. He told everyone he'd pulled out his back shooting baskets. They believed him.

🍥

*I* got pregnant my senior year. It came as no surprise; we never used protection. I didn't breathe a word to Al at first. But when I'd missed three months in a row and spent mornings dry heaving over the sink, I knew I couldn't hide it any longer. Cried myself to sleep for nights.

Al didn't worry me. I knew he'd want to get married. The snag was coming clean with Mum. She had two sets of standards when it came to sex: hers, which amounted to anything goes; and everyone else's, which were a helluva lot less forgiving. The first time Al sat in our parlor she threatened to work me over if I ever came home in the family way—her, meanwhile, heading upstairs to Vlado.

I begged Al to come with me the day I broke the news. Had

him change into clean clothes, polish his shoes, and brush his teeth with baking soda. Mum was standing at the stove, her back to us, stirring lentil soup.

"What? You're having a *baby?*" She turned around with the ladle in her hand, soup dripping on the linoleum.

I cringed as she walked toward us, footfalls loud as King Kong.

"The God's truth?" Her lips were a thin white line.

Al laid a shaking hand on my shoulder. "Yes, ma'am. But we want to get married, and the sooner the better."

She brought her face, all ugly, up to mine and spat. "Didn't I teach you nothing? You're finished, you know that? You'll have to quit school! Is that what you want? To count pennies the rest of your life, bent over a washboard"—pointing at Al—"just like *his* mother?"

"Mum . . ." I wiped her spit from my face, too frightened to answer.

"You couldn't wait until the priest said it was alright?" She started to weep. "Shame on you!"

"Mum, everything'll be okay," I whispered, taking Al's hand so she could see. "We *love* each other."

"Love?" She lifted the ladle in the air. "Don't talk to *me* about love! It's all lies, you hear me? I could kill both of you!"

We scrambled straight out the back door, fast as we could go.

🐚

*T*hat afternoon Mum—her spirits restored—dropped a fifty-dollar bill down her cleavage and went out on business. She headed first to Washington Street and haggled for a pretty lace wedding gown, then visited the priest and explained my situation, delicacy to the wind. He shook his head, offered her his condolences along with blackberry brandy, and agreed to marry us the last Saturday of the month. She kissed the hem of his garment and headed to Madame Vargas, an old gypsy living in a garage hung with scarves. For fifty cents she had her tea leaves read, then asked about my future, which cost another quarter. The predictions pleased Mum—that I'd get rich someday—so she hired the old fortune-teller's sons to play at the wedding. Twenty dollars bought four hours of their time, cheap for the best gypsy band in all Braddock. The balance of her money went for flour, eggs, and sugar, to bake a three-tiered wedding cake.

Mum hauled her purchases home. She heard Annie singing in the parlor and interrupted her song with my news. The girl didn't look thrilled. She was twelve years old, the age where you've figured out exactly what men and women do in bed. And the thought makes you gag, especially imagining someone like Mr. Hood, the school principal, trousers around his ankles.

I'd wanted to take her aside beforehand, tell her sex really wasn't so bad, just two pieces of skin rubbing together, and a mess to clean up after, was all. But I'd get tongue-tied and shy. A week before the wedding, I watched her dawdle as she hemmed her bridesmaid's gown, stopping to sip lemonade, as if she didn't care about the deadline.

"You mad at me?" I asked her, after we sewed in silence a full hour.

"What makes you think that?" She didn't look up, broke a thread and tied the ends.

"Just a hunch."

"Well, I'm *not* mad, okay?"

"Then how come you won't talk to me? You won't even *look* at me, for God's sake! What have I done to you?"

She burst into tears and ran from the room. I sat a full hour puzzling it out. Maybe it was only that she'd miss me, off and married, her best friend gone, no Lily around. I knew I'd miss her. Good God. Just awful.

It wasn't till years later, when she was so sick, I found out the truth. That back then she knew as much about sex as I did. First-hand experience with Vlado.

*And* so we were married. Fifty-two guests, mostly Al's family and friends. I'd invited only Mrs. Lemack and—at Mum's insistence—her boarders. Those louts drank most of the booze, slapped the women's backsides, and overturned tables after Al and I left. I should have known better.

Our married life started out shaky, and not just because I was pregnant. Al didn't have a red cent left, once he'd rented his tux. The man was unskilled labor and made half as much money as Granddaddy. So we did what we had to and moved in with Mum. Lived on a diet of turnips. And fought.

I hate the memories. How I filled the trash with shattered dishes, smashed furniture, wet hankies. How we slept back to back and didn't speak for days. Partly on account of money. But mostly on account of his drinking. He did plenty the first couple years of our marriage.

Strictly speaking, Al was a Saturday night drunk, sober as Carrie Nation the rest of the week. But he could raise hell when he'd tied on too many. He came home with split lips and cracked bones where he'd collided with bouncers and cops. I'd worry myself sick watching him leave. Mrs. Lemack—then Mrs. Tagliatello—would stop by to keep me company. She'd bring a deck of cards, comic books, and a can of Campbell's tomato soup. Always stayed till he staggered back home.

"You're going down, Boy," she told Al one night, wagging a finger in his face. "Just like my father, that horse's ass. Keep it up and Mash will leave you, mark my words. Why the hell should a lady like her stick with the likes of you? Huh?" She tightened the cap on the ice bag and dropped it, none too gently, on his head.

Al would have decked anyone other than Mrs. Lemack saying that. But he teared up instead and wiped his nose on a soiled dishrag. Scolding would do that to him sometimes.

She sat down then and patted his knee, the only part of his body wasn't aching. Stuck two cigarettes in her lips, lit them both, and passed one to Al. "Hey, Bub, no one's telling you not to drink," she said. "A man's got to do that. But drinking's about making friends—should be, at least—which you sure as hell aren't doing. What're we going to do with you, huh?"

She was back on Mum's doorstep next day with an idea. Walked Al down to the Moose Club, chattering all the way, and fronted him five dollars for a membership card.

"You'll like it here, lots of decent folks," she said, beating the pants off him at table hockey. "Mean drunks don't last a day, out on their ear, house policy. So reading between the lines, Bub, I'm counting on you to behave. No more fights, you hear me?"

He did. And it worked. But he never stopped tippling on weekends, as much as I begged him.

"A man's got to drink," he'd say, crumpling one beer can and opening another. "I heard it straight from your girlfriend."


Seven years later we were still broke, still fighting, and still living with Mum. I wanted my own little home, especially now we had Barb. Turned my eyes pea-green visiting Mrs. Lemack. She and Sal owned a cute little row house with striped awnings, a mud room, and wall-to-wall carpet. I'd keep Al awake, trying to convince him we could do just as well.

"Yeah, dream on," he carped. "You and your hare-brained ideas! How the hell am I gonna buy you a house? Huh?"

"I'll find a way, believe it."

"Sure you will," he yawned, stroked his full stomach, and fell asleep.

So I got myself a job, thirty-six miles from home in a sweat-shop stitching shoes. The place had no phone, no lunchroom, not even a Kotex machine. There was only one toilet behind a thin checkered curtain—and always a line and an odor.

The boss, Gus Franzone, drove me hard. He jammed forty of us ladies, mostly Hunkies, into a windowless room. He'd prowl the aisles, spilling cigar ash as we hunched at the machines, telling us bathroom jokes or panning our work. We hated him. He'd put the squeeze on any new girl, buy her black panties, and expect a payback after closing. I don't think he scored once in all the years I worked there. The women would just sooner quit.

It was a nightmare. Every Friday I swore I was through. But I'd be back again Monday, and the next, and the next. I lost track of time as weeks piled up, then months, then years. All totaled, I worked in that hellhole for thirty-nine years.

Only thing I've got to show for it is my fingernails. People always ask me about them. They're not a pretty sight, bumpy and brittle and split, from the times I stitched through them by accident. Gus didn't even pay the doctor bill.

*In* three years, I saved enough money for a down payment, part of which included a lump sum from Mum. I wouldn't describe it as a gift. She told me *she'd* find the right house, that *she* was the one in the know, and I'd do best to stick to her rear. I didn't argue. That was back before real estate brokers, so you haggled on your own, which took nerve. Or a calling.

Mum was in her element. She found something amiss with twenty-five different places—cracks in the foundations, loose floorboards, water stains, termites, doors that wouldn't close. And worse, she'd take offense at any flaws, then browbeat the owner to lower the price.

"You trying to hoodwink me?" she asked one elderly gentleman, pointing at a beam in his attic. "That's dry rot."

I started to sweat because I liked this particular house. The owner was nice, too. Downstairs his wife was baking us choco-late chip cookies.

"I think you're mistaken, ma'am," the old man said, dragging a clubfoot behind him. "It couldn't be dry rot. We had the beams replaced a year ago."

Mum popped open her purse, pulled out a thin screwdriver, and plunged it straight through the wood. A cloud of sawdust fluttered to the floor.

"What did I tell you?" she glared at him, all evil triumph. "Liar."

Then she marched straight out to the street, leaving the old fellow dodging the lightbulb in his attic, his wife at the stove with her spatula. She didn't even wish them good day.

"Mum, I *liked* that house!" I panted angrily, catching up behind her. I'd just apologized for her rudeness, and held the hot cookies wrapped in wax paper.

"Liked it? That was an outhouse! Look, Mash, leave this to me. You don't know shit from shinola. I'll find you the right house, trust me."

And she did, the very home I still live in. She'd heard that the owner just died, a widow named Litchfield, whose heirs—unmarried sisters—were anxious to sell. The puddle in the basement gave Mum just the leverage she needed. She lowballed the ladies to the tune of seven hundred dollars. Damn dickering went on all afternoon before they caved in, gave Mum a final price of thirty-five hundred dollars, and ordered her the hell off the porch.


*T*hat was the house where my kids grew up, and I grew old. Barb says the neighborhood's too depressing even to visit, maybe one reason I don't see her often. But she's right; it's drab here. The only color you see is in springtime, when dandelions poke out the cracks in the sidewalks. Or Christmas, when I hang out my lights.

Still, I loved my new house. Drove back from the settlement clam-happy, Mum and Al up front, me in the back with the kids, a coconut cake melting in my lap. Mum bounded up on the porch even before Al killed the engine. We found her painting the door with honey.

"What in Sam Hill you doing?" bellowed Al, fumbling for the key.

"You got eyes in your head, don't you?" she shrugged. No love lost between those two.

"Yeah, yeah, but why *honey?* You ever hear of ants?"

"Sure. And you can live with a few today, can't you?" She went back to her work, gabbing at me over her shoulder. "Doesn't your old man know honey's good luck? That it'll protect this place from an elephant stampede?"

"You bonkers, lady?" Al stuffed his thumbs in his waistband and snickered. "That's *Africa* you're talking about. There ain't any elephants in Braddock!"

"Works great then, doesn't it?" she shrugged, wiping her forehead with the back of her hand.

"There's things that work better than honey, if good luck's what you want," shouted a voice from across the yard. "You ever hear about welcome mats?"

It was Mrs. Kosavitch. She was young then with stiff yellow hair, penciled eyebrows, and lipstick coating her upper teeth. She vaulted over the chain-link fence, spry as an alley cat— even on her thick legs—and joined us on the porch.

"Jeez, am I glad to see it's a family with kids moving in here," she chattered, shaking hands without asking our names. "The old lady living here before—Mrs. Litchfield, guess you know about her—didn't have much use for *my* kids, let me tell you. She called up complaining my Stevie tossed a match in her trash, imagine that, the kid wasn't seven years old! And she wouldn't even answer her door on Halloween, no matter how many times I told the boys to ring her bell. Had it in for my husband, too—"

"What's your name?" asked Mum, frowning.

"Kosavitch, Mary Kosavitch. K-O-S-A-V-I-T-C-H. My husband's Stan, you'll meet him soon enough, promise. Hey, that looks like a nice cake you've got there," she said to me. "How about I bring over some plates? Coconut's my favorite. Be back in a jiffy."

She ate most of it sitting cross-legged on our porch, talking nonstop. Gave us the history of the neighborhood, her marriage, her pregnancies. It didn't surprise me Al wandered off. The Moose was only six blocks away.

"Stevie'll make good company for you," Mrs. Kosavitch said, pinching Tom's cheek. "Buzz, too. My boys are only ten months apart, you believe that?"

"Ten months only?" I said. "You sure had your work cut out."

"Not by choice, let me tell you." She licked the icing from her fingers. "I wasn't home from the hospital a day after Stevie was born before Stan was back lifting my nightgown. And I'd just got a nasty episiotomy, hurt even to breathe. 'What the hell you doing?' I asked him, as if I didn't know. 'Just shut up and pretend I'm ol' Blue Eyes,' he told me. So that's how I got Buzz."

"You always tell strangers these stories?" asked Mum. Till then, I never thought anything could surprise her.

"Strangers?" said Mrs. Kosavitch. "Lady, we're *neighbors*. And why not set the record straight? You thought I was crazy, didn't you, with two kids so close?"

"How about we go inside?" said Mum, shaking the crumbs from her lap same time she was shaking her head.

"I can't wait to see the place without all that ugly furniture," said Mrs. Kosavitch, barging her way ahead of us. "Her sisters tell you it was me who found her? Yes'm, right on the living room couch. And with a half-empty bottle of gin between her knees. She'd been lying that way just short of a week, a stroke, that's what the autopsy said."

"How'd you get inside the house?" I asked, glancing at Mum.

"Simple. I jimmied the lock with Stan's Swiss army knife.

Alright, alright, I know it's illegal, but I hadn't seen her in a week and figured something was up. And it was still winter, not like her windows were open, and I could just hang my head inside and shout 'yoo—hoo.'"

"So what did you do . . . *after?*"

"This and that. I went through the house and turned off the lights and opened the windows—it smelt a little ripe in here— and then I pulled any food worth saving out of the fridge and checked all the gas jets on the stove. I even went down to the basement to see if she'd left any laundry on. Then I called the cops and the newspaper."

Closest I've ever come to speechless. "You find anything in the fridge?"

"Just a sack of turnips and a half pound of coffee. Nothing I could give to the boys. Or the turtles, either."

"Turtles?"

She laughed. "You'll get used to me, I promise. I've got thirteen beauties in the backyard. Great pets. Here, hang on a minute."

She ran off and returned with a turtle in each hand. Waved them right under Mum's nose. "Just don't stick your finger out, ma'am, this one here's a snapper. Pretty though, ain't he? I let the boys take him in the bathtub."

And so it went for the rest of the afternoon. Took three hours to get her off the porch, same time as Al staggered back in the yard.

"Looks like you've got your hands full, Mash," said Mum, the woman barely out of earshot. "If I'd known she was going to be your neighbor, those sisters couldn't have *paid* me to take this house."

"How about we feed her a poisoned cake?" I said, not trying to be funny.

Mum laughed. "Her? There's no killing that kind, just like the bugs in my rosebushes." She checked her watch. "Looks like time I got home, Kids. You in good enough shape to drive, Al?"

"Of course I am," he grumbled, straightening his hat. Then he grinned out of nowhere, straight at Mum. "You were wrong, by the way, Lady. That honey didn't keep away the elephants."

$\mathcal{M}$rs. Kosavitch was right about one thing: Stevie and Tom made good company. The two were thick as thieves, shoplifting at Woolworth's before either made it through the night in dry pants. I never knew what goodies I'd find in Tom's pockets.

By fourth grade they moved on to arson. Boys tossed matches out back of Rudy's Market and triggered a three-alarm fire. I whipped Tom with a wooden spoon, then stuck him in parochial school, which we couldn't afford. The kid lasted less than a week. Nuns tossed him out for vandalizing a statue—he'd painted tits and a bush on St. Theresa the Little Flower.

In high school, with Elvis the rage, Stevie and Tom changed their style. They dressed identical in peg-leg pants and T-shirts, hair brushed in greasy swirls, cigarettes behind one ear. I snipped Tom's hair off one night with shears. Surprised me he slept through it. Didn't surprise me when he lifted twenty-five dollars from my purse next morning and stayed out all night.

And then there were their girlfriends, tramps with white lipstick and dirty sneakers. The boys would bring them by our house during school. I'd find the bedspreads wrinkled up like a mole got loose underneath and long bleached hairs on the pillows. It didn't surprise me Stevie knocked up his girlfriend. Mrs. Kosavitch found an abortionist, cheap, hollered the news across the yard as she paid the paperboy. And asked me if I wanted the number.

$O$f course, she had troubles of her own. Told me every single one of them with her elbows on the fence, starting with her husband. It's true I never saw Stan he wasn't stumbling down tavern steps. He kept a beer keg on the kitchen table while she and the kids ate standing at the sink. I'd see Stevie and Buzz—still toddlers—lapping up whatever leaked out of that keg on the floor.

I can't think why the woman piss-moaned on my porch the day Stan dumped her. And for a fifty-year-old nitwit who boasted she was still a virgin, just hadn't found a man good enough until him. If I'd been Mrs. Kosavitch, I'd have packed him his bags, a box lunch, and a map of New Zealand long ago. Danced on the table like a Cossack.

Not her. She sulked in her bathrobe and nipped Jim Beam. It didn't help she got infested with cockroaches that summer. She'd pound on our door at midnight, a bug tangled in her hair, hacking away with a steak knife. For weeks I let her sleep on the living room sofa. But Al got tired of that arrangement since he couldn't slop around in his skivvies. He sent her packing.

She hadn't seen the last of Stan, either. He called from every drugstore, crying to come home. Turned out his girlfriend dumped him. She'd found a niche selling Amway and didn't want him showing up whiskey-breathed and spoiling her sales.

"You think I should take him back?" Mrs. Kosavitch asked, following me from one side of my car to the other as I swept out the floorboards.

"Lordy, ma'am, don't ask questions like that," I shrugged. "How would I know?"

She needn't have asked. Stan was back next day, stuffed in a lime-green leisure suit and drinking diet soda on the porch. He parked a new Lincoln in her garage and swore up and down he'd reformed. Not so. Wasn't a week before the repos found him and hot-wired his car.

This time she kicked him out. He found work—a short-order cook at Newberry's lunch counter—and moved to a one-room apartment. Probably skunk-drunk the day he drowned in his bathtub. This happened when Mrs. Kosavitch and her sister were down at the shore. And it was August, hot as the summer Mum died. The stench got so bad his neighbors called the cops.

The real trouble started at the morgue. Stan, it turned out, was the second drowning victim of the day. An hour earlier the cops had brought in another, some fellow named Benny they'd fished from the river. The coroner—famous for tippling— switched toe tags by accident and loaded the bodies into the wrong hearses, Benny headed for the funeral home of Mrs. Kosavitch's choice, Stan to Benny's crematorium. That very afternoon, Stan went up the chimney in a puff of smoke, just as Mrs. Kosavitch was writing a check for the most expensive casket in the undertaker's showroom. No telling how they figured out that Benny wasn't Stan. But Mrs. Kosavitch didn't waste time, called that lawyer you see smirking on all the bill-boards in Braddock, and started a lawsuit. She'd never tell me how much she got—about the only thing she hasn't told me— but I figured it was more than change. I noticed new aluminum siding on her house, air conditioning units in every window, and the Bug-Away truck parked at her curb. The lady got rid of those roaches for good.

The crematorium sent her Stan's ashes. They'd swept him into a porcelain vase, Chinese, top quality, so she boasted. It wasn't on her kitchen counter a day before she buried it out front. She plunked down that plastic Virgin on top the very spot, then invited the neighbors over for a wienie roast to mourn him.

 

*E*ven with Stan gone, her sorrows weren't over: her sons were still living at home. Buzz was harmless enough, but not many people, including the cops, were willing to pay him no mind. He'd get crazy for weeks and sit drooling in doorsteps, dangling a string, and talking to hydrants. It took her years to think of putting him on a bus to California.

Still, Buzz was small change next to Stevie. That kid was downright evil. He torched the brassieres on my clothesline, a couple stray dogs, and the bundled magazines I'd left out for the Red Cross. His talents got him work with Pittsburgh thugs—until he trapped himself inside a burning warehouse. Doctor said he'd never seen anyone survive such bad burns. Kid lost all his hair, his eyebrows, his toes. Even his ears got melted, judging from Mrs. Kosavitch's Polaroids.

The judge had no pity. He sent Stevie to prison for twenty-five years with bandages still on his face. According to his mother, he's become a model prisoner—even got a girlfriend through the prison pen-pal program—and quotes the Bible, chapter and verse, from memory.

By my calculations, he'll be out in two years and itching to set a new fire. Hell's bells. Just another thing to worry about, as if there's not enough.


$O$nce we were settled in our new house, me and Al got on better. Gone were the days of broken dishes and nasty comments and worrying afterward what the neighbors might think. We didn't care; we seldom spoke anymore. Sundays after church, he'd still trail me to the bedroom like clockwork. I'd be a good sport, lie still as he'd go about his business, and drape him with an afghan afterward. Then head to the week's worth of laundry growing mold in the basement.

Even with our new house, his real home was the Moose. I'd see more of Mrs. Lemack than my husband, weekends especially, when she'd drag me to flea markets and the bowling alley. And out for pancakes after.

Maybe that's why I don't miss him so much. He left me years ago, for his barstool and buddies and catnaps. He didn't even curse or slam the door or find a fancy gal. Too much bother.

# $\mathcal{E}$xit 16—$C$arlisle

"$\mathcal{W}$e're coming up to HoJo's in another five miles," says Mrs. Lemack, turning down the volume on Bessie. "You working on your hunger yet?"

"It's only 10:30! You're not famished *already*, are you, Mrs. Lemack?"

She drums her fingers on the steering wheel. "That a question that needs asking?"

"Well, is this snack-machine hunger? Or empty-the-fridge hunger?"

"Three guesses, Mrs. Kuzo," she smiles, wet around the mouth. "How about some fried clams?"

"You're the driver," I shrug, rubbing my slipped disc. "And the wallet, if I recall."

She pulls into HoJo's and parks between two semis. The woman's fascinated by them. Drivers, too. She eats lunch alone at a truck stop once a week and comes home full of boastful tales. Swears she was a trucker in an earlier life. Which doesn't make sense because trucks weren't around before she was born. Or for some time after.

We head to the toilet and tap our kidneys. The housekeeping at HoJo's isn't what it used to be. There are no paper towels, and the hand dryer's broke. But Mrs. Lemack makes do, wipes her hands with a roll of one-ply toilet paper, then heads for the machine that sells Kleenex and sewing kits and maxi-pads. She pulls the lever for the thimble-sized bottle of lilac cologne, twists it open, and douses herself.

"That's better," she sighs, sniffing her wrists and offering me the little that's left. "You ready for a real meal?"

🦋

*I*t was a lousy few months deciding what to do with the lottery ticket. Just thinking about it gave me heart palpitations, hiccups, loose bowels, dandruff. I was in and out of Dr. Gibson's office with a list of complaints.

I've been his patient thirty years. He's probably the only GP in Braddock still wearing a white coat and head mirror. Man whistles along with the waiting room muzak and laughs at his own goofy jokes. I can't complain about his bedside manner. He listens to my list of symptoms, brows knotted with concern, and agrees something needs to be done. The only thing wrong with him is he can never find a thing wrong with me.

"Take a deep breath, Mrs. Kuzo, no more talking," he said, touching the icy knob of the stethoscope to my back. "You under any unusual stress? Family problems? Unpaid bills? Loss of a loved one?"

*My basement is wet, for starters.*

"Lawsuits? Criminal assaults? New neighbors? A recent birthday?"

*I found a feather on my engine block. The bird was real.*

"How about the anniversary of your husband's death, perhaps? Or your mother's?"

*I dreamt I was wrapped in the China silk rug.*

"Dieting? Purging? Change in any of your habits?"

*I have a winning lottery ticket that scares the bejesus out of me.*

"You're fit as a fiddle!" He pulled out his ear pieces. "Those are lungs of a woman half your age, Mrs. Kuzo, you know that? Seems to me you just need to relax and eat healthy. And try getting out a little more. Meet some new gentlemen. Shake a leg."

So I drove home with a prescription for Xanax, an appointment with a licensed nutritionist, and a referral to an older women's therapy group. Hang it all. The doc thinks I'm crazy.

❁

*T*he fried clams at Howard Johnson's used to come piled sky-high on an ironstone plate with salty french fries, tomato wedges, and coleslaw. I never could finish it and always passed the plate to Annie, my pantsuit grown tight in the crotch. The girl didn't refuse my leftovers. She speared the last of the clams, sponged off the plate with a biscuit, and washed it all down with ice tea. I figured the extra helping was her due. She always paid for my lunch and any souvenir I wanted from the gift shop.

That was back in the days when I traveled the turnpike three times a year, when Annie was married and living outside Philadelphia. I'd drive down and spend an overnight, then haul her back to Mum's house for a week. And when the time came to go home to her husband, I'd stick her on Greyhound. Annie didn't drive. Nerves, she said. And I didn't doubt her, not with all the nicotine in her blood. And all her shock treatments.

The clams were better back then, plump and crisp and nut-flavored. Nowadays you get half the amount, twice the oil, at three times the price. I pull an orange from my handbag and grimace. To think it was clams got me headed to Bessie's grave in the first place.

Even Mrs. Lemack's disappointed. "You win some, you lose some," she says, pouring ketchup on her clams and eating them anyway. "Try to cheer up, Mrs. Kuzo. I'll buy you a hot fudge sundae, you game?"

❀

*A*nnie wasn't always so helpless. For two years after high school, she waited tables at a diner in Braddock and saved every penny. It was a busy place, right around the corner from the high school, and popular at lunchtime with teachers. Embarrassed the hell out of her, slinging hash at the very people who'd told her she'd someday make her mark on the world. They weren't so impressed anymore and rarely left tips or called her by name. She was just another Hunkie in a hair net warming their coffee.

"For Pete's sake, why not get out of there?" I said as we folded the boarders' laundry. "Get yourself a real job. With your looks, you could be a salesgirl at Kaufmann's."

She stiffened. "I'm too tall, they'd never hire me. Besides, I like where I'm at. And I get all my meals free."

It was true, she'd gained weight, got curvaceous as Betty Grable. The diner was famous for milk shakes and Dutch apple pie.

"Alright, so they feed you," I said. "But don't you want to make more money?"

"Sure," she smiled. "Someday."

I wondered whether she had a sweetheart, maybe one of the busboys. I'd noticed a few of them wiping off tables, their taut little haunches inches from my face. She'd never had a fellow before, not even a single date, sat on her bed dry-eyed the night of her senior prom reading Sinclair Lewis.

"So who's the guy?" I asked.

"Huh?"

"Jeez, Annie, own up! You have it bad for one of those busboys?"

"Ed? Dickey? Those dummies?" she giggled. "You've got to be kidding!"

"Boys don't have to be smart to show you a good time," I smirked.

She colored, chewed a fingernail. "Maybe I'm not so easily entertained."

"Oh yeah? They don't entertain with their brains. Try thinking south. Or maybe you know about *that* already."

"For God's sake, Masha!" she snapped, shaking out a pillowcase. "You ever pull your head out of the gutter?"

It felt like she'd kicked me in the chest. "Jeez, kiddo! What's eating you?"

"Nothing's *eating* me. It's just some things aren't funny. Period."

She picked up the linens and left the room, me feeling queer as a bug. I followed her to the top of the steps and watched her pull on her coat in the doorway.

"Maybe we'll have to find you some nice professor," I called out, snottier than I'd intended. She didn't answer. Slammed the door.


*B*ut it turned out she did have a fellow. He'd been coming by the restaurant every Saturday for lunch, dressed in a porkpie hat and a suit he'd ironed himself, scorching the fabric shiny. He slipped her big tips and notes asking for dates, and had daisies delivered to the kitchen. Mike Gallagher. Irish.

I sighed, first time she brought him home. He was damn good-looking, a strapping six-foot steel cutter. Kid didn't say much, sat stroking Annie's hand while I peeled peaches for a cobbler. But he worked his jaw later putting down dinner, three loaded plates and half my cobbler when it came steaming out of the oven. He called me a good cook. I like men with big appetites.

He knew how to woo her, too. He brought her scented soap and boxed chocolates and spent every blessed dime he earned showing her the town. His parents were dead ten years, tuberculosis, so he had no other obligations. I figured his people must have taught him good manners. He even knew how to hold up a woman's coat behind her so she could slip her arms through the sleeves. That's a real gentleman. Unusual among steelworkers.

"So when're yuns getting hitched?" I asked as she dressed for a date, in another of Mum's castoff frocks. It was short even with the hem dropped, but she had the bosom to fill it.

"I'm not marrying him," she said, blotting her lipstick on a tissue.

"Baloney! He's a good boy. Good job, good appetite, good manners. Seems pretty sweet on you, too. What're you waiting for?"

"Look, Mash, there's more to life than marriage and babies," she said, picking lint off the bodice. "I've got a list of things this long"—she stood on tiptoe, her arm stretched to the ceiling— "that I want to do *first*. And I couldn't do any of it if I were married—especially to Mike. Can't you see? He's not going anywhere. The mill's his life!"

I let pass that Al worked there, planned to stay on, too. Counted to ten before I spoke. "So you planning to run for President or something?"

"What if I am?" She frowned at her reflection in the mirror and sucked in her stomach.

"Seems a little ambitious."

She spun around angrily. "Okay, I may never be President. But I'm not going to spend my life washing Mike's laundry and fixing his soup and raising his kids. Or worse"—she shuddered—"keeping boarders. Huh-uh."

The doorbell rang then, and off she galloped. I heard her laugh on the porch and invite Mike inside. He'd brought her a dozen red roses and a bottle of Blue Grass cologne. I'd normally go down to greet him, then close the door as they left. But I was still miffed with her, telling me what little she thought of my life. How she wouldn't make the same fool-headed mistakes.

So I put Tom to bed, still peevish. Pulled on pajamas and spread out my crocheting on the sofa. It was only eight o'clock; Al wouldn't be home from the Moose for another couple hours. The night was so warm, I dozed in the middle of my work. Woke to the sound of a heavy slap.

"I said *no*, didn't I?" It was Annie's voice, indignant, alongside the house. "How many times do I have to tell you? Good*night!*"

It was hard to resist peeking out the window. About time Mike made some moves, as many months as he'd been waiting on that girl. I heard the front door slam, then Annie sniffling on the stairs. Decided to leave her alone; advice could wait until morning. Al wasn't home yet, so I lay down and dozed once again. I woke a second time to the sound of her voice, muffled but pleading. Directly below. In her bedroom.

"Why, why are you doing this? Can't you see, I don't want to? No, no, no . . ." Damn, what was she up to now? She smacks him, then lets him back in the house, then invites him to her bedroom, then gets cold feet. Al had a name for that. Cocktease.

But she was sobbing, frantic enough I got worried. I climbed down the stairs, tying the belt on my housecoat, and knocked on her door.

"You okay in there, Annie?"

It was thirty seconds before she answered.

"Yeah . . . please, Masha, *please*, just go back to bed."

I did as she said and waited by the window to see Mike leave. He never did. And in a few minutes, I heard the groan of bedsprings in her room, faster and faster, then the whole house was quiet. Sly vixen, I thought.

⁂

*N*ext day they broke up. She told me the reason, red-eyed, over breakfast. Said she wasn't ready to get married, not to Mike. He was a nice guy, but he couldn't make change for a nickel, or read without stuttering. She wanted a man she could respect.

I bobbed my head sympathetically, thinking I knew the real reason. Sex. It hadn't sounded like she was much interested from what I'd overheard. I felt the same way, of course, my first time with Al. Sat in Sunday school next day, shamed to death, my legs twisted around each other. So it seemed to me she owed her boyfriend another chance. Said so.

"Another chance?" she cried. "To prove *what?*"

"That he can make you happy." I stirred my oatmeal and smiled slyly. "Things do get better, if you know what I mean."

She colored. "For God's sakes, Masha!"

"Alright, then, but why burn all your bridges?" I said, remembering him stroking her hand over peach cobbler. "Tell him to call you in a month, once you've had time to think. Annie, honey"—I stroked her hair— "any fool can see he loves you."

"Oh Masha, leave her alone," said Mum peskily, pouring coffee. "She knows what she's doing. That boy was shanty Irish and nowhere near smart enough for her. Good riddance!" Mum never did like the Irish. Ranked them one rung above Italians.

That was when Vlado slid through the door, smelling like sweat and cheap hooch. He sat next to Annie, grinning at nothing I knew about, and drizzled honey on top of his oatmeal. He never once took his bloodshot eyes off my sister.

"You lovesick, Chickie?" he asked, grinning. "Need a new boyfriend?"

She fled the room, overturning her chair.

⚭

*T*he Xanax Dr. Gibson gave me didn't help. It put me to sleep twenty-four hours a day and gave me nightmares, vivid as Hollywood, about the bird and Lily and Mum. I remembered Mrs. Lemack saying that if you've got a pimple, squeeze it. So I threw out the Xanax. And decided to get rid of my ticket.

The possibilities, of course, were endless: burning, tearing, marking, crumpling, cutting, flushing, peeling, shredding, swallowing. That's what Mrs. Kosavitch did with her first will, the one that left everything she owned to her husband. She'd had a change of heart about his inheritance the day he dumped her for his ladyfriend. Gal stopped me on the steps of Rudy's Market and asked me over that morning for hot chocolate. And, she smiled, to help her put her affairs in order.

I didn't like the sound of it. Made me think of the way people talk when they're expecting a visit from Dr. Kevorkian. I asked for a rain check.

"No," she said, her hand on my sleeve. "You're coming, like it or not. I need a witness."

"For what?"

"To see me screwing Stan. Oh, stop making faces, Mrs. Kuzo! I'm not talking about *sex,* good God! I'm just revoking my will, so he doesn't get a red cent. And I need someone to say they saw me do it."

I joined her in her kitchen, not that I could refuse, her dragging me with her thumb in my belt loop. I watched her tear the will to confetti, soak the scraps in hot chocolate, and chew it all like cud. I warned her the paper would give her the trots, last thing she needed with her spastic colon.

"Don't you understand anything, Mrs. Kuzo?" she said. "I *want* it to hurt! And bad enough I'll never forget what that

125

sonovabitch's done. Then when he comes scratching on my screen with a box of Whitman's chocolates, begging me to take him back, telling me I'm sexy, I'll pump him with my .44."

I crossed myself. "You keep a piece like *that* around?"

"Hell, yes. I loaded it just this morning." She wagged her finger in my face. "So you mind your p's and q's, too, Mrs. Kuzo, you hear?"

But she was all talk, never shot him or anyone else. She took the old boy back, his hair reeking of Grecian Formula, the day his girlfriend split. They invited the neighbors for a Welcome-Back-Stan barbecue, bring your own steak. Love-birds drove to Jacoby and Meyers next morning, sneaking kisses at every red light, and forked over twenty-five dollars to have the identical will prepared. Of course, she swallowed *that* will, too, after Stan's creditors hot-wired his car. Which she didn't need to do, being's he ended up drowned.

Still, the story inspired me. I boiled up water for chocolate, dusted a mug with Nestle's and tore open some marshmallows. Even left the phone off the hook in case Mrs. Lemack called.

But I lost my nerve as the teakettle whistled. Started to cry like a newborn. I just couldn't destroy it. And I didn't know why.

❦

*W*ith Mike Gallagher gone, Annie laid plans of her own. She was all ambition back then, hiding every penny she earned under a loose floorboard in Mum's gardening shed and counting her stash at night. She was going to college, full-steam ahead. Filled out applications by the light of the stars and listed the diner as her return address. She didn't breathe a word to anyone, not even me.

She got into Penn State. Full-tuition scholarship. They even offered her work in the dining hall to pay for her books and her toothpaste. The night she got word, she wrote a short letter and tucked it under Mum's silverware—then scadoodled to the library before the boarders sat down to dinner.

Mum read the letter over a bowl of buttered turnips. She laid it face up on the tablecloth, her forehead wrinkled, and turned to me. "You knew about this, Masha?"

I shook my head and reached for the note.

Mum grabbed my wrist. "You see *your* name on that anywhere?"

"No, but—"

"Hands off, then. And don't lie to me. I *know* you know all about this. What's Annie told you about going off to college?"

"*College?* Not a word!" It stung me that my sister had shut me out. I'd thought we were best friends. And ten to one Mum'd blame me, that I'd somehow put her up to flying the coop.

"She's planning to become a schoolteacher," said Mum, rereading the note.

I shrugged, still sore. "That so?"

"That all you can say?" Mum threw her face in her hands and came up seconds later— unbelievably—laughing. "Annie's going to college. *My* daughter! And on scholarship! Think about that, Masha. The very first Tulevich!"

I thought better than to bring up the fact Annie wasn't a Tulevich. Grunted instead and slathered my bread with Oleo.

"There's no keeping us back any longer," Mum was saying. "We're going somewhere at *last*. And it's Annie who's pulling us up!"

Labor Day weekend, we waved the girl off at the bus station. She carried a little frayed suitcase packed with all the clothes she owned, three patched dresses, a pullover sweater, four sets of underwear, a yellowed slip, and her hairpins. She climbed on board the bus and sat on the opposite side from where we could see her. I knew she was crying.

"By God, I hope she gets what she deserves," said Mum, wiping her own eyes as the bus rolled out of its berth, shooting hot smoke in our faces. "And a nice boy, too."

She found a boy, alright, but I'd hardly call him nice. Good-looking? Smart? Rich? Some women might think so. But Ted was a cocky bastard. I felt it in my bones first time I laid eyes on him. The curl of his lip didn't suit.

She'd been seeing him awhile, hinted in her letters about "a special someone," but wouldn't tell us his name. When she came home at Christmas, I barely recognized her. The girl had lost twenty-five pounds, forever sworn off apple pie. She passed the time smoking and waiting by the phone for his calls. I didn't like it. She wasn't Annie anymore. She'd stopped singing.

"Why don't you invite him—whatever his name is—to Braddock?" I asked.

"Here?" she frowned. "No thanks!"

Ashamed of us Hunkies, I thought. Held my tongue. "Then how can I meet him?"

She brightened. "Come up to State College, Mash. We could have a good time."

I held her to her word and took the bus up the week of spring break. Mum agreed to watch my kids on condition I report back everything that happened. I'd never seen her so curious about anything.

When I got there, Annie was waiting on the platform, arm in arm with her boyfriend. I limped the full distance to where they stood, dragging my luggage, my spine stiff from the bus seat. She threw her free arm over my shoulder without letting go of him and crushed my nose against the bones in her neck. Damn, she was looking good. Her throat smelled of clean perfume. First time I ever saw her in gloves, silk stockings, and a hat. Any king would want her.

"Masha," she gushed, standing aside. "I want you to meet someone *very* special."

His name was Ted Hinterteil. Gave me pause, sounded like a bathroom fixture. It surprised me he was shorter than Annie.

Skinnier, too. He had a thick thatch of blond hair that skirted his forehead, snow-white teeth, dimples, and eyes as blue as Annie's. Boy was American head to foot, no steelworker's son. Better than us, and he knew it. I hated him.

"Looks like you need help with your bags," he said breezily, considering he'd just crushed every bone, shaking my hand. "Allow me?"

"You sure you can handle all that?" I had my own suitcase and two big boxes of baked goods for Annie.

The boy ignored me, picked up the luggage, and took off at a clip. He was stronger than he looked. I found out later he'd once been the welterweight champion of Central Pennsylvania and worked out hours each day with weights and a punching bag.

"What do you think?" whispered Annie as we tagged along behind him, his narrow butt in full view.

"He's cute," I said indifferently.

"Is that all? Just cute? Mash, he's perfect!"

"You two in love, by any chance?"

"*I* am," she whispered. "I just hope to God *he* is!"

Ted flagged us a taxi out front, helped the driver load my luggage, told him where to take us, and then paid our fare with a ten-dollar bill from Annie's wallet.

"Aren't you coming along?" I asked him.

"No, I have other commitments," he said, glancing importantly at his watch. "Annie can explain, if you're interested."

She did, couldn't wait. Cupped her hand to my ear, tickled it as she whispered. "Ted's got an interview tomorrow with a Philadelphia law firm. For a summer internship. It's a big deal . . . he needs to get home and rest . . . he's nervous about making a good impression, can you *believe* that?"

No, I thought sourly as the cabbie hustled us inside. That boy's type doesn't sweat. He's an ivory statue. No pores.

She poked her head out the window and touched Ted's hand before we drove off. "Good luck tomorrow, Sweetie! Call me tonight, will you? Please?"

"If I have time," he said. He turned on his heels in the opposite direction and disappeared in the crowd. I noticed he hadn't even squeezed her hand.

🐚

*S*he heard nothing from him for days. Sang his praises dawn to dusk, how he was third in his class, president of his fraternity, on his way to law school in the fall. But nighttimes she trembled in bed beside me, her fist in her throat, stifling sobs.

"What's with Ted?" I finally asked after three sleepless nights. We were eating egg salad sandwiches at a luncheonette. "You sure he's alright?"

"Of course he is!" she answered briskly, reaching for her Lucky Strikes, her food barely touched.

I couldn't bear seeing her so upset. "Can't hurt to call him, you think?"

"Nah. He probably just stopped off to see his folks on his way back from Philly. He'll call. I *know* he will."

Then she described how she'd met his parents, good folks, Methodists, from Blue Ball, Pennsylvania. His father was a high school principal, coached track; his mother taught piano and played the church organ. There were four kids, Ted the second, the rest of them girls. His sisters were wild about him, even fought over his medals from debating tournaments and boxing matches. Every week they mailed him gingerbread and peanut brittle and shoofly pies in tissue-lined cardboard boxes.

"I love them all," said Annie. "They didn't ask me a thing about myself or my parents or Braddock, just treated me like one of the family. And his sisters are all so pretty! Petite types with tiny hands and feet. Ted's always telling me to lose weight, but they told him I'm fine the way I am. That all I'd need was a decent hairstyle and new clothes cut for my figure."

"If they're your friends, then why don't you call them?" I

urged, wondering what kind of friends would suggest Annie's figure needed flattering. "Maybe they know where Ted's at."

"No, no," she shook her head hurriedly. "I couldn't do that, absolutely not!"

But call him she did, ashen-faced, the morning of the fifth day. She dialed his fraternity while I stood outside the phone booth trying to read her lips. He must have answered on the first ring and kept the conversation short. I swore I heard her apologizing. But she bounded out of the booth, peachy cheeked and bright-eyed.

"Everything okay?" I asked doubtfully.

"Of *course* everything's okay! He just didn't want to bother us while you were visiting. Which is what I thought all along, even with you turning me into a nervous wreck!"

I hid my anger. "So what's he have to say?"

"Good news. He got offered the job in Philly, isn't that wonderful? And he's going to meet us for dinner tonight, to celebrate. That okay with you?"

"Sure."

She stooped and kissed my cheek. "Oh, Mash, if you could only know how happy I am!"

I wished I could share her excitement, but I couldn't. Something stunk. My sixth sense told me he'd been celebrating already. With another woman. Or two.

❀

*U*nlike Mike Gallagher, Ted didn't finish the food on his plate. There was nothing the matter with it, really, just a flank steak a little well-done around the edges. He paid more attention to the busty waitress and the olives in his martinis. After chugging a fourth, he started talking, his elbows on the table, staring me down as he spoke.

"So, Masha—may I call you Masha?—I assume Annie's told you our news, hasn't she?"

"No, I haven't, Sweetie—" she interrupted, her hand on his wrist. I could see she was trembling.

"Why not?" he asked irritably, pulling his hand away. "You've had five days to do it! Isn't that how long she's"—indicating me—"been here?"

"I . . . just . . . wasn't sure now was the time."

"I *thought* we discussed this already."

"I know, I know. I'm sorry, Sweetie."

"Well, then," he said, turning my direction, one corner of his mouth curled. "*I'll* break the news. The fact is, Masha, Annie and I are married."

I choked on my T-bone steak and grabbed a glass of water. "Married? You're kidding! Since when?"

"Since Friday two weeks ago."

I turned, outraged, to Annie. "Why the heck didn't you tell me this? What's Mum going to think?"

Ted skewered the olive in his glass and poked my shoulder. "How about congratulating us first? I mean, isn't that the custom? Among *Americans* at least?"

"Alright, congratulations, then!" I shrugged and turned back to Annie. "Kiddo, what's with the secrets?"

"Oh Masha," she whispered, her pale skin throwing off heat. "It's too complicated to explain. We just didn't want to wait! Please, please don't tell Mum! I'm coming home next weekend to tell her myself. Well, not the whole truth, only that we're *planning* to get married. Listen, we intend to go through it all again in June. She doesn't need to know, do you think?"

"Not unless"—I considered switching to our language, abandoned the idea—"you *had* to get married."

"Had to get married?" Ted sneered, tilting back in his chair. "Are you asking Mrs. Hinterteil if she's pregnant?"

I faced him. "Yes. I am."

He let out a ballpark whistle. "What kind of people do you

take us for, Sister?" I could see in his eyes he knew I'd marched down the aisle with a full belly.

"You can go to hell," I said quietly.

"Oh, Masha!" cried Annie, wringing her hands. "Don't talk like that. He's my husband! He's family!"

Family. I started to weep. Fact was, she was my sister, and I was losing her, just as I'd lost Lily. Only this time to *him.* She took me in her arms, both of us crying like open spigots, kissing each other's hands.

"Everything'll be alright, Mash, I promise," she wept. "Try to understand, I love him! But I love you, too! We'll never drift apart, you and me, will we?"

"Good God," laughed Ted, sitting up in his chair and snapping his fingers at the waitress for the check. "What the hell have I got myself into? What kind of family is this?" He peeled off some bills and threw them on the table. "You coming, Annie?"

She nodded. Kissed me one more time and stood up.

$\mathcal{D}$ear Abby says to contact your clergyman when you've got problems she can't answer. I figured the lottery ticket was one of them. If I'd ask anyone what to do with two hundred thousand unwanted dollars, they'd laugh till they'd emptied their bladder. A clergyman, at least, is paid to keep a straight face and dry pants. So I called Father Serge.

It wasn't my day; his answering machine came on. I hoped it wasn't a sin hanging up, but I've never talked to one of those nasty contraptions. That's why I don't bother phoning Barb's house. Her machine screens all her calls.

But I had to talk to Father Serge, couldn't put it off. Recalled he heard confession starting at three each afternoon. I hadn't been for ages, not in the eighteen years since Annie died, when I gave up on God. But that day I was going. The absolute last resort.

*F*ather Serge was ten minutes late. I couldn't decide whether to lay claim to him at once or give the other old ladies—who'd arrived after me—front seats. Problem with going last was I might wait hours. The gals around here love the confessional. I've seen them take sandwiches, juice boxes, needlepoint, and knitting inside. Then march out two hours later with the better part of a baby sweater over their arm. I've always kept it short, five minutes at most, time enough to describe how I cursed Mrs. Kosavitch or wished I was dead. I'm a boring sinner.

Father Serge nodded as he passed. He's a tall man, six feet, with one shoulder higher than the other. He never smiles, just as well, with those pointed teeth. He's covered with moles, some black, some purple, that he scratches during Mass. Shingles, the old gals whisper. Syphilis, says Mrs. Kosavitch.

Everyone gossips about him, how he vacations at the shore with his housekeeper or picks up hookers in the lobby at Harrah's. Mrs. Yuhasz, the worst of the parish motormouths, swore up and down she'd seen him at Asbury Park playing miniature golf with a Dolly Parton look-alike. She followed them down the block to Dairy Queen, then through the front doors of the Best Western Motel. Of course Mrs. Yuhasz also claims she spent a week in a UFO circling over Braddock. So I don't listen to her garbage anymore.

I can't see Father Serge with a woman, anyway. His hobby is collecting insects. He's got a glass case of them at the rectory, hundreds, flattened and labeled with typewritten cards. God's most beautiful creatures, he calls them. Even the cockroaches.

🍺

*I* never liked the confessional. Smells like the last occupant, equal parts sweat and Jean Naté. You have to grope around in pitch blackness to find the kneeling bench. Then ease yourself down, joints popping, without a handrail. I once felt a spider shoot up my arm.

Father Serge opened his screen and threw in some light. He was sitting in profile, chin propped on his fist. I cleared my throat.

"Excuse me, Father . . . but I'm not here to make a confession today."

"So . . . ?"

"What I'd really like . . . I mean, what I really *need* . . . is advice."

He sighed. Probably expected me to whine about my gall bladder or about how Mrs. Kosavitch pinches a roll of toilet paper from my bathroom whenever she comes to call. And it was getting near dinnertime. His stomach was talking.

"It won't take long," I promised. "In fact, if you like, I'll come back whenever's convenient."

"That won't be necessary," he sighed, gently but bored, settling back in his chair. "Take as long as you like."

"Okay then. It all comes down to . . . a really *simple* question."

"Such as?"

I took a deep breath. "Well . . . I've come into some money. More than I'm accustomed to, and I need to know—"

"Money? How did you get it?"

I couldn't answer truthfully. "Just let's say . . . through someone else's generosity."

"I see. Then you inherited it?"

"Not exactly. But that's all beside the point. What I need to know is—"

"How much money?"

"Probably enough to put a new roof on my house. And then wrap the rest of it in aluminum siding. But—"

"In other words," he cleared his throat, "a substantial amount."

"Not to some people." I wasn't lying. What was two

hundred thousand to Donald Trump or Mike Tyson or that goofy purple dinosaur on TV?

"So you're looking for some guidance on how to spend it, is that it?" He touched his fingertips together, one by one.

"No, not at all. What I want you to help me with—and this might sound strange—is *whether* I should spend it."

"Come, now, Mrs. Kuzo. It *is* Mrs. Kuzo, am I right? You're not giving me anywhere near enough facts."

No surprise he knew who I was. Barb always said I had a voice you'd never forget. Didn't know whether to be flattered or not. I'd recognize Diane Sawyer's silky voice anywhere. But then, too, Wilma Flintstone's.

"Why are the facts so important?" I asked, gritting my teeth.

"Because I suspect—and correct me if I'm wrong—the money you're speaking of is tainted in some way."

"Of course it is!" I gushed with relief. "Isn't all money?"

"No. At least not money we choose to donate to a higher purpose."

"A *what?*"

"Come, come, you know what I mean. No? Well, on a local level, think, for example, of the Carnegie Libraries. Surely you agree that's money spent for the benefit of others."

So he was getting around to it at last. A sales pitch to save St. Stepan's.

"But Father—I don't want to donate it! Look, there's something so bad about this money it might be a sin even *giving* it away."

"Does this money have anything to do with your son?" he asked sharply.

I didn't like the question. "My son? I'm not following."

But of course I was. Tom had just been arrested growing pot in a plastic kiddie pool behind his trailer. As far as everyone around church was concerned, the kid was the same as Ted Bundy. It didn't matter he owned his own auto body shop and worked on their cars—even Father Serge's Chevette—and gave them all a discount.

"Let me be direct, Mrs. Kuzo," he said. "I'm asking you to level with me. Is the money you're speaking of . . . stolen?"

"By Tom?" I said indignantly. "Is that it?"

"It's just a hunch."

I bolted out of the confessional, opened the door to his compartment, and wagged my finger in his face. "You think I'd come here asking you to help me run a laundering operation? For Christ's sakes, Father Serge!"

"Ma'am," he said quietly, "perhaps I should remind you this *is* the house of God."

"Yeah, but maybe I should remind *you* I've tithed 10 percent of what I get from Social Security every year since I retired—"

"I'm aware of that—"

"And what I get from Uncle Sam is maybe enough to feed me pork and beans. So give me a little respect!"

"No disrespect intended, ma'am. But the holes in your story didn't leave me much of an alternative."

"All I was *asking* was what I should do with the money!"

"Then you've come to the wrong place," he yawned and stood up. "What you need is an investment counselor. They're in the yellow pages."

🌸

*A*nnie took the bus home to Braddock the following weekend, dressed in a shapeless wool jumper Ted's sisters had sent her. She called Mum into the parlor, crossed her hands in her lap, and broke the news that she was engaged. It didn't go down well.

"What about school?" asked Mum. "You thought about that?"

"Of course. And I'm putting it on hold. I'll need to work while Ted's in law school."

"That mean you're going to quit?"

"For the time being, yes."

Mum sent an ashtray into orbit against the wall and shattered it. "You crazy? What the *hell* do you think you're doing?"

"Isn't that what you wanted?" wailed Annie. "That I'd marry a successful man?"

"Of course I do! But your boyfriend's not successful yet. And if he's a good man, he'll want you to finish school and be successful, too. What happened to your plans? Don't you want to teach school anymore?"

"Yes, Mum, but I love him. Can't you understand? I don't want to wait!"

"You sleeping with him?"

"Mum!"

"Go ahead, sleep with him!" she shouted, throwing up her big hands in disgust. "You don't need to quit school to do that. Think of it as part of your education."

"Don't talk cheap like that!"

"Cheap? What's cheap? Rent a hotel room. Take off your clothes for an hour. Then stick your nose back in your books and finish your degree. Mark my words, Girlie, you leave school now, you'll end up his maid."

"You don't know a thing about us!"

"No? Okay, suit yourself," said Mum, sweeping the broken glass into the palm of her hand. "But remember what I'm about to say. It's no use making sacrifices for a man; they can't be trusted. Believe me, Girl, I know."

"Yes, I believe you," said Annie bitterly. "With all the men you've had coming and going."

Which was when Mum popped her square in the face, then dragged her by the hair out the pocket doors and through the foyer. Pitched her out the front door and down the steps. I found her an hour later, crying on her knees. Her beautiful face was bruised, her stockings torn, her hair disheveled. I brought her inside, packed her an ice bag, and boiled tea, both of us weeping.

Next morning Ted arrived, a bouquet in either hand, roses for Mum, tulips for Annie. The boy was immaculate in his linen suit and starched shirt and silk tie. He behaved like a gentleman, even to me. No surprise Mum fell in love with him. She sat cross-legged beside him on the Duncan couch, asking him all about himself in her broken English. Later that day, the three of them shopped for wedding clothes. Mum picked—and paid for—a double-breasted pinstripe suit for the groom, a gunmetal-gray dress for Annie, a tight purple sheath for herself.

They got married a second time in June, both families in attendance. Held the ceremony in a Philadelphia hotel because Ted's mother, who had female problems, wouldn't travel to Braddock. I've kept all the wedding pictures, but not on the wall, can't bear the sight of my brother-in-law. Particularly the five-by-seven of him and Mum, arms entwined. She's grinning.

They didn't take a honeymoon. But Annie honored her end of the bargain and put Ted through law school. He found them an attic apartment on the Main Line and negotiated free rent in exchange for Annie cleaning the rest of the building. The landlady knew every drunk divorcee in the neighborhood and introduced Annie all around. Girl spent the next three years on her knees scrubbing their floors and freshening their drinks.

🍍

"*T*wo hundred thousand? That's all?" said Mrs. Lemack the day I showed her my ticket. "You've probably spent that much playing Super Seven all these years. What are you going to do with the loot?"

"Not a thing. It was a mistake. I shouldn't have won."

"You're not making much sense, Mrs. Kuzo. Set me straight, will you?"

"Okay, then. The money's dirty. There's something wrong about it—gives me the heebie-geebies. And don't ask why."

"Sounds like you've pretty much made up your mind. That ticket's going to stay sitting on your dresser, true or false?"

I nodded, relieved to make a clean breast of it.

"Then what the heck are you telling me about it in the first place?" she bristled.

"You don't think I'm crazy, then?"

"Crazy? What you do's no concern of mine, Mrs. Kuzo. I never judge a soul. Now, how about I show you my bowling scores? You're not going to believe them. I mopped the floor with everyone last night, the very people who said I was past my prime!"

# $\mathcal{E}$xit 21—$\mathcal{L}$ancaster

$\mathcal{T}$he last time I saw Vicky was three months ago. Easter weekend, to be exact, just after Barb filed for bankruptcy and Tom left the hospital. I'd got a letter from her asking me to dinner. She and Sidd were driving out to Pittsburgh.

*You don't need to put us up*, she'd written. *I know you're having your troubles. So we'll be staying with our friends Sam and Purna. Maybe you remember them.*

Shoot, did I. Seven-foot fellow and the roly-poly Indian wife he'd met digging ditches in the Peace Corps. Vicky brought them by one night when I'd barbecued hamburgers. Whispered in my kitchen Sam never ate anything cooked, always carried raw food around in a knapsack. She wasn't lying. He sat on my porch chewing carrots and crabgrass.

*I insist you let us take you to dinner. How about Saturday night? We could have a real celebration, with good food and interesting atmosphere—so no Leonetti's Diner, please! And remember, the treat's on us.*

Irked me to read that. I like Leonetti's, the only joint around here that feeds you the amount you've paid for, pound for pound. Years ago Vicky would beg me to take her, back when Annie got strange and I had custody. She'd order breaded veal cutlet, two kinds of pie, and still demand ice cream on the way home. And now she's too good for all that.

*Otherwise, things are moving right along. In another six months, I'll sit for my orals and—depending on the outcome— join the ranks of unemployed Philadelphia psychologists. Of course, my career won't concern me if we get pregnant. Sidd and I agree a child needs the full attention of at least one parent— something, if I recall, I never had. And if there's one thing I believe, it's that children deserve the best their parents can provide—morally, spiritually, and metaphysically.*

Damn right. And Vicky got all that malarkey she was talking about from her mother. Not that she'd remember.

*We'll come by for you at seven, barring an Act of God. It's been ages since we visited. This should be fun!*

I didn't share her enthusiasm. Still irked me she hadn't bailed Barb out of bankruptcy. I don't care for her company, either, all the ugly things she says about Annie. And it just keeps getting worse and worse, the longer my sister's dead.

❀

*W*hen Ted finished law school, he got hired at a silk-stocking Philadelphia firm. The partners gave him a gum-snapping secretary, his own paneled office with a view of Camden, New Jersey, and a bottomless bottle of Chivas Regal. He spent the first of many paychecks on clothes, natty as Cary Grant in his silk shirts. They never wrinkled in front, not at all like Al's, which bunched like opened parachutes no matter what size I bought him.

Ted made lots of money, grew a thin mustache, and gained weight. He specialized in personal injury, had a knack for picking good plaintiffs, most of them old folks. He'd sue their surgeons for cutting out wrong organs or leaving sponges in their bodies. Cocky kid settled most of his cases over the phone, feet on his desk, tie loosened, cracking his knuckles over his head. He'd offer his gum-chewing secretary a shot of Chivas to celebrate.

Three years into practice, Ted bought a big house on the Main Line, same neighborhood as the partners. Annie sent me snapshots, a drafty red brick barn with oak floors, six bedrooms, and a kidney-shaped swimming pool. Stuck-up neighbors, too, the types that wore argyle vests and kept sailboats in Maine. Annie saw them only once a year, at the neighborhood picnic. She invited me along a couple times to keep her company while Ted worked the crowd. Darndest thing I ever saw, rows and rows of cedar picnic tables, all covered with starched gingham cloths, everybody standing around drinking martinis out of picnic thermoses, chatting about cricket matches and prep schools and Paris. Ted fit right in.

He had to work eighty hours a week to keep himself in style. His version, anyway, why he never was home. Annie got accustomed to eating alone under the chandelier, a book in her lap. She'd climb into bed every night at nine with a hot water bottle and her Lucky Strikes. Ted never called to tell her when to expect him. He stayed away days at a time.

It's true he was clever and brought home the bacon. Made close to six figures before he was thirty. Still, Annie never asked him for a cent. He frightened her. So she dressed in yard-sale clothing her entire marriage.

"Why the hell don't you buy something new for a change?" I snorted, thinking about Ted's income. "It ever occur to you you deserve better?"

She laughed bitterly, ash crumbling off her cigarette onto the parquet floor, and started to cough. Girl couldn't get her breath back till I'd thumped her hard between the shoulder blades and brought her a Dixie cup of water. I couldn't see the humor.

But when it came to dressing Vicky, Annie went first class. She drove the girl to stores in Bala Cynwyd, sale or not, and turned her loose with a credit card. Vicky had more clothing than Princess Di. Silk lingerie, too.

Not that she spent much time in those skivvies, at least after she left home. She went to college at Swarthmore, then dropped out and worked as an artists' model, even in winter, sprawled out naked in front of a class, with a space heater blowing up her backside. Annie and I visited her one weekend when she was living with hippies in that Germantown commune. She'd decorated the walls of her bedroom with sketches the students had done of her, every one of them buck naked. Annie didn't say a word on the way home. Stared at the white line on the highway, blinking back tears.

❦

*V*icky and Sidd took me to a restaurant called "Marrakech," upstairs from a beatnik bookstore in a crummy little alley in Shadyside. We spent half the night finding it, Sidd driving the wrong way down one-way streets and side-swiping trash cans in the Jaguar. He asked every wino for directions and never got more than a grunt. The last drunk heaved an empty bottle at the car, then chased us down the street, cursing camel jockeys.

"Look, Kids," I said, teeth chattering, once the welcoming committee disappeared from the rearview mirror. "I've got a six-pack of Coke and stuffed cabbage in the fridge. What do you say?"

"You know we don't eat red meat," said Vicky briskly, "so relax. This is our night on the town, remember?" Then she flagged down a couple of girls, got them to draw us a map on some junk mail once we'd dropped them at a biker bar.

Twenty minutes later, we found Marrakech. There wasn't a chair in the joint, only low tables and lumpy cushions. Everywhere you looked were professor types with bushy eyebrows and black turtlenecks and nasal voices, hunched over wineglasses, forehead to forehead with girls half their age.

It wasn't the first time I'd seen that kind of lopsided pairing. Vicky had a middle-aged boyfriend once, her history professor at Swarthmore, an Englishman named Trygve Wiggins-Bugg. He wore smoked glasses like a blind person and a lapis lazuli bracelet.

"That man's older than her father," groaned Annie. "There should be laws against robbing the cradle like that!"

I kept my comments to myself, that Vicky wasn't coming out smelling like roses, either. She was robbing the grave.

I finally got to meet Tryg, as he called himself. A Sunday afternoon in Annie's hospital room, last few weeks of her life. She'd lost all her hair from chemotherapy and didn't bother with wigs anymore. Had me prop an old picture of herself on the bedside table, still in high school, radiant, on horseback at Kennywood Park. It made me weep to look at it.

Vicky, meanwhile, sat in her boyfriend's lap, lighting his pipe and tweaking his mustache, him prattling cheerfully about politics and wine. He was dressed all in black, except for a paisley scarf knotted girly-style at his neck, and white sneakers, no socks.

"Tryg's a Marxist, you know," said Vicky, earnestly, to her mother. "Do you know he did his doctoral thesis on the labor movement in the American steel industry?"

"Bet the only steel he's touched is the fender on his Saab," I whispered in Annie's ear, shaking out her blanket.

That was the last time I saw her smile.

*A*nnie tried for years to get pregnant. She called me, honking in a Kleenex, every time she'd get her period. When I brought her to Braddock, Mum suggested she visit Madame Vargas, the old gypsy who lived in the garage draped with scarves. Mum didn't take a new lover or invest any money without visiting her first. Swore by the woman's skills.

"I don't believe in that sort of thing," said Annie, arms crossed.

"You don't, do you?" Mum rolled her eyes. "Well, then, stop crying in your beer! Maybe you should be counting your blessings. You want your legs to look like this?" She lifted her skirt, showing the varicose veins that had thickened with each pregnancy. "You've got a good-looking husband, a nice house, and time on your hands. Why not go back to school? Finish that fancy degree you always wanted. And just keep your husband interested, he'll get you pregnant, mark my words!"

Annie sat there, tears in her eyes, biting a thumbnail, and flicking cigarette ashes into the conch shell I'd brought back from Florida. She had the ugliest hands I've ever seen, fingertips yellow with nicotine, cuticles torn and bleeding. They'd get infected from her saliva, swell to the size of a punching bag and have to be lanced at the ER. She'd laugh about it afterward, pitching cigarette ash around on my afghans.

But Annie followed Mum's advice and enrolled at Swarthmore. She studied so hard she ruined her eyesight and had to get glasses—which she later sat on by accident in philosophy class. Ted refused her the money for a new pair, so she taped the broken pieces with Band-Aids.

She did get pregnant. Quit school for good and bloomed like a hothouse flower. She gained forty pounds, her hair turned to spun gold, her skin to cherry cheesecake. She was the only pregnant woman I've known who could still turn heads, even up to the day her water broke. Which, for her, was the day all hell let loose.

*A*nnie had postpartum depression after Vicky was born. That's what the nurse told Mum anyway, wrote it down on an index card and pronounced it three times slow. She made Mum say it back. We'd neither of us heard of it before and scratched our heads.

Mum and I had driven straight to Philly soon's we got word Annie was down in the mouth. I couldn't stay long, had to get back to the factory, but Mum jammed six suitcases and a hatbox in the trunk of my Dodge and told me she'd stay till Annie got better. It shocked the bejesus out of us seeing her flat on her back in the hospital bed, hair tangled, face turned to the wall. Her pajamas were dotted with cigarette burns, her wedding ring loose on her yellowed finger.

"Annushka!" cried Mum, pitching the snake plant she'd brought along into the nurse's hands. It was tied with a huge blue ribbon, no secret Mum had hoped for a grandson.

Annie tried to speak but couldn't, sucked on her scaly knuckles, blinking back tears. Mum sat down and covered her face with noisy kisses. Poor kid looked even more pitiful after that, an escapee from a carnival kissing booth.

"You okay?" I asked, handing her a tissue to wipe off Mum's mess.

"I'll be alright," she whispered with effort. "I just need . . . to get back home."

"You've really got to talk to her, Mrs. Tulevich," the nurse said as if Annie wasn't in the room. "It's not uncommon for new mothers to be depressed, of course, but your daughter doesn't seem to have the slightest interest in the baby."

"What you expect me to do about it?" asked Mum sullenly. "She comes to this hospital to have her kid, she's paying you good money. And then you tell me she's got problems you can't take care of?"

"We're only asking you to help us," the nurse said evenly,

as if she were used to all kinds of personalities, crummy ones especially. "Try talking to her, please."

"I'll do what I can," said Mum, pushing past to hang up her fur coat. "But all my kids were born in the bed where they were made. No need for hospitals back then. I ain't never seen a mother all teary-eyed like this. You been feeding her okay?"

"Mum, they've been feeding me fine," said Annie, embarrassed, up on her elbows, the color coming back into her face.

"They can't be, you look like a bag of bones! What's your husband going to say, you coming home so skinny? You want back in his bed, don't you?" She lifted Annie's chin in her hand. "Here, Mash, fetch my makeup. This girl needs all the help she can get."

Annie smiled bitterly, eased herself down on her back as Mum flicked open her compact and unscrewed the mascara.

"There, take a look at that," said Mum to the nurse. "She can smile, she can talk, she's fine. Now go get my little granddaughter, would you please? I've been sitting in the car all day, see these swollen ankles?"

"We only bring the infants to their mother's rooms at feeding time," called the nurse stiffly, heading out the door. "But you're welcome to walk down to the nursery, ma'am."

"What *she* needs is a good screw," Mum said in our language. She pulled up a chair next to Annie's bed and stroked her hair. "Girl, what the hell are you boo-hooing about? You're through the worst of it, you hear me? Dry those tears! Now, how's that good-lookin' husband of yours? He home cleaning house for his mother-in-law?"

🪷

*F*or the next few years after Vicky was born, I didn't see much of Annie. We'd gab once a month on the phone—always me calling her—about our kids or Mum or Jack Kennedy. We never mentioned our husbands. I'd still fetch her three times a year, and always for Russian Easter. She'd come along to church and over to Mum's for baked ham. But she didn't take communion anymore.

Near as I could tell, her life was peaches and cream. Ted became the firm's managing partner, doubled his income, and bought himself a second house on the Jersey shore, a big place with picket fences and shutters facing a rocky beach. She begged me to bring Mum, but I had only two weeks vacation a year, and I always took it with Al—who wasn't interested in Annie's company. He said she'd got too uppity for her Braddock family, and he'd rather go to Vegas. I made it down at last over Labor Day, while Ted was meeting some important clients in Chicago, and Al was at the Moose picnic. Perfect timing.

She was waiting out front, hand-in-hand with Vicky, both dressed in sneakers and pedal pushers. Gave me pause to see Annie up close. She'd got horribly thin, chicken bones, every ring in her neck exposed, her bosom gone. I found out later she was smoking three packs a day, even in the bathtub.

"You okay, Kiddo?" I asked as we sat in her kitchen.

Her hand shook as she fingered a place mat. "Do I look that bad?"

"No," I lied, "just tired. Motherhood wearing you down?"

"Of course not," she frowned. "Vicky's a *gift*. Can't you see it's her keeping me going these days?" She parted the cafe curtains and waved to her daughter on the swing set.

"Then why the long face?" I asked as gently as I could.

"God, I can't hide anything from you, can I?" She ran a hand through her brittle hair and dropped her chin to her chest.

"You're not pregnant, are you?"

"*Me?*" She laughed unpleasantly. "No, Mash, I'm not pregnant." She lit a cigarette and opened the refrigerator, her back to me. From the rear she was a shoestring, no hips, no haunches. "What can I get you? Baloney, Velveeta, olive loaf, peanut butter and jelly . . . ?"

"Coffee's fine," I said. "With milk, if you've got any."

"It's gone bad," she moaned, pouring what was left in the sink, clotted as cottage cheese. "God, I'm sorry."

"Relax, Kiddo," I said. "We can all walk down to the store in a bit and get more. I promised Vicky a Snickers bar, anyway. And in the meantime, I can drink coffee black."

She slid into the seat opposite me, grabbed a dirty saucer, and ground out her cigarette. Then teared over, blotting her face with a tea cozy. She was waiting for me to say something and sat a full minute.

"It's Ted, isn't it?" I said at last.

She nodded, then hid her face in her gnarled hands. "Please don't breathe a word to Mum. Promise. You know how fond of him she is."

"Word of honor." I reached over and squeezed her shoulder. Then settled back in my chair, expecting her to run him into the ground over the way he treated her.

She didn't. She got up from the table instead, measured instant coffee in my cup, and lit another cigarette. And suddenly grinned, ear to ear, a whole new person. "Vicky's downright wonderful, Mash. I never thought I could love anyone so much. And she hasn't had a teacher who wasn't crazy about her. Precocious, that's the word Ted uses. I'm sure she gets it from him. Vicky?" she called out the window. "Come here, sweetie! Want to show Aunt Masha the mobile you made at school?"

The kid, up to her elbows in mud pies, was chafed by the interruption. "Go away! I'm busy!"

Annie turned to me, smiled crookedly. "That's kids for you. Hey . . . how about we go out for ice cream? Bet she'll go for *that*. And I want to hear everything that's happening in Braddock, okay? *All* the gossip. And before you get started, where'd you get that hair cut? It's darling!"

That was how the rest of the visit went, her cooing and chirping and gushing over nonsense. Not another word about Ted. We hiked up and down the boardwalk, fed Vicky frozen custard, sloshed around in the surf. I felt I'd never known her at all.

🏵

*I* let Vicky order for me. The menu was in English, near as I could tell, but I didn't recognize a blessed thing except the price column. I didn't ask the waiter if they had anything simple, like steak or fried chicken or tossed salad. Questions like that could get you drop-kicked out the door of this kind of joint. And the waiter looked peevish to begin with, tapping a pencil while Vicky dawdled over her menu.

"How about living dangerously?" she asked me as if he wasn't there. "There's things on this menu to *die* for."

"Thanks but no thanks," I said, picturing snake meat kebabs. "I'd prefer to stick with something plain."

"Plain? In a Moroccan restaurant?" She tugged on her braid and grimaced. "It's a wonder you Tuleviches ever made it to America, you know that? No moxie!"

I cringed. Thought she had a lot of nerve, patting herself on the back, that she was somehow better than Mum and Annie and me, just because she'd eat cow plops in a clip joint.

"Well, then, have it your way," she said, rolling her eyes and flipping back to the front of the menu. "Hmmm . . . there's Chicken á la Moracaine"—she pronounced it with a French accent and a straight face—"which is about the least daring entree."

"Sounds fine," I mumbled.

"Same here, too," said Sidd, snapping the menu shut.

"Wimp-out!" she teased, tickling his ribs. And, as if to impress me with *her* moxie, she ordered pomegranate drink, potato-stuffed phyllo, and barbecued squid wrapped in palm leaves. I watched her reach across the table for the wine bottle, hold it between her knees, and pop it open as effortlessly as Barb. She poured, sniffed, then swirled the booze in her mouth like Lavoris, muttering something about *legs*. Started yakking next about her infertility tests and basal body temperature.

She'd long since lost my ear. Too many distractions. Like the professor and his student to my left. Lovebirds were getting awful cozy on those lumpy cushions. He had his tongue in her ear, a hand up her skirt, a tent in his pants. I leaned back on my elbows, joints cracking, and watched. Damn if I wasn't about to see a baby conceived.

❦

*T*he year after Mum died, Ted called on a Friday night. I was standing in the bathtub wiping mildew off the shower curtain.

"Masha, we've got a problem here," he announced without even first saying hello.

"A problem?"

"Yeah. Your sister. If I could get her to come to the phone, I would. But she won't get out of bed. And it's been three days now."

"She sick?" My stomach was lurching. Wished I'd gone easier on the pepperoni pizza I'd brought home for dinner.

"Listen, I don't have much time, so I'm going to be frank with you. Annie's been having mental problems. Serious problems."

"Good God," I whispered. "How long?"

"Months. I've been taking her to a psychiatrist. You know what that is, don't you?"

Ticked me off. "*Yeah*, Ted, I do."

"Well, congratulations. But let's get to the punch line. Her doctor's suggested hospitalization, but she's put up such a fight I dropped the idea altogether. Until today. I don't have much in the way of recourse with her behavior this unmanageable. Unless, of course, you get involved."

So that was it. He was dumping her. "What the heck do you expect me to do?"

"First, let me give you the facts. She's not eating. Or sleeping. Or bathing. She barely speaks anymore, except to some imaginary person called Lily. She's no use with the housework or cooking, and she can't take care of Vicky. To put it bluntly, I don't have the time or patience to be handling her. There's no explanation for her behavior. I want you to know I'm packing her bags and bringing her to Braddock tomorrow. Assuming you'll take her."

"Here? But—"

"I'm *expecting* you'll help me out. I think the best thing for her right now is to get back to her family."

"Her family? *You're* her family, Ted!"

He let ten seconds pass, then lowered his voice. "I'm talking blood, Masha. Or doesn't that rate with you anymore?"

Bastard. "Let me talk to her, Ted. *Now.*"

"You haven't been listening. I told you she won't come to the phone. So let's start over again. We've got a problem. Understand?"

The blood banged at my temples. "I know damn well *you've* got a problem, Ted. And maybe Annie does. But I'll have to talk to her before I decide whether I've got one, too. So cut out this *we* business."

"You want to talk to her? Excellent. I'll bring her by tomorrow so you can see for yourself. By one o'clock. And remember, I'm punctual."

"Ted—"

"Yes?" Irritably, probably checking his watch.

I lowered my voice. "I can keep her here a few days, but—"

"That should be more than enough. If that doesn't bring her around, then maybe you can have her committed to the state hospital nearest you. My secretary can get you the number. Or, if you prefer, you can check in the phone book yourself."

$T$ed was on my doorstep next afternoon. Vicky, too, seven years old, lugging her own little set of ballerina luggage and dressed in tights and pink toe shoes. She clutched a tightly rolled sleeping bag and a naked Barbie.

"I thought your sister would do better with Vicky along," announced Ted as I opened the screen door. "I know I didn't mention it on the phone. But just throw down a pillow. She can sleep anywhere."

"I'm hungry," said Vicky, dropping her Barbie on the sofa. "Can I have an Eskimo Pie? Daddy said you'd feed me. And I'd get whatever I wanted."

"Sure, Doll," I said, quietly cursing her father. A six-figure income and he wouldn't even stop on the turnpike to buy his kid a cheeseburger. "I'll fix you something soon's we get your mom settled. That's a deal, okay?"

"You got soda?"

"Sure do." I patted her cheek and turned to Ted sullenly. "So where's my sister?"

"She's still sitting in the car," he said. "And she won't budge. I might need your assistance."

I followed him, trembling, to the curb. I wouldn't have recognized her. She was not only thinner, she was filthy. Her forehead was covered with pimples, no makeup, not even her trademark red lipstick. I noticed fever sores clustered in the corners of her mouth, a dusting of dandruff on her shoulders. She was wearing one of Ted's old shirts, wrinkled as if she'd slept in it for days. The worst part was the smell of her, stale body odor, not the strong, healthy stench Al gave off after a hard day's work at the mill. It was the smell of sickness, just like Mum had the last few weeks of her life, that hung in her nightgown no matter how often we bathed her.

"Let me handle this," said Ted, opening the car door. "Annie? I'm telling you the last time. Get *out!*"

She didn't move, so I opened my arms to her. "Sweetie, it's

Mash." No answer. "You want to come in for some lunch? Please?"

"Out of the way," growled Ted, forcing me aside. "I'm sick of this farce."

And then he did the thing for which I'll always remember him. He pulled my sister out with both his hands on her neck, threw her down on the blacktop and kicked the door shut.

"Get moving," he said, lifting his foot under her back.

She wouldn't let me help her to her feet, scrambled ahead of him with her shoulders hunched like a vulture, straight to the porch. She perched herself on the arm of the glider and lit a cigarette, eyes downcast. Her hands trembled so bad she dropped the match on the plastic cushions and left a burn mark I can still see when I'm sitting out there evenings.

"Annie, *please*," I wailed. "For God's sake, what's the matter?"

"He's says I'm bad," she said, pointing at Ted. "That I'm ... shit. And that he'll take Vicky away and get me committed for good and—"

"What did I tell you?" said Ted impatiently, turning to me. "That's absolute nonsense. She's been like this for weeks, and I just can't keep her any longer. I've got a trial coming up—with a lot of money at stake—and I can't have her carrying on like this. It's an embarrassment. You understand?"

I ignored him and threw an arm over her shoulder.

"Maybe you can talk some sense into her," he continued, watching Annie. "When she's ready to stop this play-acting and become a real wife again, sure, then I'll be happy to take her back. You hear me, Annie?" He brought his face up to hers. "*Yoo*-hoo. Anybody home?"

"You got some potato chips?" asked Vicky, shaking my pant leg. "And Coke? My Mommy never buys any."

"Here's my number at work," said Ted, handing me a card. "Call me when she's better. But not one minute sooner."

"*R-r-r*-ruffles have *r-r*-ridges," said Vicky, rolling her r's. "*R-r-r*-ruffles have *r-r*-ridges, r-r-ruffles have *r-r*-ridges . . ."

"You need any help over there?" shouted Mrs. Kosavitch over the fence. "I'd be glad to lend a hand!"

❀

*A*nnie didn't get better. Not for a long time, anyhow, and then it didn't last. I took a couple days off work, got her into the shower and fresh clothes, but she wouldn't eat or sleep or speak. Just watched game shows, hours on end, smoking and burning holes in my new floral slipcovers. I was getting crazy right along with her, weeping my way through a roll of paper towels over the kitchen sink.

"What the hell's going on?" asked Al, pawing through his lunch bucket Monday morning to see what I'd packed. He tossed out the banana and replaced it with Oreo cookies. "Your sister gonna stay with us from now on? What about the kid? This here ain't some hotel, you know. You tell that to her tight-ass husband? Oh, stop crying, for Chrissakes, will you?"

That's when I got Mrs. Lemack on the phone. She'd had one of her in-laws committed, knew the ropes, and pulled up in her Lincoln ten minutes later. She sent me upstairs for luggage, took Vicky to a neighbor's, and then drove us helter-skelter to Braddock Hospital, right up to the Emergency Room doors. She left the Lincoln parked in the ambulance slot, flashers blinking.

The place was bedlam, thanks to a six-car pileup. We sat in the waiting area as they wheeled the gurneys past, me stroking Annie's ponytail, Mrs. Lemack reading *True Confessions* out loud. Her voice drowned out the overhead TV, same as her chatter about how she planned to donate her body to a medical school—false teeth, acrylic nails, spinal fusion, and all. This turned a few heads and got poor Annie wincing. The nurse finally called our name, took us back a narrow hallway, and pushed Annie down on an examining table.

I wasn't sure whether to be relieved or not when they admitted her to psychiatry. Observation only, the doctor told me, seventy-two hours maximum—and then, hopefully, she'd be sent home to her husband. Hopefully.

🍞

She wasn't sent home. And since Ted wouldn't pay for a private hospital, Annie got sent to the state institution. She stayed there eighteen months. I'd visit her every weekend, bring Vicky, peevish and whining and tugging at my elbow for soda pop. I was now the kid's legal guardian.

I never knew much what happened in the hospital, only that Annie got lousy meals and shock treatments. They'd zapped her hard enough to fracture both arms. Still and all, she started looking better—gained weight, combed her hair, plucked her eyebrows. She was talking, too, mostly reminiscences about Braddock and Mum and Nicky. But I didn't like her stories; they gave me a chill. I didn't know whether to believe her or not.

"Remember Granddaddy's cats?" she asked one sunny afternoon.

"Lord, who could forget them?" I laughed, thinking of Al.

"He kept three dozen till the day he died, you know that? I counted them after the undertaker left."

I nodded. The old man had a stroke a year before he died and lost all his speech and the use of his limbs. Mum stuck him on the porch behind the kitchen, had a carpenter enclose it with glass and make a sickroom. It always surprised me how gently she treated him. She changed his linens and bedpans and spoon-fed him split-pea soup. Even fetched his cats, laying them at the foot of his bed with yarn and a box of catnip.

That was the summer Nicky spent in boot camp just before he went off to the war. He came home to visit a few weeks, cocky in his uniform and meaner than a shark, especially when he'd drink. Mum was having health problems herself, uterine fibroids, and had to go in for a hysterectomy. And with Annie still in high school, and me and Al just moved to our own home, that left Nicky in charge.

"You don't know what happened, do you?" Annie whispered, twisting the sleeve of her hospital gown.

I shivered. "What are you talking about?"

So she told me. How twice a day, around noon and again in the evening, Nicky loaded up two plates with meat loaf or chicken or pork chops. He carried them out on the porch, set his plate down on the table, then balanced the other on Granddaddy's chest. Nicky ate first, washed it down with beer, then called in every cat, ringing the little dinner bell Granddaddy'd always used for them. The animals were ravenous—Nicky hadn't fed them—and followed their noses straight to the old man's bed. Nicky stood by crowing with laughter while the cats climbed on Granddaddy, fighting over his food, the old man frozen helpless on his back with dozens of cat butts crowded in his face.

Annie watched it all through the window, shaking in her shoes. She never told anyone because Nicky had threatened to kill her. He'd nicked her throat with the tip of a Bowie knife, just so she'd understand he meant business.

So Granddaddy starved to death. It was Mum who found him, out on the porch in the twilight the day she came home from the hospital. She screamed for hours, clutching a pillow to her incision. Then turned around and blamed it all on Annie.

❀

She finally went home to Ted, but she was never really better again. She'd go for stretches of a year or two, then end up back in the hospital. Each time Ted brought Vicky to live with us. I managed only with Mrs. Lemack's help. She'd walk the kid back and forth to school and bribe her with Ring Dings to finish her homework. The two got to be friends.

I'd put Vicky in public school, same place me and Annie'd

gone, only now everyone was American, even the teachers hadn't heard the word Hunky. Vicky was popular, with her honey-blond hair and blue eyes and fancy clothes. Not much of a student, though. She got bad grades, hung out with hoods, and sassed all her teachers, which infuriated her father. He blamed me and Mrs. Lemack and called my friend a nut case— as if we'd put Vicky up to misbehaving.

It was after she lost her virginity in the rear of the Mr. Softee truck that Ted got tough. He stuck her in Catholic boarding school out in the country, nothing male for fifty miles except livestock. She got kicked out for sneaking some farm boy into her room, then went to live with one after another of Ted's fakey sisters, all of them married to ministers. Vicky didn't last a month with any of her aunts. Hated their airs. She'd call me in tears, begging to come back, promising to behave. But I couldn't cross Ted. The morning I found her asleep on my porch, tears still in her lashes, I called him to come fetch her. She'll never let me forget that. How he dragged her away, clawing and screaming and calling my name.

Ted finally moved out on Annie for good. Broke her heart, but she wouldn't admit it, sucking on cigarette after cigarette, tearing her nails with her teeth.

I often wonder what her life might have been if she'd never left Braddock. Stuck with me. And married Mike, her steel-worker sweetheart, who'd stroked her hand so tenderly over peach cobbler.

🍃

*T*he restaurant bill came to sixty-nine dollars for three people, disgraceful, and Sidd even left a ten-dollar tip. I wouldn't let them buy me dessert, not at those prices. Insisted we go back to my kitchen for fudge ripple ice cream and nut roll. This time they didn't argue.

"I could eat this all night," said Vicky, her mouth full of

both. "You've been promising me your nut roll recipe for years. How about writing it down?"

"Sweetie, you'll just have to watch me make it sometime," I said. "I couldn't tell you how much butter or sugar or nuts to use. I don't even own a measuring cup."

"Can't you approximate?"

"Not tonight," I said. "I'll send you the recipe at Christmas."

"I've heard that one before. Why do you always do this to me?"

"Do what?" I asked. "Do *what?*"

❧

*V*icky's always wanted something from me. Most of all my ears. To fill with tales of her mother, and nothing I'd want to hear, either.

She couldn't keep secrets. Passed on how Annie and Ted slept in separate rooms, how Annie whittled her arm with a penknife, how Annie swore the wrong twin had died—should have been her smashed on the sidewalk, not Lily. And above all, what a bad mother she'd been.

Girl's habit bottomed out the day we buried my sister. We were driving home together from the cemetery—Vicky at the wheel of her unwashed Toyota, empty beer cans rolling around on the sticky floor—when she let loose a blue streak of cuss words. I figured she was speaking of Ted. He'd neglected to come, or even send flowers.

I was too tired to listen, all the weeping I'd done, and put up my hand. "Sweetie . . . please. Don't."

"Why not?" she spat, trying to light a cigarette with shaking hands. "Are you *defending* that prick?"

"Defending him? You crazy?"

I thought it was common knowledge I hated the man. He'd put my sister in a nursing home the last few weeks of her life and left written instructions prohibiting visitors. She'd died alone, hoses running in and out of her body, surrounded by strangers and beeping machines. The nurses called me at work with the news since Ted couldn't be reached, not on Valentine's Day. And Gus wouldn't give me the rest of the day off. He sent me back to my machine.

"Surely *you* know the scoop, don't you?" Vicky whispered, swinging a hard right into the parking lot of a miniature golf course. "All about him and his girlfriends?"

"I had my suspicions," I said wearily.

"Then why didn't you tell her? Jesus, you think I could? Her daughter? He had dozens of women, hundreds, maybe, even screwed a couple of my high school friends, you know that? God, I could throw up!" She pounded the steering wheel. "How could she be *that* stupid?"

"Sweetie, I can't explain. There's things about your mother I never understood, either."

"Bullshit, Masha! What's to understand? She brought it on *herself*. No one made her hang around with that scumbag."

I bolted out the door and charged across the parking lot. Sat down doubled over on a wet park bench, my guts in spasms, from hearing her spit on her mother's grave. The girl chased me down like a rabid dog.

"You know where my father is today?"

I covered my ears, had enough. "*No.* And I don't care."

"You're *going* to hear, like it or not!" She sat next to me, spoke low. "He's in Key West. Working on his tan with some dumb cunt from his office. He wouldn't even come to the phone when I called."

I jumped to my feet. "Alright, alright, it's the shits! But why the hell are you telling me this?"

She lifted her face, eyes full of tears. "You're family, aren't you?"

# Schuylkill Expressway

"This sure is one helluva road," says Mrs. Lemack, both hands gripping the wheel for a change. "You ever see so many potholes?"

She's talking about the Schuylkill Expressway, the snaky highway that takes you from the turnpike into Philly—two narrow lanes on either side of a sagging chain-link fence, bumper-to-bumper traffic, and roadkill every few feet.

She's not the only one who's nervous. I shake out a brown paper bag and dig in my purse for Rolaids. Take some deep breaths like they tell you to do on the airplane and pray we're not sideswiped or rammed from the rear.

I've panicked here before. Thirty years ago, the summer

Mum got sick, when I was on my way to fetch Annie. I'd lit a candle at church just that morning, too, praying the car would hold out and that Mum would recover. But God had His own lousy plans. He killed my fuel pump right along this stretch of road. And abandoned poor Mum.

"You got any idea where's the next exit?" Mrs. Lemack pants, face drenched with sweat.

I hand her a hanky. "Dunno . . . maybe a mile?"

"Let's take it." She shoots into the right lane and picks up speed. "There's *got* to be an easier way to Bessie's grave."

I don't argue, not today. I've got too much to think about. And she'll do what she damn well pleases, anyhow.

🍀

*M*um's last years, even before she got sick, were disastrous. Just desserts, according to the ladies at church. But I still have my doubts.

It started with each of us leaving her—me, Nicky, Granddaddy, Annie. Even Vlado hit the road, in the clutches of another woman. Loneliness was new to Mum. She loathed an empty house—or worse, an empty bed. So she picked fights with anyone, anywhere.

Vlado's desertion was the biggest surprise. He'd left her for Mrs. Stefanko, a widow from church. She was no peach—in her mid-fifties, owned a dry cleaning business, and never brushed her teeth. She'd been watching Vlado for years, sending him scented notes and little gifts, like electric razors and battery-operated back scratchers. While Mum was having her gallbladder out, the lady cleaned his clothes for free and brought him hand-cranked ice cream.

I guess they fell in love. The day Mum got out of the hospital, he taped a farewell note—in Mrs. Stefanko's handwriting—to Mum's boudoir mirror. She found it at bedtime, shattered a window, and cut up her hands. The neighbors called the cops and me, don't know in what order, but I came in my nightgown and pin curls.

She was lying in a heap on the floor. Sat up to show me the note, then fed it to a candle flame once I'd bandaged her hands and wiped her tears. It nettled me, all her hysterics over Vlado, but I kept my nasty comments to myself. I fixed her a plate of buttered turnips and put her to bed.

Mum survived. She coddled herself with a new wardrobe, a brand-new Packard, and a mink stole. But she was in her mid-forties then and showing it. She'd thickened in the waist and sagged in odd places. Men began to keep their distance. Which didn't go down well.

She had good reason for her tantrums, I suppose. Especially after Vlado sent her snapshots of the party gags store he'd opened with Mrs. Stefanko in Buffalo. Lout posed himself beside his hottest-selling item—a life-sized inflatable female with enormous breasts.

⚘

*T*he first exit off the expressway isn't far from the stuffy Bala Cynwyd neighborhood where Annie used to live. Or from Manayunk, the other direction, where Princess Grace grew up. The two neighborhoods are worlds apart: Annie's rich, all smart shops and big houses, Grace's overrun with auto body shops and custard stands. It used to make my sister chuckle, being they had the same birthday.

That was the only pleasure, of course, Annie got from that date. Otherwise, her birthday was a day to be dreaded, at least till she moved out of Braddock. Mum had a strange way of celebrating, which she forced on my sister—me, too—first thing, birthday morning. I've never leaked the details to a soul.

"Whew!" says Mrs. Lemack, parking the Firebird in a road construction area. "Let's have a look at the map."

I'm not too keen about being here, and getting a ticket's the least of my worries. The pavement's torn to shreds, and there's nasty-looking sewage seeping from an exposed pipe. I haven't forgot it was in Philly they had that outbreak of Legionnaires' disease. Mrs. Lemack doesn't care; she's got the map spread out on top of her stomach, tracing a zig-zag route with her fingernail and a felt-tip pen. Any fool can see she's planning a detour that takes us past Vicky's. She's even marked the street with an X.

"Think you can navigate?" she asks, handing me the map.

"Look, how about I drive?"

"You? How come the change of heart?"

I hide a smile. "Mrs. Lemack, I *know* this city."

"You're on then, Girl," she shrugs, climbing out her door. "Can't argue with a generous soul."

But she does. The minute I cut the wheels and head back to the Schuylkill Expressway. As far away from Vicky as I can get.

❈

*A*fter Mum lost Vlado, she lost her money, too. It took awhile and required some assistance. But her pockets weren't emptied at gunpoint; Nicky didn't do things that way. He worked her good and slow.

They'd been chummy for years, since the day he brought his bride to Braddock. Phyllis took all the credit, boasting about it when I visited her in Florida, her hand in a box of chocolate-covered cherries. She told me she'd lost her own parents, knew all about grief, and that I should listen up.

"I'm telling you this so you see how important it is to *forgive*," she said, standing up to check her hairdo in an heirloom mirror. "Up till the day Daddy got sick, we fought like tigers, can you imagine, little old me? But I forgave him! So I wasn't interested in those awful stories your brother told me about Mrs. Tulevich—she's *still* his mother. Kiss and make up, I always tell him."

Phyllis's efforts worked to Nicky's advantage. The summer Mum had been ten years by herself, he called her with a business proposal. Told her he was out of the shoe-selling business for good, plumb tired of rude customers and unwashed feet. He wanted to start his own business, a liquor store—which couldn't go wrong in Ft. Lauderdale, not with so many retirees. Folks there had time, thirst, and money on their hands.

Mum didn't mince words. "You asking me to put up the cash?"

"Yeah," he said, unfazed. "But I'm asking a *helluva* lot more. How about you come down to Florida and help out?"

"Me? And leave Braddock?"

"Why not? That place is a fucking dump. What's keeping you there? Vlado come back?"

"I'll have to think about it."

"Well, don't think too long. I've got other ideas that don't include you. Remember that."

Mum didn't think long. An hour, maybe, not even enough time to consult Madame Vargas—or me. She called next morning to say she was selling the house and moving down south, to find a new man and do business with Nicky. The news soured my stomach.

"How much's he asking you to put up?" I asked.

"That any business of yours?"

"No, but I'm a little worried. *He* doesn't have a thing to lose."

She hung up. Didn't call back until the day before she left and only then to ask for a ride to the train. I'd already heard the full scoop from Annie, how Mum had accepted a low-ball offer on the house, then wired the money to Nicky. And how she'd sold off the furniture and draperies and appliances, even the China silk rug where Lily died. The only thing that didn't go was Mum's bedroom set, for sentimental reasons. Dad had kept it on lay-a-way the year before they married, and she wouldn't part with it. She shipped it to Florida in crates.

Al and I drove her to the train. She was radiant that day,

weighted with jewelry, doused with cologne, swaying on four-inch heels. I tagged along in the rear, shoulders hunched, fighting tears, and baffled by it. I had every reason to rejoice, bossy and blaming as Mum had always been, and now she was out of my life. But my heart and my head were in two different places.

"You crying, Mash?" she asked, almost gently, as her train was announced.

I couldn't answer, looked away, but she crushed me in her arms, all the sharp surfaces of her buttons and jewelry bruising my skin. We were bawling in unison.

"You girls should have done all this kissy-face back in the car," grumbled Al, dropping Mum's suitcase with a thud. "That train won't wait forever, Lady. Here, take your luggage."

So she left, the clatter of her heels echoing in my ears. I smelled her perfume on my clothes for hours. And the bruises from her jewelry—turning first red, then blue, then yellow—lasted a long time. Mum, it seemed, always left her mark on you.


*I* got used to the idea of Mum living so far away. Distance made her nicer. She called once a week and sent little gifts for no reason—seashell earrings, crates of plump oranges, and a stuffed baby alligator I gave to Mrs. Lemack.

Over Easter she came up to visit. Something was wrong; the woman looked weary. She didn't want to talk, never got round to it, anyhow, too busy being a grandmother. Annie and Vicky were up at the same time, and Mum fell head over heels in love with that kid. I still don't understand it; she'd never paid much attention to Tom or Barb or her own children, and Vicky had always been spoiled. It irked me, watching Mum play peekaboo for hours. She and I never had a grown-up conversation the entire visit.

It wasn't till much later, when Mum was sick, that I heard

the truth about the liquor store. That Mum had financed it top to bottom—the building, the inventory, the advertising—with the money she'd made from the Braddock house and the sale of all her stocks. She'd made zero-interest loans to Nicky—unrelated to business—which were never repaid. Phyllis kept the company books and wouldn't let Mum have a peek. It came as no surprise the business folded; Nicky, it turned out, had sold the inventory on the sly.

So that was how Mum lost her money. She never blamed Nicky, just headed back to Braddock once she'd sold her bedroom set for train fare. I met her at the station the week before Christmas. The woman looked like hell. But her mood was as merry as the season, and she whistled and chirped all the way to the car. She couldn't wait to tell me her news.

And that was the first that I heard of it. The opal ring.


She'd found it the day before in the Amtrak washroom, stone-side down in a slimy soap dish. The jewel was enormous, mounted in platinum, with fireworks exploding inside. No one would know if she kept it, of course, but Mum had some scruples. She took the ring to the conductor, explained the situation, then clattered alongside him in her scoop-necked dress and open-toed mules while he looked for the owner. Nobody claimed it, which was strange. The train was an express from Miami to Pittsburgh and hadn't discharged any passengers.

"Well, Sonny," she said, "I guess that makes it mine."

The man—according to Mum—spat on the stone, rubbed it dry, and turned it slowly in the overhead light. "Sorry, ma'am," he said without looking at her, "but it's company policy to hold lost property thirty days."

She stamped her foot. "You take me for a fool? That ring doesn't belong to *nobody* on this train!"

He kept examining the stone, smiling to himself. "And you heard what *I* said, lady. Now go take your seat. I'll give you a form to fill out that says you're next in line if no one else claims it."

Mum, as always, was ready to fight. She spun him around, snatched the ring, and dropped it down her dress.

"You want it?" she taunted, straightening her pillbox hat. "Well, Sonny, you just come *get* it." Then she marched past him, swaying her hips wide. He didn't follow her.

I can still see her, all grins, spreading her big bony fingers on my dining room table, showing off that trinket. My hair stood on end—"an *opal?*"—but she called me an old world fool. It tickled her she hadn't paid a penny for it, not that she had much else to celebrate about. She was broke.

"My luck's gonna change, I know it," she said, twisting the jewel on her finger till it caught the light and sent rainbows dancing on my wallpaper. "Just you wait and see."

She never took it off after that, couldn't, not even with soap. The band was too tight.

*A*fter she'd been back in Braddock a week, Mum found a railroad flat in East Pittsburgh and a job waiting tables at the Coconut Grove, a smoky bar famous for brawls and live polka music. It was backbreaking work, and Mum was near sixty. I never knew her real age—she'd adjust it, always downward, to the age of her current boyfriend, but it broke my heart to see her hoisting trays, her ankles so swollen. She never turned down any invitation to dance, either, haggard as she looked. At the end of her shift, she'd limp home in the dark, carrying her waitressing shoes. She paid for everything, including her rent, with loose change. Her tip money.

She was still on the prowl for new men. Set her sights on Joey Wancho, the dishwasher. At the end of his shift, he'd move to the bar, still in his undershirt, and drink up his wages, winking at Mum each time she'd skim foam off his beer. He'd been fired from the mill and bragged how he'd beat the foreman unconscious. I didn't believe a word, but the tale amused Mum.

They started keeping company. Threw my stomach in an uproar, not that Mum asked for my blessing. He was half her age, unwashed, and dumb. He'd been born in Braddock, but spoke pidgin English and couldn't tell you which came first, World War I or World War II.

She took him home for good when she heard he was living in his car. I'd find him slouched in her Naugahyde Lazy Boy, beer in hand, scooping Good 'n Plenty from the crystal candy dish Dad gave Mum the day I was born. He'd brought along Jeannie, his teenage daughter, who camped in the kitchen. The girl stayed out all night and came home smirking and splay-legged from all the exercise she'd got in the backs of cars. She never lifted a finger to help with the housework and cussed out anyone who asked her to clean up.

"Disgusting," I said to Al once as we left Mum's apartment. "What can we do?"

"Not much," he shrugged. "Joey's got her bamboozled."

He was right. In April, they got married.

So we stopped going over there, saw less of Mum and more of our new color TV. I missed her, but then again, she had changed.

*M*um started losing weight after her wedding and shrunk two sizes in a month. She didn't have money for a new wardrobe, unless you counted the cash she could get for the ring, which she swore she'd never sell. She claimed she didn't need new clothes anyhow, spent her evenings in a waitress uniform, days in a housecoat. And even after she lost all that weight, the ring wouldn't budge off her finger, not that she was tempted to part with it.

I invited her one Sunday for meat loaf, just the two of us. Slipped Al ten dollars beforehand with instructions to head for the Moose. He was hung over from the night before, not in the least interested in hooch or table hockey, but I couldn't relax with the two of them bickering. I wanted her alone.

She came an hour late, dressed in capri pants and sneakers. Barely said a word. Left her appetite at home, too.

"Mum, what's the matter?" I asked. "You sick?"

"No. Tired, maybe."

"*Tired* don't make you stop eating. I'm tired, see?" I cut off a knob of kielbasa, chewed noisy, and washed it down with cherry pop.

She turned her face sideways and held up one hand. Moaned like an animal caught in a trap, then showed me the lump on her back. She'd noticed it months earlier, bending down to tie her waitressing shoes. The damn thing had since doubled in size and hurt like hell. She couldn't sit or eat or sleep.

I was terrified. It was the first time I'd really thought about losing her. I held her a full fifteen minutes, neither of us speaking, our hearts banging out of sync. Couldn't stop crying, neither of us.

The next morning, I drove her to the doctor. She didn't have a cent of medical insurance, so the doctor put her in the county hospital once he was certain it was cancer. He started her on cobalt treatments, which burned her pretty skin. When Joey came to fetch her a few weeks later, I did as Mum requested, told him it was just gallbladder problems, not to worry. And no sex for six weeks.

"You *got* to be kidding," he groaned, rubbing his stomach.

"Hell no," I said. "And I'm not repeating myself, you hear me? Keep your grubby hands in your pockets."

*I* started checking on Mum before work every morning. It surprised me how happy she was to see me. She'd set out stewed prunes and Frosted Flakes and stroke my hand as we yakked. We never discussed her illness. But for the first time she talked about Dad.

She'd met him at a dance when she was working in a glass factory. Left at dusk every day with bandaged hands, blood seeping through.

"Sight of it broke his heart," she said. "He walked me home that night and promised to rescue me. And he did . . . at least those few years I had him. He was a *good* man, Mash . . . and you know something? He'd be awful proud of you."

I stroked her cheek, hearing that. We were friends.

Then one morning, she didn't answer the bell. I got scared, crossed the street, and rang her from a public phone. Still no answer. So back I went, heart in my mouth, and jimmied her lock with a nail file. It turned out she wasn't dead, not even asleep. She was lying sideways on the sofa, wrapped in the afghan I'd knitted for her wedding gift, face bruised, hands clutching her belly. The house was a wreck.

"Mum?" I cried. "*Mum?*"

She wouldn't talk at first, then let loose. It'd been Joey, alright. He'd come home the night before, skunk-drunk and hungry for sex. Slapped her when she resisted, then had his way anyhow. Before he left he helped himself to anything of value—her fur coat, pearls, tortoiseshell mirror.

"At least he didn't get my ring," she sighed, twisting it on her finger, too tired from radiation to cry. And that was all she had to say.

But I rounded Al up from work, handed him a baseball bat, ordered him to kick Joey's ass. No luck. Years later, I heard the louse had hopped a bus to Youngstown, married another older woman and died of a stroke in her bed.

*M*um went back to work a few weeks later, chatty and cheerful, but the cancer had grabbed her for good. On Fourth of July she quit, trudging home with an extra five dollars the cook had slipped in her pocket. By August, she couldn't leave bed even to use the toilet. So I went and got Annie. And Vicky.

We managed Mum's care, swapping off twelve-hour shifts, so I could still work in the factory. Mum went down fast, grew lumps on her head and couldn't keep a thing in her stomach. Nighttime, I'd sit by her bed peeling stick after stick of Juicy Fruit gum, pulling the wads from her mouth as they lost their flavor. She couldn't even spit them out.

The heat was the worst of it. Record high, and Mum had only one fan. I'd sit it on a rickety card table alongside her bed, noisy as a freight train, and lay her out naked. It never made the place cooler, just lifted the dust and shook the dried palm leaves she'd tucked behind a print of *The Last Supper* on the wall.

Maybe it was just the heat, but I started wanting her to die. Praying for it, even. The sooner the better.

$G$od answered my prayers, alright, but He raised a little hell in the neighborhood first. He started a fire in the house catty-corner that spread halfway down the block. I watched it all from Mum's sunporch, shivering in the heat. Knew damn well the fire was no coincidence—sent straight from hell, a taste of what poor Mum could expect if we didn't call the priest.

"So soon?" asked Annie, toweling the sweat off Mum's face. "She ate some cereal this afternoon, remember?"

I didn't have time to argue. Dialed Father Serge, begged him not to waste a minute. That's how Mum had last rites at midnight, sirens squealing in the street, all of us weeping and covered with sweat. At least I did that much for her. And got her safe to purgatory.

Next morning, Vicky sneaked down the fire escape, still in her nightie, and headed straight for the steaming rubble. She fetched a doll from the ashes, face blackened, hair singed.

Brought it back to the breakfast table and tried feeding it Juicy Fruit gum, a napkin tied around its melted neck.

"What in the hell are you doing?" Annie whispered, grinding out a cigarette in the sink. "Where'd you get that thing?"

The kid hung her head and wouldn't answer. But Annie was all motion. She grabbed the doll by its hair, tossed it down the air shaft, then washed her hands furiously in the dishwater. Vicky, meanwhile, pitched a temper tantrum right on the linoleum. I couldn't calm either of them.

It was somewhere in that chaos Mum died down the hall. Annie found her, a few minutes later, her mouth gone slack, her skin cold. Still makes me weep. I should have been holding her hand. Warming her feet. Asking her forgiveness for Lily's death and a thousand other things.

Didn't.

$\mathcal{M}$um had a small policy that paid for her funeral. The viewing lasted three rainy days, nowhere near long enough, given the number of visitors. They came in droves, young and old, shaking out boots and umbrellas and rain bonnets in the foyer of Shankey's Funeral Home. Mum had a reputation, of course, but I'd no idea she was famous. I counted hundreds of faces and recognized only a handful. Almost no one sent flowers.

That bothered me. But not so much as Mum's appearance. Laid out, she wasn't much to look at. She'd been wasted by the cancer and weighed under eighty pounds, but that wasn't what bothered me. It was her outfit. Everything about it was wrong—color, style, and fabric. She would have hated it.

Annie and I were to blame. We'd shopped for a dress with the best of intentions, wanted Mum looking herself. But we hadn't slept for days and lost all our sense in the store. We tried clothing on ourselves, sheaths and furs and broad-brimmed hats. I forgot to wipe off my lipstick and left a smear down the front of a cocktail dress. Honest Annie insisted we buy it, which cleaned out our cash.

"Now what?" I said, peeking in the shopping bag. "We can't bury Mum in *this*."

"No . . . but hold on"—she dug in the bottom of her handbag, grinning triumphantly— "Here, I've still got an extra five dollars. Why don't we try a secondhand store?"

That's where she found a size four powder-blue gown, two dollars, draped on a bald mannequin. I didn't have time to run it through the washing machine, just dropped it off at the funeral parlor on the way home.

And that's what Mum wore to the grave, that and the opal ring. Vicky wanted it bad, begged for it, but I took a hard line, which really made no difference. The ring had shrunk right along with Mum, as tight on her finger the day she died as it'd been in my dining room a year before. No one could pry it off her. Not with soap or cooking oil or tears.

$\mathcal{T}$he day after the burial, Annie and I did what we most dreaded. We went back to Mum's flat, aired the rooms, beat the rugs, caulked the tub. And then we got down to business, sorting through her belongings. Joey, of course, had walked off with anything of value. But Mum was a pack rat who barely parted with Kleenex and never with coupons.

The job took us thirty-six hours. It amazed me how much she'd hoarded, boxfuls of lingerie, table linens, teacups, near-empty bottles of cleaning fluid. She had stacks of ice cube trays, hundreds of rusted coat hangers, empty shoe boxes, jelly jars. And a whole shelf of unlabeled canned goods from Food-land, marked down to a nickel, and no telling just what was inside. I started to weep. That must have been how Mum afforded to eat.

We hauled most of the junk to the curb, then divided what

was left between ourselves. We didn't squabble; in fact, neither of us wanted any of it and just couldn't admit it. I kept offering Annie pillowcases or teapots, as if it were some kind of sacrifice. The worst part was the jewelry. Joey, shrewdly, left only baubles. Yet more than anything, that junk was Mum—vulgar, but it caught your attention. We didn't throw it out. Set it aside for Vicky.

Near the end of the second day, Nicky pounded on the door. He'd shown up in Braddock the last day of Mum's viewing, and drank at her grave from a brown paper bag. The man barely acknowledged me and ignored Annie altogether.

I never knew where Nicky stayed those few days. Or cared. But I cringed at the sight of him, unshaven, standing in Mum's door. He limped past Annie and me, headed straight for the desk and rattled through Mum's unpaid bills, lease agreement, bank statement, unfilled prescriptions.

"What are you looking for?" I asked at last. But I knew.

"She leave a will?" First thing out of his mouth.

"*Mum?*" I could barely stifle my laughter, as superstitious of wills as she'd been. "You kidding?"

He stared me down. "Then we'll have to get the county to appoint an administrator. To divide up the property and pay the bills."

"Yeah," I said. "I *know* about that. But what use's an administrator? Mum didn't leave a damn cent."

"That's a *lie*, and you know it!"

"It isn't a lie," Annie said quietly, approaching him. "Here's the passbook to her savings account. Have a good look yourself."

He snatched it from her, scanned a page, and threw it on the floor. "It's all lies, goddam lies! Having fun, Ladies? Screwing me out of my money?"

"No one's screwing you out of anything," I said. "She didn't leave diddly-squat. Just take a look at this dump!"

"Yeah, it's a dump. But the mistake *I* made was not getting here soon enough. Mum was the type to stash ten thousand in cash between her sheets—Hunky banking. That where you found her money? Huh?"

"There was no money," sighed Annie. "She spent every cent she had on your liquor store."

"What the *hell* do you know about that?"

"Enough," she said. "More than enough, really. Like how the inventory disappeared. Right under Mum's nose. And no one seemed to have any information about it. Least of all you."

"You calling me a thief? That it?"

"Yes," she said, her lips trembling. "*And a bastard.*"

He grabbed her chin between two fingers, let out a hoot. "Bastard? You calling *me* a bastard?" He switched to a whisper. "Only bastard I know of, Pussycat, is *you*. Did Mum ever get around to telling you your Daddy's name? Or she take it with her to the grave?"

"Get out," I said, hands turned to ice.

He paid me no heed, kept his eyes fixed on Annie. "Can't imagine why Mum would tell me and not you. How much's the information worth to you, huh? I'll give it to you cheap, cross my heart. Just hand over what's mine, sound like a square deal?"

"You go to hell," I said, pushing past him and grabbing Annie's hand. I steered her right out the door and down the steps.

He didn't follow us. But I could hear him from the street smashing plates, pounding furniture, cursing. He was searching for Mum's hidden treasure.

🍥

"*R*elax, Mrs. Lemack," I say, knuckles white on the steering wheel. "If we'd taken city streets like you wanted— why, hell, we'd be on the road till midnight."

She's been sulking the last twenty minutes, since I short-circuited her plans to visit Vicky. I can't say I care for driving on this crazy expressway, but it brings us as close to Bessie's grave as any road in Philly. And about as far from Vicky as I can get.

"Just take a look at the signs," I say gently, don't want her mad at me the rest of the afternoon. "We'll be there in ten minutes. Want to be friends?"

She ignores me and turns up the music, Bessie singing "Take Me for a Buggy Ride." But I figure she couldn't be mad anymore. She's beating time slapping her thigh. And getting ready to roll.

# Mount Lawn Cemetery
## Sharon Hill, Pennsylvania

"Cut the engine," says Mrs. Lemack, once we're off the expressway. "I think I see a florist's."

Guess she's serious about buying Bessie flowers. It's not a good idea in this heat; they'll wilt in an hour. But plastic flowers aren't her style—except in her house—and it's good just to get out of the car.

The shop's small inside, only one salesgirl and a couple teenage boys buying corsages. The kids stop and gawk as we hobble through the door like they've never seen gals with bouffants. Mrs. Lemack doesn't notice; she's shuffling toward the flower cooler. There's not much selection this late in the day—roses and sickly carnations—and the prices are twice what you pay in Braddock.

"The roses are prettier, but they'll break the bank," she frets, her nose against the glass. "On the other hand, when's the next time I'll be paying Bessie my respects? Think I should splurge, Mrs. Kuzo?"

"Make up your own mind," I grumble as the salesgirl boxes the boys' corsages and rings up their bill. They pay in loose change, probably their lawn mowing money.

She tries her luck next with the salesgirl, who recommends the roses, fifty-five dollars a dozen. My friend counts her bills twice and swabs her face with a hanky. "Maybe I'll go half roses, half carnations, then. But still . . . this *is* for Bessie Smith."

"Who?" says the salesgirl, handing the boys their boxes.

My friend thumps her palm against her forehead. "You mean to tell me, Hon, you've never heard of *Bessie Smith*?"

The girl shrugs, examines her lacquered nails.

"Well, this ring a bell?" She breaks into "You've Got to Give Me Some," like a scene from a corny musical. Only what she's singing isn't family fare; it's Bessie at her dirtiest, something about round steak and raw meat.

"Hey, party *on!*" shouts one of the kids, clapping in rhythm. "You're terrific, lady!"

Mrs. Lemack finishes, sweeps a bow. "Wanna hear more?"

"Go for it!" says the kid.

I can't bear watching her play the fool. Tug on her oversized T-shirt and point to the door. There's still time for her to save face. And to stop at K-Mart for a plastic arrangement.

"Whoa, chill out!" says the kid, one hand on my shoulder. "Let the lady perform! We've got a national treasure here."

I'm furious. Flick off his hand and face my friend. "Okay, Mrs. Lemack, you want to show off? *Fine.* But give me the car keys. I'll meet you outside."

She winks at the boys, overturns her handbag on the counter, and finally shakes the keys loose from a pile that includes Band-Aids, chopsticks, and a Slinky. I snatch them and head out the door. The sun's gone behind a clump of ugly clouds—best news of the day, kills the heat.

Twenty minutes later, she's tapping on the driver's side window, all grins. It looks like she bought the biggest arrangement the salesgirl could gouge her for, a rose-covered jungle gym that takes four people, including the boys, to load up. I have to scrunch down in the backseat just to get the door closed, and even then, half the frame is hanging out the window. Gal pokes along ten miles an hour so's not to disturb a single petal.

I grit my teeth, thinking evil thoughts. Still and all, I've had a minor victory. Flat out refused to let those jerky kids come along, much as they begged. It doesn't matter Mrs. Lemack tried to shame me, calling me names like Wicked Witch of the West. Far as I'm concerned, it's water off a duck's back.

෯

Still, the roses smell good. Makes me think of Mum. She grew roses for fragrance, not looks, and never left them hanging on the bush. June and July, our house was full of them, in drinking glasses and jelly jars and paint cans, anything she didn't use to bottle moonshine. I got married clutching a dozen. And afterward, she'd bring me bunches wrapped in wet newspaper.

I missed those roses once she moved to Florida. Begged Al to buy me a dozen, at least on our twenty-fifth anniversary. He didn't come through, but he had his own reasons. That was the day he got laid off for good from the mill.

I was heartsick, and the roses were the least of it. I'd been hoping for years to quit the factory and work part-time. Dreamt about running the register in a stationery store, pencil in one ear, chatting with customers. But with Al out of work, we needed my factory income. That's why I stayed there another twenty-five years. And even that barely paid the bills.

Al wasn't ready to sit at home, either. He was forty-eight

years old, no kid, but not about to be put out to pasture. The man was old-fashioned, too, when it came to a woman paying his way. He took the only job he was offered—as a high school custodian—and at half his old salary, but we needed every nickel.

He hated the work. Mornings, he bagged Trojans in the parking lot, Kotex in the girls' room. Afternoons, he fixed broken windows, swabbed hair from the sinks, scrubbed smut off bathroom walls. The man came home in moods as foul as the smoke from the mill. He drank twice as much and ground his teeth in bed.

Annie knew our situation. She'd send us money stuffed inside four or five envelopes, just like Russian stacking dolls, then slap on twice the amount of postage required, as if to make sure the package wasn't returned. I'd always call her the day I got it.

"You talk this over with Ted?" I'd ask, nervous as a pigeon. "I mean, it *is* his money, isn't it?"

"Ted hasn't got a thing to do with this," she sniffed. "It's between me and you. So not another word."

Al didn't like taking Ted's money. He said Annie had no business stealing it, even if her husband was a pantywaist. Al was all flapjaw, of course; he didn't know how much we needed Annie's help. I'd always balanced the checkbook and paid the bills and shopped for groceries. He couldn't add columns of figures, not even with his fingers.

So I made do without roses, except the summer nights I couldn't sleep. Then I'd prowl the neighborhood with a paper bag and scissors, and clip as many blooms as I dared.

❀

"*H*oly moley!" crows Mrs. Lemack. "We're here, Mrs. Kuzo! You awake?"

She swings a hard right, slams her brakes, throws me up

against the door. But even from the backseat I can read the sign. Mount Lawn Cemetery.

The woman's all business. Once I'm out of the car, she pulls her jungle gym out through the window and tosses it my direction. She unlocks the trunk, hauls out the ten-pound bag of peat moss, throws it over her shoulder, and heads north at a clip.

"Hey," I say, panting to keep up with her, my heartbeat haywire. "Where the heck you headed? How about we *find* the grave first?"

"And make two trips? Hell, no! Have faith, Mrs. Kuzo! God'll lead us to the spot, mark my words."

I chase after her, dripping sweat and cursing. After twenty-five minutes, we still haven't found Bessie's marker. This is a nasty place, too—burnt grass, broken bottles, wadded Kleenex. And I swear I just heard thunder.

"How you going to know her grave when you see it?" I shout.

"Lordy, Mrs. Kuzo, you don't remember? The epitaph? I must've told you a hundred times—'The Greatest Blues Singer in the World Will Never Stop Singing.'"

"Then why the hell isn't she singing now?" I pant. "She could lead us straight to her grave!"

*A*nd then God opens the heavens. Serves up a hailstorm that sends us scrambling back to the Firebird, ducking hail and flying branches. We scrap the peat moss and flowers. Count our blessings to make it back to the car. This has got to be doomsday.

"If only we'd left earlier," shouts Mrs. Lemack, over the roar of the storm. "We'd have missed all this. Heck, we'd be back at the motel feeding quarters to Magic Fingers."

"There wasn't a word about this in the weather forecast," I

moan. "I've got a crummy feeling we're not *supposed* to be here."

"Enough of that silly talk, Mrs. Kuzo! There's been storms this bad in Braddock."

"Not like this. Someone—something—is telling us to leave," I say, more and more agitated. "Either that . . . or trying to *kill* us."

She clucks her tongue. "Baloney, Mrs. Kuzo. Best thing to do's just wait it out."

"No. Let's leave."

"You're crazy," she says, throwing the almanac in my lap. "Want to quiz me some more?"

I won't let her boss me this time. Thump my hand on the dash and rattle Bessie's picture. "Let's go, Lady! *Now!*"

"Alright, alright, calm down, will you?" She fumbles with her key, races the engine, throws the car in reverse. But it won't budge an inch, even with her full weight on the accelerator, her rear wheels spinning. We're stuck in the mud.

Which is how I know the howling out there isn't God.

It's Annie.

❀

"*D*id you know my mother really could drive?" asked Vicky, the last time, ten years ago, I took her to Leonetti's Diner.

Of course I knew. I'd taught her myself in Al's '39 Ford, then coaxed her through her driver's exam. She gave up her license the day she got married. Ted's idea. He didn't want to pay insurance.

"She ever tell you how we went for a spin in Ted's Corvette?" prodded Vicky, picking ham out of her chef's salad. "All the way to State College?"

I knew about that, too. Heard it straight from Annie's mouth, her last Christmas, when I hauled a half-dozen poinsettias to the hospital, and she joked her funeral wouldn't be for another few weeks.

"Did she tell you about the mud?" asked Vicky. "Hey! Look at me, will you? How much do you know?"

Enough, I thought, hairs standing up on the back of my neck. Enough.

"*T*here's something I need to unload," Annie told me that chilly afternoon, pushing away her hospital lunch, creamed beef on toast points and apple brown betty. "I'm not interested in last rites. Oh, don't look so hangdog, Mash. Sure, there's virtue in coming clean with God. But why spill your guts to a priest? A stranger?"

I puzzled it out. "Maybe . . . to make double sure God hears?"

"Oh, Mash, just listen to yourself!" she laughed gently, squeezing my hand. "God hears *everything*, you forget your catechism? Besides, what I'm looking for is *your* forgiveness. Not His."

"Why?"

She paused, fighting tears. "Because I'll never get it from Vicky. And what I've got to confess concerns her. Please, Masha!"

I sighed, pulled up a chair. She started with a rundown of her suicide plans, a subject that had fascinated her for years. How she'd listed every method in a notebook—poison, pills, rope, burning, bullets, falling, drowning—and ranked them in order of appeal. The first on the list was always the same. Driving Ted's car off a cliff.

"And not just any cliff, either," she laughed, rolling a cigarette between her fingers. "I've always had a taste for irony. I picked a mountaintop where Ted and I used to park before we got married. God"—she rolled her eyes—"all the promises he made me in the backseat! Lies, every last one of them."

"But you didn't do it," I said hoarsely. "I mean . . . you didn't drive off the *cliff.*"

"No. And not for lack of trying, either. I drove back four different times, and the first three I didn't come close. Know why?"

I shook my head, praying she'd stop.

"I flat out lost my nerve. I just couldn't die alone. So I headed back home and lay on the bathroom floor."

"You said you tried it *four* times."

She closed her eyes. "Yeah. That's when I took Vicky along, to steady my nerves—but nerves weren't the problem. It was . . . an unforeseen obstruction."

"Huh?"

She flicked ashes into a bedpan and laughed. "Talk about irony! My rear wheels got caught in the mud, right at the edge of the cliff. You believe that?"

"What about Vicky?"

"She slept through it. Remember how car sickness did that to her?" She laughed crazily, tearing at what little hair she had left. "Jesus, Mash, can you forgive me? For nearly killing my own child?"

Of course I did. But I didn't believe a word of her tale. It was the cancer talking. Or her madness. Not her.

※

"*D*id she or didn't she tell you about the mud?" Vicky repeated, pushing aside her chef's salad.

"The mud?" I was sweating. "What do you know about it? I thought you slept through it all."

"Oh, Jesus, is that what she told you? That I was *asleep?*" She thumped the table, brought the waitress running. "Bullshit, Masha! I was sitting right beside her! And I saw *exactly* what she was doing. She was trying to kill me!"

"Not your Mom," I said, looking for the exit. "She wouldn't harm a hair on anyone's head."

"No?" She tore her napkin down the middle. "There's a helluva lot about her you don't know. She tell you how she kept flooring the gas even with me begging her to stop? That sound familiar?"

"*Vicky—*"

"Or how I bolted out the backdoor? And ran down the road?"

I was ready to slap her. "This is a public place," I hissed, waving the waitress away. "Stop airing your dirty laundry."

❀

"*S*top crying, for God's sake," says Mrs. Lemack as the storm dies down. "We're not the first people to get stuck in the mud. Here, take the damn wheel."

She jumps out her door, tries pushing the car from the rear, and gives up. She shakes the rain out of her bouffant and grabs the cellular phone from under the dash. "Let's call Triple-A. You got your card, don't you?"

I don't. Search my handbag inside out. And I swear I saw it in my wallet back at HoJos.

"That's funny," she smirks. "I don't have mine either."

"What the hell's going on?" I ask, indignant. "You stopped by Triple A just before we left, remember? For the Trip-Tick and all those tourist brochures? Don't tell me you left your card on the counter!"

"'Fraid so," she says, shaking her head. "My noggin ain't what it used to be."

"So what are we going to do?"

"We could"—she smiled—"call Vicky."

"That so?" I turn my back on her. "Over my dead body!"

❀

*V*icky's line is busy the first four tries, and when I finally get through, one of Sidd's aunts picks up. I can barely hear her over the sputter of whatever's frying on the stove. Once she hears I'm Vicky's aunt, she makes a fuss and passes the phone all around. I end up yakking with another dozen Hindus—all asking about my health in choppy English—before someone fetches Vicky from her study.

"Masha?" she cries at last. "I don't believe it! What are you doing in Philly?"

"Good question," I snort, can't decide whether to rejoice she's at home or to hang up for the very same reason. "And I'm not in Philly exactly. You ever hear of Sharon Hill?"

"Sure. But what're you doing *there?*"

"Let's just say it's a long story, Sweetie. I'll get Mrs. Lemack to tell you. She's with me. But first, we're going to need a lift. And a bed for tonight. Think you can come pick us up?"

"What a silly question! Of course! But just exactly where are you?"

"Mount Lawn Cemetery. The main gate."

"Jesus Christ," she says. "See you in fifteen minutes."

🐚

*I* can't hide a smile as she runs out from her car. She's wearing a green surgical scrub suit, ballet slippers, and no bra. It's her hairstyle that kills me. A top knot twisted around a pencil.

"Ladies!" she laughs, crush-hugging both of us, then pointing at the Firebird. "What gives?"

"Car trouble," I say, glaring at my friend. "We'll need to get a tow truck."

"Well, get in, get in!" She opens her trunk, throws in our luggage, and pushes me up front. "Now first things first. You hungry?"

"Yes'm," says Mrs. Lemack. "My tummy's talking awful."

"Good. I know a great Burmese place right around here. Or how about a Jewish deli? You like potato latkes?"

"Not me," I say, checking the dash for air bags. "How

about you drop me at your place first? I need to rest up for the trip back home. *Tomorrow*."

"You can't be serious," she cries, turning down the sitar music. "You ladies just got here! C'mon, Mash, hang loose. I've been working my buns to the bone on that dissertation—you couldn't have timed this better! How about a few days in the country, just the three of us, up in Bucks County?"

I'm in no mood to be bullied into another trip, particularly to some cutesy country inn with four-poster beds and dust ruffles and muffins baking all hours. "Maybe next time," I say, anger in check. "I wouldn't make good company, anyhow."

"That's not true," she persists. "Why do you always say things like that? There's no one I'd rather spend my time with!"

"Yeah, that's what your mouth says."

"*Stop* it, Masha. You're sounding like Groucho Marx. No, let me rephrase: one part Groucho, one part curmudgeon."

"Cur-*what?*" Sounds like a dirty word.

She laughs and tweaks my cheek. "Look it up in the dictionary when you get home."

"So how's your family?" Mrs. Lemack bellows, chin on the back of Vicky's seat.

"Prima—and everyone's home tonight except Sidd. He just got called to the hospital."

"What for?" asks my friend.

"Good question. But at least the ER beeped him early. Most of the time it's right when we're . . . we're . . . well, getting *cozy*. And Sidd's so goddam polite, he'll talk with the intern an hour. I don't need to tell you"—she winks over her shoulder at Mrs. Lemack— "it's been *murder* on my libido!"

I swivel around too, not to wink but to scowl. "You were planning this all along, weren't you, Mrs. Lemack? Weren't you?"

❦

*V*icky likes to stake out the parking space in front of her house with a couple homemade parking cones. Tonight she's in for a nasty surprise. Someone's carted off her contraptions and parked a rusted Oldsmobile out front. We have to leave the Jag seven blocks to the west on a street lined with stripped cars.

Small wonder the girl's in a snit. She scrawls an evil note on the underside of a Light Days pad—closest thing to paper she can find in her handbag—and shoves it under a busted windshield wiper on the Olds. She kicks the hubcap, too, sends it flying down the gutter with a crash. Mum all over again.

We follow her up the steps to her house. It's a spooky old Victorian, something Stephen King might live in, with stained glass and witch's hats and sealed rooms. Vicky spent a day at the Philadelphia Historical Society researching its history. Seems the place is famous. Two suicides the night of the stock market crash and things going bump in the night ever since.

But size-wise, the house—four stories—is just right. There's thirty-five people jammed inside, not counting Vicky's out-of-town "guests," backpackers from all over the world. She's listed in a special directory and never turns anybody away, not even runaways from New Jersey. She tosses them sleeping bags, tells them to eat anything they find in the fridge, and to please hold down the noise if they're having sex—her husband's a doctor and needs his sleep. Then she patters up to her study and stays up till dawn, twirling her hair and banging on a computer.

⚜

*T*he Hindus are just finishing dinner. Darndest eating arrangements I've seen. There's a row of high chairs against the dining room wall—just like at Burger King—and picnic tables lined up end to end down the middle of the room. We weave in and out behind Vicky, from brothers to sisters, aunts to uncles, in-laws to cousins, shaking hands. The men wear the same outfit—short-sleeve cotton shirts buttoned to the neck, dark double-knit slacks, and enormous Timex watches. The women wear either saris or loose-fitting paisley pajamas and plenty of jewelry—sitting ducks for muggers. Everyone's got black plastic glasses, oiled black hair, and the same lousy barber.

The aunties insist on feeding us, even over Vicky's objections. They won't hear a word when I offer to help, and they chase me out of the kitchen with a dishrag. It's just as well. The room's crowded, flies everywhere, and even the ceiling's sweating from humidity. Noisy, too. Those gals can sure talk, *chippy-chippy-chippy* as they load our plates with food I plan to eat with my eyes closed.

"Go ahead, Mash, it's only the pig's sphincter," whispers Vicky, smirking. "You don't want to insult these good folks, do you?"

I do as I'm told, careful to pick out the peppers. And to grin at the cousins and sisters and aunties lined up behind my chair.

🍩

*T*his isn't the first time I've tasted their cooking. A half dozen occasions is more like it, starting with the party Vicky threw after she and Sidd got back from Bombay. They'd just been married in a Hindu ceremony, but Vicky wanted a second wedding—American style. She packed all her friends under a canopy in the azalea garden behind the Art Museum. And loaded the tables with curries and rice.

I'd brought Barb along, who left George at home pulling teeth. She'd just got her breast implants and tested the waters that day in a V-necked dress, keeping track of the stares. Wasn't a single Hindu didn't stick to her like crazy glue, shirt buttons loosened, glasses steamed. Their womenfolk were furious. Gave Barb the evil eye.

Not that she cared; she'd just come for the entertainment. And she didn't have to wait long, either, once Judith and Mark—Vicky's best buddies—arrived. They'd brought a cage of white doves, planning to free them the moment the bride and groom kissed. "It's the poetry of the moment," Judith explained to each guest. "And Mark's going to capture the magic on videotape."

"Birds? That's the stupidest idea I ever heard," I sputtered as Vicky rewrapped her sari one last time behind a bush. "And bad luck, too."

"Bad luck? Oh Masha, give me a break! I agree, it's silly, but Judith's an old friend. How can I hurt her feelings?"

"Girl, what you don't know about birds," I shivered, thinking of Lily. "But never say I didn't warn you."

"Yeah, I've been warned," she laughed, taking my arm. "And we'll all be buried in volcanic ash. Or someone will poison the punch. And Armageddon's on Thursday. Now, are you ready to lead me down the aisle?"

I did, to a tape of tinkling Indian music, stepping over guests sprawled on blankets or beach towels or on top of each other. I'd agreed against my better judgment to give the bride away. Vicky hadn't invited her father—hated him—and with Annie dead, I was, as she put it, next of kin. Or as Barb put it, stuck.

The ceremony was mercifully short, ten minutes, Vicky and Sidd taking turns reading poetry that didn't rhyme or make sense. Then the minister mumbled a few words, nothing about God, and told the newlyweds to kiss. It was at that moment Judith clicked open the cage and shooed out the birds with a popsicle stick. They took off, but not toward the heavens: started flying in circles instead, catch-as-catch-can, over the heads of the guests, straight out of that Hitchcock movie.

Barb laughed all the way home. She said it was worth scooping bird poop from her cleavage, just to see the look on Vicky's face, all her guests screaming and scrambling for cover.

"And the *food*," she said. "Did you ever taste anything so awful?"

I chuckled along, all agreement. Lucky thing she couldn't

hear my pounding heart. Not even Barb knows what I think about birds.

❦

*M*rs. Lemack puts away her third helping, licks her plate, and lets out a loud, smelly belch. She's been the center of attention the past hour, not only for her appetite, but for her stories. She's just finished telling Bessie's history to my wide-eyed niece. "No way!" Vicky gasps. "Now *that's* some woman!"

I shake my head. Don't know what's to admire in a gal who chugged corn liquor, bedded both sexes, busted up hotel rooms, spent her off-hours in buffet flats. And then died like a dog on the highway.

But Vicky writes it all down and says she's going to work the stories into her dissertation. And that she'd like to take pictures of Bessie's grave tomorrow, me and Mrs. Lemack posed on either side.

"You're looney tunes, both of you," I grumble, checking my watch. It's past my bedtime.

"You know better than to say a thing like that," says Mrs. Lemack, winking at Vicky. "Alright, Bessie doesn't run to everyone's taste. But you've got your odd moments, too, Mrs. Kuzo."

"Not like *that.*"

"Oh yeah?" she bristles. "Worse, maybe."

"Such as?"

She lets a couple seconds pass, then gets evil. "How about how you spent your lottery money?"

"Lottery money?" says Vicky. "What lottery money?"

"Nothing you need to know about," I say sourly, glaring at my friend.

"What's going on here, Masha? No, sit down! You didn't really win the lottery, did you?"

"There isn't much to say on that score," I say, standing up anyway. "And Mrs. Lemack's got a lot of nerve shooting off her mouth. Good*night,* ladies."

"Not so fast," says Vicky, grabbing my arm. "I'm dying to know! How about I brew up a pot of tea? We can drink it in my study, just the two of us, no interference."

"Go on, Mrs. Kuzo," shouts Mrs. Lemack, carrying her plate to the kitchen for more. "And if you don't tell her the truth, *I* will."

# 45th and Spruce Streets
# Philadelphia

*Vicky*'s study is a lopsided attic room with water spots and warped floorboards. As usual, it's a mess.

"Have a seat," she says, pointing to a sagging sofa covered with the afghan I crocheted for her wedding. "You notice anything new?"

I scout it out. The room looks unchanged, same undusted photos of Sidd standing in the Ganges, same Mexican weavings—including her favorite of humping donkeys—and the same sickly plants. Then I see it, propped on her desk. An eight-by-ten glossy of me from last Easter.

"Crumps!" I groan. "Why'd you stick that thing up?"

"You don't like it?"

It's awful. I'm standing stoop-shouldered in front of my pussy willow bush, hair a fright, nose nearly touching my chin. Only thing missing is a cat and a broomstick. I tell her so.

"Jesus, Masha! What a thing to say about yourself!"

"Take a good look. It's true."

She throws herself down on the sofa, all petulance. "Annie was the same, by God. Did you know she wouldn't even pose for pictures once I finished high school? That's the last one I've got of her."

She fingers a snapshot of mother and daughter on graduation night. Vicky's mugging for the camera, her mortarboard askew, one arm clutching Annie in aggressive chumminess. Annie stands stiff and stone-faced, and no wonder: she was already sick with the cancer. But she's still beautiful, in her shapeless Goodwill dress, plastic handbag, and red lipstick. My throat's too tight to swallow.

Vicky doesn't notice. She's busy propping my picture high on a shelf I can't reach without stilts, like she's worried I'm planning to steal it. She's gabbing all the while about her new computer and the smut she can pull off the Internet. Then she breaks open boxes she's brought back from India—fabric and jewelry and perfume—and insists I help myself. The girl knows I hate gifts, but tonight I'm flexible. I choose a simple silver necklace for Tammy.

"Let's have some music before we get started," Vicky says, squatting in front of a cardboard box of cassettes. She picks through a hundred before she finds what she wants, something called "Sausalito Symphony."

"There, isn't that soothing?" she purrs, tape running. "It's whales. Mating songs, really. I get my best work done"—she nods at the computer—"with this in the background."

*O*ne of Sidd's sisters sweeps into the room carrying a teapot, cups, and Sweet 'n Low. She sets it all down on a low teak table covered with crumbs and pours tea for two.

"Thanks, Dira," says Vicky, sniffing the steam. "You're a doll."

The woman smiles, pats the girl's head, and pads out the door. She even closes it behind herself, just like a servant.

"Don't look at me that way," Vicky says, pulling up a chair for me. "I know I'm spoiled. But it's a recent phenomenon, believe me."

I leave unsaid that she's always been spoiled. Watch as she pries open a tin of butter cookies she's hidden under the sofa, the kind filled with white cupcake papers.

"Okay, Mash, now we've got the right ambience, let's get down to business. You're going to tell me about the lottery, of course. And I've got some juicy news, too—a regular *quid pro quo*. You want to start?"

"Nope." I swat a mosquito. Can't fathom why she doesn't have window screens.

"Okay then, me first," she shrugs, curling up on some Indian-print cushions, the cookies at her elbow. "I just got a phone call from Ted."

"Your father? What's *he* want?"

"Money. Thirty thousand, rock bottom minimum." She grins wide. "It's poetic justice. He's broke."

"Did you rescue him?" I ask sourly, thinking how that money could have saved Barb's house.

"Me?" she scoffs. "Masha, give me some credit, pu-leeze!"

"So . . . ?"

"Let's say I told him—politely, mind you—to swivel on a well-greased thumb."

❀

*I* can't help chuckling. It was two years ago Ted gave up practicing law. He thought his true calling was running a restaurant. An *elegant* restaurant. He invested all his money in this scheme—plus whatever he could borrow from his creditors—and built the joint from the ground up, shouting directions from the sidelines in a cashmere coat and hard hat. He called the place *Mandy's* after his buxom little girlfriend—half his age—with crossed eyes and a baby-doll voice. Vicky heard the details from the lady herself, who calls up drunk whenever Ted stays out all night. The girls are friends. Or so Mandy thinks.

"What the hell does Ted know about running a restaurant?" I asked Vicky the first I heard of his plans.

"Beats me. But he doesn't intend to dirty his hands in the dishwater. Mandy says he's hired a manager, the same guy who ran that resort in St. Thomas where the rock stars dry out. You're coming with us to the grand opening, aren't you?"

"You've *got* to be kidding."

"Mash, this is family history! I *insist*."

So I crocheted seven hours on the Greyhound bus to Philly, then waited out front of the terminal half the afternoon before I spotted the Jaguar. Damn car was leading the limo Vicky had hired to haul all the Hindus along. I dashed straight to her car, backed in fanny first, and fell in her lap. Counted six aunties sitting in the rear clinking jewelry and singing Beatles tunes off-key. Sidd was driving.

"It's about time Ted meets my new family, no?" Vicky said. She was balancing a mirror on the dashboard and dotting her forehead, dead center, with nail polish.

"He's expecting . . . all of us?" I asked, counting up the Hindus on my toes.

"Who knows, who cares?" She painted her fingernails next and waved them under my nose to dry. "But Ted needs to learn that when he invites me, by implication he invites my *family*."

It took an hour to get there. Worth the bother, though. The place was enormous, all skylights and girders and glass, two levels built around an outdoor patio with fountains and tropical plants. Ted expected brisk business, judging from the size of the parking lot, big enough for Disneyland. Except in Disneyland you don't see lawyer-types climbing out of Volvos any which way you look.

"Yeah, he's invited the entire Philadelphia Bar," winked Vicky, "including those sleazy judges they indicted for bribery. But hey, the food's free. Those boys'll show."

Ted stood in the doorway greeting his guests. It was eighteen years since I'd seen him; pleased me he was showing his age, and so poorly. I'll grant, he could still dress. He wore perfect gray pinstripes, a starched linen shirt, and a fresh boutonniere. Cologne, too. Mandy was cheap in comparison. Gal's tits and guts hung out of a black bandage dress, and her breath reeked of mouthwash and gin.

"Why, Masha! What a *pleasure* to see you," Ted drawled, pressing my hands to his heart like an old friend. "And Victoria? Is that really you?" He hadn't seen Vicky in years.

"Yeah, Ted, the one and only." She rewrapped her sari as he bussed her cheek and didn't kiss him back. "And this, by the way, is Sidd. My husband."

"Well, Victoria, you always knew how to make an entrance," he chuckled, same time he shook hands with Sidd and the City Solicitor. "But quite honestly"—he lowered his voice and nodded toward the Hindus— "I wasn't expecting the United Nations. We don't serve much in the way of international foods here, except for a couple Thai dishes."

"What makes you think we're interested in your food?" she said loudly, turning heads in every direction. "We're only here to marvel at the money you've wasted."

He continued shaking hands behind and in front of her, not missing a beat. "Maybe we'll have time to chat a little later . . . catch up with each other, as they say."

"Yeah. Come look for us," she said, passing through the front door, muttering *asshole* loud enough for him to hear.

He didn't come looking, of course. Not until he needed her money.

"*Y*our turn," says Vicky, brushing crumbs off her lap. "And let's cut to the chase scene. How much money did you win?"

I sigh. "Two hundred thousand. Just about a year ago."

"That's wonderful!" She pours more tea and pops her knuckles. "Why didn't you tell me?"

"Must have slipped my mind."

She rolls her eyes. "Oh, bull, Mash! You're always keeping secrets."

"Secrets? What secrets?"

"I'm not going to respond to that," she laughs. "Did you spend it on yourself?"

"Hell, no."

"Your house?"

I cluck my tongue and deliver the lines I've prepared. "Look, it's not anyone's beeswax, really. The money's gone. Kaput. That's all you need to know."

"Stop infantilizing me, Mash! You want me to ask Mrs. Lemack?"

Her face is so pink and so restless, I pause. What the hell. She's not going to bite, and she already thinks I'm a fool. And there's no telling what blarney Mrs. Lemack might serve up.

So I grab a couple cookies and start my tale at the beginning. Eight months earlier. With Gus Franzone.

❀

*G*us never looked so good as the day they buried him. That's what everyone says at funerals, of course. And at weddings, too, only about the bride. I've inched along hundreds of receiving lines, past bridesmaids and ushers and aging parents. And when I finally face the bride, I gush all over her and tell her she's gorgeous. It doesn't matter her teeth are chipped, she needs a shave, or she peers through cat's-eye glasses. She believes she's a knockout, and so do you, until your film comes back from the drugstore. Then you scold yourself for telling such bald-faced lies.

But Gus *did* look damn good. Movie star handsome, to be exact, not a wart or mole or blackhead. His skin was powdered the shade of ripe peaches and smelled just as fragrant. They even clipped his nose hairs and scooped out the half-moons of dirt under his nails. And he lay on a pillow plump enough to hide what killed him.

How good Gus looked was only half the attraction. The other half was the funeral home. I'm accustomed to places with velvet drapes and sticky plastic sofas and temperatures set so low you lose feeling in your hands and feet, then get to wondering who's really dead, you or the customer. But this place was *cheerful*. The viewing room was all windows and skylights and snug fabric chairs with good back support. A door on the left opened to a little walled garden with white wicker furniture and a trellis of morning glories. And the funeral director was a young woman, fetching in a tailored linen suit.

I scanned the room for old coworkers. Recognized a wrinkled few. I'd retired seven years earlier and lost touch with most of the gals. Heard Gus had been replacing them with Mexican illegals, got them dirt cheap and worked them to the bone, threatening to call immigration if they missed a day's work. It burned me up at first, him looking so doggone handsome, after all the lives he'd ruined.

I wasn't huffy long. Couldn't begrudge him his glamour, given how he'd died, which made front-page news and a "Top of the Hour" item on CNN. I swear I never heard so much snickering at a funeral before. And believe me, I've been to hundreds.

🌺

*G*us had been crushed to death by a ninety-pound block of flying ice. But not just any ice. You could call me an expert on the facts.

Two Saturdays before Thanksgiving, just before midnight,

Gus stopped by a sex shop in East Pittsburgh. He bought some dirty magazines, a six-inch French tickler, and a movie, *Take Your Hand Off My Mojo*. He drove next to SevenEleven for the morning paper, Hostess Twinkies, and a two-liter jug of Coke Classic. This, according to witnesses, was his usual pattern.

Halfway home, he stopped at a red light. He never got any farther. A block of ice fell straight from the heavens, crushed the roof of his car, and splintered his skull. A man out walking his rottweiler saw it happen and called the cops, but Gus was dead by the time they arrived. It was just a matter of cutting him out of the car.

The cops recognized this as no ordinary accident, not with an oversized ice cube still perched on the roof. They took dozens of photographs before they pulled it off, wrapped it in Glad Bags, and hauled the hunk down to the police lab. A crowd gathered on the sidewalk, laying bets it was Haley's Comet, thrown off course and crashed to earth.

The rubbernecks were wrong. This boulder had nothing to do with the heavens. Techs at the lab unwrapped, weighed and measured it, then stood it on end in the sink. By morning, the building stunk worse than a kennel. Seems Haley's Comet wasn't ice after all, but a frozen hunk of human waste. Techs came up with a theory that sold copy like hotcakes. That the comet was actually the slosh inside an airline septic tank, accidentally ejected midair as the plane approached Pittsburgh. The sewage froze as it fell to the earth, into the ninety-pound boulder that crushed Gus's skull.

*A*t the mourners' meal, I recognized Mrs. Podeslenko, one of the factory gals. Shuddered to think I looked as weather-beaten. She was probably the same age as me, but walked with a three-legged cane and a mouthful of nitroglycerine tablets. The gal never gave up on the rouge, though—perfect circles— or the corkscrew curls in front of her ears.

"Masha Kuzo!" she shrieked. "I could have sworn I'd heard you died!"

"Yeah? They've been saying the same about you," I laughed, hugging her bony back. "Good God, ma'am, how long's it been?"

"Thirteen, fourteen years, maybe?" She gripped my shoulder for support. "I left the factory right around the time my colon got infected, remember?"

"Sure. They hauled you off in an ambulance. You any better?"

"Hell no!" she snorted. "Do I look it?"

"You look about the same."

"Ha! Lies like that'll cost you ten Hail Marys," she said. "But enough about me. You got any news? Your husband still alive?"

"Nope. Not for seven years. Just after I left the factory."

"Shame, isn't it?" She clucked her tongue. "I lost my Eddie, too. Last winter. Alzheimer's. How about yours?"

"Stroke."

"Well, you don't look any the worse for it." She brought her face close enough I could see her cataracts and smell her old-lady perfume. "You got a boyfriend?"

"Huh?"

"Don't play games," she leered. "I can always tell. It's all in the walk. A waddle, I call it."

"Pshaw! Why would I need a man? I've picked up enough wet towels off the bathroom floor. No thanks."

"You always lie this much?" She poked my ribs. "Well, you got yourself another ten Hail Marys, Mrs. Kuzo. Just promise me you'll tell your little boyfriend that if he's got a brother, I'm still in the phone book, you hear me?"

"Sure, sure." I was ready to say anything.

"Good. Now let's grab a table. That one, there, near the ladies' room. No sense walking any further to tinkle than we have to."

A good-looking waiter slid the chairs under our fannies and filled the water glasses. I loved the linen tablecloths and fresh flowers and porcelain place settings. Even loved the voice of Johnny Mathis crooning over the muzak. It didn't matter to me this place was popular with the Mob. I'd dine here every night if I could. I sighed as I shook out my napkin.

"Did you ever see such a spread?" Mrs. Podeslenko asked, pulling down a drink off a waiter's tray as he passed by.

"It's a beaut alright," I said, checking the silverware for water spots. None. "Not that Gus did anything to deserve it."

"He sure didn't, that slob," she scowled. "He got just what was coming to him, getting his head cracked open by flying shit . . . but come now, Mrs. Kuzo, we're not here to jessie the dead."

I nodded, tearing open a Parker House roll. Oven fresh.

"I only wish when my time comes I could put on a show like this," she said, pocketing the sugar spoon. "How much you think this all cost?"

"Haven't the foggiest. Ten thousand?"

"Go on! It cost me sixty-five hundred to bury Eddie. And that was a *pauper's* funeral—cheapest casket I could buy, no memorial service or limos or mourners' meal. But *this?* I say thirty thousand, minimum."

"Could be," I shrugged. "Guess it's only rich folks can go out in style these days."

"Well, what better way to spend their goddam money? It's the last chance they'll have to make friends out of enemies." She chugged a Manhattan and smiled, her lipstick sticking to the glass. "And come to think of it, fancy funerals *do* make you charitable. I can't say I hate Gus anymore, not after this meal. Do you?"

I started a coughing spell, couldn't answer. Not that anything I had to say interested her. She was busy making eyes at a man two tables over, a jelly-bellied catch in a plaid suit and string tie. She staggered to her feet and moved his direction, clutching a fresh drink and winking.

I didn't feel abandoned; preferred sitting alone, so I'd have all the Parker House rolls to myself. And she'd served her purpose, God bless her, given me ideas I would have paid good money for.

So I smiled. I wasn't afraid of my lottery ticket. Not now.

🌸

"*I* didn't sleep three nights after they stuck Gus in the ground," I say to my niece. "And then I finally called the Gaming Commission. Headed up there on the 8 A.M. Greyhound."

"But what you're describing happened in November," cries Vicky. "I thought you won in *July*."

"Yeah, yeah. I was just having some difficulty . . . figuring out what to do with the money, that's all."

She dunked a cookie in her tea. "That's a pretty unusual problem. You mind expanding on that a little?"

"Look," I snort. "You want to hear the rest of this story or not?"

"Alright, alright. So you took the bus to Harrisburg . . . and?"

"And I handed them the ticket. It near killed me they couldn't pay up in one lump sum. But the lady explained I could assign my winnings. That's how I was able to spend the money outright, kind of a loan arrangement. On gifts for Tom and Barb and George and Tracey."

"You spent the money . . . on them?"

"I *tried* to. Day after Thanksgiving. The last time I had them all for dinner."

🌸

*I*'d double-checked the turkey that afternoon. Groaned. The wing tips were already singed, a bad sign given the bird was only half cooked. Barb would notice for sure, and give me her caterer's number. I thought about running the bird by the homeless shelter and serving stuffed cabbage instead. But I'd promised my family a turkey. And it was the day after Thanksgiving, when we normally celebrate together.

I'd called everyone that morning to remind them. Mentioned to Barb I had special news, so please be on time. She was god-awful curious, but I wouldn't give her a clue. I hung up and lined a pie shell with apples, scrubbed the turnips, boiled the giblets, and walked over to Rudy's for pop. That's all the drink I serve when Tom and the Greek come over at the same time. The boys hate each other, and I don't need a fight.

By six o'clock I had the table set, the bird carved, the gravy bubbling on the stove. I'd told everyone five-thirty, but my kids are always late—as bad as Liz Taylor, and they've been raised better. They'll march through the door muttering excuses, an hour, two hours late, tracking in mud like puppies.

That night was no different. Tom and Tracey showed first, ten minutes till seven.

"Where've yuns been?" I asked, trying to hide my irritation.

"Go ask your goddam Braddock cops!" bellowed Tom, grabbing the ash tray. "They pulled me over on the Avenue, third time this month! Breathalyzed *both* of us!"

I kissed them anyway, not to mind, told them to make themselves comfortable while I fetched the TV trays and Planters Peanuts.

"That crazy Greek coming?" asked Tom, still irritable, turning on the news.

"I couldn't *not* invite him," I said helplessly. "Why don't you just try ignoring him?"

"Yeah," said Tracey. "Do what the woman asks. Ain't any skin off your teeth, Tom-boy."

"Just keep him out of my face, then," Tom said, glaring at me. "Hey, you got any beer?"

"Just Pepsi. Regular and Diet."

"*Jesus*, Ma." He checked his wallet for cash, headed muttering toward the door. "See you gals in a minute. I'm off to Rudy's."

Tracey pulled off her boots and curled up barefoot in front of the TV. Crossed her legs Indian style, in skin-tight Levis that must have pinched her privates awful. She got hold of my conch shell and flicked her ashes inside.

We watched the news in silence. I never could think of much to say to her, not that she's bothered. She prefers smoke to talk.

Ten long minutes into the war in Bosnia, the doorbell rang again. My daughter and her husband.

"Bad traffic," Barb murmured, handing me the bottle of Riunite only she would drink.

"Oh, cut out the lies," said George. "Tell Mama what we were *really* up to, Barb. On the floor in the sauna with your legs—"

"How about you folks make yourselves comfortable?" I said, taking their coats. "Help yourselves to some snacks?"

Barb glared at George, grabbed a handful of peanuts. She was dressed in cycling shorts and a loose T-shirt, her hair gathered in a top knot, not a flattering style when your roots need retouching. I swore she could stand a shower.

"We were working out all afternoon," she explained, tying her Reeboks. "These holidays are murder on my cholesterol count."

"I'll say," said George. "Barb's grown a pair of love handles that could use some serious pruning."

"You kids want some pop?" I asked.

"*Diet* Coke for Barb," said the Greek, then turned to Tracey with a grin. "So Trace, where's your old man? He out visiting his girlfriend tonight?"

"What the hell you talking about?" she answered, blowing smoke in his face.

"Well, you're here, Tom's not. And you know the old saying, cat's away, mice will play . . ."

"Keep talking like that," she said, cigarette in mouth, "and Tom'll lay you flat the minute he's back."

"Oh, Trace, relax. Like the man says, 'Don't worry, be happy.'"

"*George*. . ." groaned Barb.

He turned to me smirking. "Mama, you mind telling me why we got so many uptight gals here tonight?"

"You kids want to play some cards?" I asked briskly. "How about pinochle? Till Tom gets back?"

"Only if we can lay bets," said George. "Just watch me demolish all of you!"


*M*y timing could have been better, but that was the only night I had all of them under my roof. I broke the news I'd hit the jackpot just as we sat down to Dutch apple pie. I left out a few details, like the bird and Bessie and Gus, but I told them what mattered. Like how I'd cashed my ticket. And spent it on us. All you could hear was the water bubbling through the guts of Mr. Coffee.

Barb was the first to speak up. "You've had that ticket since *July*? Why on earth did you take so long to tell us?"

"Sweetie," I sighed, "it's nothing you'd ever understand."

The Greek patted her knee. "Relax, Barb, not to worry. Mama already said she's spent it on us."

Tracey lit another cigarette, turned to Tom. "You hear what the lady just told us, Tom? Two hundred thou, hers for nothing. Holy shit!"

"So, Mama, don't keep us waiting," said George, poking my stomach. "What've you done with your booty, huh?"

I took my time cutting another wedge of pie. Then counted

to ten and drew a deep breath, all jitters. "I've spent the money on something . . . that most people don't bother thinking about. You kids ever heard of . . . pre-need funeral plans?"

Dead silence. I started to sweat.

"You're getting the best there is, that I can promise." I was up on my feet by then, rummaging through my china closet until I found the contracts. "For example"—my hands shook as I unfolded them—"you'll each get a fiberglass casket, a ten-by-six-foot funeral plot, a waterproof grave liner, dry-cleaned burial clothes, an Italian marble headstone, perpetual grave site care, limousines"—I swear I was hyperventilating—"funeral home fees, the placing of obituaries in the newspapers, flowers in case no one else sends any, and a mourners' meal in a Pittsburgh area restaurant to accommodate three hundred mourners."

"What the . . . hell?" George said, picking up a contract. "You really spent your money . . . on *this?*"

"I don't believe you!" cried Barb, slapping one hand to her forehead. "For God's sake, Mom, didn't anyone tell you these funeral plans are nothing but rip-offs? I thought you watched 'Sixty Minutes!'"

"Your crazy friend put you on to this?" asked Tom.

"This takes the cake, Lady," said Tracey. "That's the best you can do for your son? Spend your money *burying* him?"

George jumped to his feet and took me by the shoulders. "What in the hell's the matter with you, huh? Nuts? Just like your sister?"

"George . . ." said Barb, her hand on his arm.

"I'll tell you what I'm going to do," he shouted, spraying spit across the table. "I'm getting us a smart lawyer and getting you committed! Jesus H. Christ!"

I was weeping awful and wiping my eyes on the edge of the tablecloth. My beautiful plan—that seemed *so* perfect—hadn't worked at all. They didn't want any of it. Or me.

"I should have known you couldn't be trusted with money," George was saying. "Like mother, like daughter!"

"Shut up," growled Tom, fist in George's face. "Nobody talks like that to *my* Ma." Then he turned to me, scowling. Crumpled his napkin and finished his beer, one hard swallow. "Thanks for the dinner, Ma. You haven't forgotten how to feed a man. But do me a favor, will you? *Keep* your goddam funeral."

"And the same," cried Barb, "goes for *me!*"

❀

"*W*hy, Masha, why?" asks Vicky. "I just don't get it! I mean, why didn't you just give them the money outright? Or stick it in a trust?"

I can see I have a lot more explaining to do, and this is the hardest part. She needs to hear the truth—the whole truth—for Annie's sake. So I suck in my breath. "Your mother ever tell you . . . about Lily?"

"Lily?" she stiffens. "Yeah. Plenty."

"Then maybe you know the story about the day she died. When the bird flew in the room?"

"What bird?"

So I tell her—in tears—about that terrible morning. And the morning, just last year, when I flattened the same bird on the turnpike.

"That's why that money scared the bejesus out of me, don't you see? It was evil! So I had to use it in a way that wouldn't harm a hair on anyone's head—which meant we all had to be dead *first*."

"Oh, Masha, it was only money! How could you be that superstitious?"

"Because . . . I've already got enough on my conscience." Girl's not cutting me an inch of slack, but I've got to spill it all. "Didn't you know I was supposed to be minding your mother and Lily that morning? And I went inside the house instead?"

"That's what Annie always told me," whispers Vicky, forehead in knots. "That it was *you*—and not *her*—who took the heat."

I nod, face in my hands.

"Oh Jesus," she says, her hands clutching my shoulders. "Why didn't Annie ever tell you the truth?"

I turn to her, choking. "What the . . . hell are you talking about?"

"That it wasn't *you* who killed Lily." Her voice is a whisper. "It was *her*."

I'm speechless, then angry. "Stop it! You're lying!"

"I'm not," she says, pulling away and groping for Kleenex. "When you went inside the house that day, Annie and Lily started fighting—over a ball they were playing with. You remember it?"

Of course I did. India rubber that left a queer smell on your hands.

"It was really Annie's ball," says Vicky, her voice sounding like it's bubbling up from underwater. "She'd got it from Mr. Kurtyak, her godfather. And she was pretty possessive about it. So when Lily took off with it across the yard, Annie chased her down. And ended up pushing her off the wall. No homicidal intent, of course."

I can hardly breathe. "No. That *isn't* how it happened."

"Yes it is." She lays her hand on my cheek. "I got it straight from Annie's mouth, just another one of her bedtime stories. I wish to God she'd told you!"

🐚

*I* don't have time to catch my breath. Mrs. Lemack's banging on the door hollering nonsense, something about laying a bet. Vicky puts down her teacup, smiles at me as if we never had this discussion, and opens the door. My friend tumbles in with Dira on her heels.

"I don't believe it," Mrs. Lemack wheezes, from climbing

four flights of steps. "She says"—pointing at Dira—"that you wear a sari without hooks or buttons or safety pins. And I say bull. Who's right?"

"Go ahead, Dira, we're all girls," says Vicky, fully recovered. "Show her."

Dira smiles and unravels her garment. She's not embarrassed standing in her petticoat. Mrs. Lemack lifts the sari off the floor and runs her finger along the edges, searching for hooks, snaps, buttons, or tape.

"Well I'll be danged. This has got to be magic. You mind putting it back on for me, Hon?"

Dira smiles again, wraps the silk around herself once, then pleats another three feet of it between two fingers and stuffs it all inside her slip. She throws the last yard over her shoulder and stands tall.

"What do you think, Mrs. Lemack?" asks Vicky. "That something you might want to wear to the bowling alley? I've got a couple extra in my drawers downstairs if you're interested."

My friend rolls her eyes. "Missy, you got any idea how much I weigh?"

"No—and don't tell. It doesn't matter. Saris are the one garment where it's absolutely true: one size fits all. Just keep your panties on."

"Well, hot diggidy-dog! You want to join us, Mrs. Kuzo? A little game of dress-up?"

"No," I whisper, heading out the door, my heart in tatters.

"You been crying?" my friend calls after me. "Hey, Girl! Chin up!"

# Cathedral of the Archangel Michael Philadelphia

*I* come to this church every time I'm in Philly. It's not that I won't miss Sunday Mass, gave up that habit a long time ago. It's privacy, actually, I'm looking for—and church is the only place Vicky and Mrs. Lemack won't tag along. They'll have me by the collar after lunch, count on it, when we head back to Bessie's grave. But this hour's mine.

It took me two trolleys and a brisk walk to get here. Northern Liberties, they call this part of town. It's as seedy as the neighborhood around St. Stepan's—busted sidewalks, hell-hole bars, more potholes than pavement. I walk with my eyes on the ground, hop-scotching over broken glass.

The church, at least, makes it worth the trip. It sits on a whole block, slathered top to bottom in blue paint and gold leaf, a Slavic Taj Mahal. There's icons by the hundreds and polished marble floors inside. Can't figure where the money comes from. I've never seen more than a few dozen folks here at Mass, most of them toothless and lame.

The best part's the choir. Two dozen crystal-clear voices, both sexes, and no roller-rink organ drowning them out. I need this kind of music today. Spent the night standing in line for the toilet, chatting fakey with Hindus, cussing out the side of my mouth. Not so Mrs. Lemack. She slept the night through, arms extended, smack in the middle of our bed. But she hadn't heard Vicky's bombshell, either. That would have kept her hair curled.

The Mass here is old-world style, sung in our language, which raises my spirits. But not enough to take communion; my throat's too scratchy, and I don't like plum wine. Still, I owe this place something. I leave all my coins in the collection basket, three jingling dollars' worth, plus the Canadian change Mrs. Lemack got back at HoJo's.


Once Mass is over and the choir's gone, I tend to my usual business. Hobble to the altar rail and kneel, knees cracking, in front of the candle rack. I light four votives—old habit—for Annie and Lily and Mum and Al. Shake out the match and reach for Mum's rosary.

I start praying in whispers, asking God's help, not that He's been too attentive. The Man's busy, I suppose—never had time to answer my prayers about money and health and good looks. But He's cold-shouldered requests that weren't half so silly, like helping Tammy walk again, or saving Barb from bankruptcy, or healing Tom's broken skull. And every single prayer about Annie.

So he owes me. *Quid pro quo*, as Vicky would say. Only this time I'm not asking for favors. Just answers.

So Annie's to blame, if I can believe her daughter. It wasn't an accident at all. Lily ended up just where Annie wanted her, facedown on the sidewalk. Not my fault.

She took her punishment. Must have. And alone. Not a day passed Mum didn't keen over Lily or order us to pray for her soul. Got so we cringed at the sound of that poor baby's name. Just wanted to forget her.

That wasn't Mum's inclination, especially on Annie's birthday. *Lily's* birthday, she'd always correct me, scowling. Poor Annie never had candles or cake or presents. Mum wouldn't allow it. She had her own grim ritual she enforced till the girl left home. And it was always the same. Mum woke us at dawn, the only day of the year she didn't sleep late. Once we were dressed, she fixed dry toast and coffee—our only meal for the day—and ordered us out to the porch while she clipped some white roses, one for each year of Lily's life. We'd hike to the bottom of the block, wait for the number 10 trolley, and shiver at the sound of its bell.

The last stop was the cemetery.

"You sure you want to get out here?" the driver always asked. "It's a little early for visiting hours. Spooky, if you ask me."

Mum would ignore him, push us out the door and straight uphill to Lily's grave, me leading the way, all of us choking on the sulfurous air from the mill. I could never find the exact spot. Except in my dreams.

"There it is," Mum would say, first words all morning, her hand heavy on my shoulder. "Go on, now. Both of you."

We took off our shoes and knelt on the mound face to face. Stayed there all morning, praying and weeping and aching all over, Mum moaning that Lily might still be with us. If only.

*I*'ll admit that I'm pissed—could have done without

Vicky's news flash, at my age especially. Sleeping dogs should lie. But the worst of it's that Annie did me wrong. She kept a secret that could have changed my life.

And why? I loved her. She was always my child, even after she'd grown up, grinding out one cigarette as she lit another. I'd carry her ashtray to the trash, holding my nose, then dream a thousand dreams of her as a little girl, learning to tie her shoes, to play jacks, to chop onions so she wouldn't cry. She laughed a lot when Lily was still alive.

It always worked. Those were the dreams that got me through the hospital visits and the meetings with her doctors and her own strange behavior that I never understood. And now I feel I never knew her at all.

Mrs. Lemack, of course, wouldn't cotton to that.

"Stop crying in your beer!" she'd say, all pesky. "That was oodles of years ago. And six to one, you'd have taken the blame even if you'd seen her push Lily. Look, you *had* to protect Annie—no telling how your mum would've punished that kid. So what the hell difference does it make?"

Gets me crying, the truth of it. But funny thing, for once the tears don't hurt.


*T*hey're closing up the church. The janitor's been by twice, pushing a mop and pointing at his watch. Just as well. I promised Vicky I'd be back by noon to help her pack the picnic basket, even offered to fry chicken legs, just the way she likes them. So I need to dry my tears and finish up.

I do what seems right. I cross myself with Mum's rosary beads and thank God for touching my life. Vicky's news hurt, alright, but it let air get at old wounds.

I never knew till last night what turned my sister on herself. Girl had everything God forgot to give me, so it never added up. I knew about Nicky and Vlado and Ted, but men alone can't ruin women's lives. Always knew there was something else. Always.

So I pray for her soul. As long as it takes for her votive to burn itself down.


$\mathcal{V}$icky's sitting at the bottom of the cathedral steps, fanning her face with a newspaper. She grins and cups her hands around her mouth.

"Yo! Mrs. Kuzo!" She's as loud as a foghorn. "Want a ride?"

I wasn't expecting her. And certainly not looking so cute. She's dressed in a loose cotton sundress and sandals, and brushed her blond hair down her back. Girl's beautiful, just like her mother, even if she doesn't tweeze or shave.

I take my time going down the steps, one hand holding my sore hip. It's hot out here, high nineties, and the Jaguar doesn't throw down any shade. No wonder Vicky's face looks so red.

"What're you doing here, Sweetie?" I ask. "You didn't need to come, you know."

"What? In this heat? And leave you to melt in the trolley?" She's almost indignant. "Believe it or not, Mash, I'd *like* to keep you alive."

"Where's Mrs. Lemack?" I ask, peering in the back of the car. As if she's the type to sit quietly knitting.

"I left her at home frying chicken."

"Her? She'll *ruin* it!"

"I don't think so. Sidd's sisters are helping out. They're fixing us a picnic. Your choice of location."

I think of mangoes and curries and queer sour pickles. "What do those gals know about breading?"

She smiles. "You think you can give up control for a change?"

Smart aleck. I fetch a hanky from my purse and swab off the sweat. "When did I ever control *you?*"

She sticks both hands on my shoulders—big hands, like Mum's—and peers straight into my face. "Look, Mash, I'm doing this for *you*. I figured I owed you as much after last night."

I try to twist out of her grasp. "What're you talking about?"

"For God's sake, level with me, just this once! You haven't forgotten about the skunk I threw in your lap."

Fair's fair. "No," I whisper. "I haven't."

She releases me, sits down on the steps, picks up the paper, and fans herself. "I'd like to apologize for acting like a jerk. Pick me apart, will you?"

I sigh and sit down next to her. The air from her paper feels good on my face. "Naw. It had to come out. I just wish I'd known about it earlier."

"I thought about telling you lots of times." She reaches for my knee. "I mean, you had a *right* to know—it's your history, isn't it?"

"Then"—devil's advocate—"why didn't you?"

"Because I knew how you felt about my mother," she says, her lower lip trembling. "I guess in some half-assed way I wanted to *protect* you." She throws her face down on my knees, clutches my pant leg, and lets out a sob. "God, I blew it."

"No, you didn't." I can't stop myself stroking her hair, the same feel and texture of Annie's. She'd wanted to protect me. To protect *me*.

"I know you won't believe it," she whispers, her lips moving against my knee. "But I really *did* love her."

"I know you did, Sweetie." I can't stop my tears. "I did, too. And what you told me really doesn't matter."

"How can you say that?" she wails. "I betrayed both of you!"

"Huh-uh." I'm rubbing her shoulders. "It's okay, Sweetie. Really."

And I mean it.

She wants to be my friend. Says she's always wanted to be my friend. I guess I believe her. Who else but Vicky calls on my birthday or sends little notes or asks about my gallbladder? I get a box from her twelve times a year, Fruit-of-the-Month Club, apples and oranges and perfect black grapes, half of which I share with Mrs. Lemack.

"She's a treasure," the woman tells me, picking seeds from between her front teeth. "You lucked out, Girl, you know that?"

I didn't, back then. And I'm not even sure now. The girl's still a mystery with her odd taste in men, her cob-webby house, those funny words she's learned in grad school, more letters than anything I've seen in a crossword puzzle. But she says she loved her mother.

She's next to me, gabbing about the picnic. How Sidd's sisters are packing macaroni salad, homemade biscuits, cold watermelon, and a jug of sweet ice tea. Only thing Mrs. Lemack fetched from the store was a Pepperidge Farm chocolate cake, which she didn't have time to make from scratch. I'll admit, I'm glad they've done the work. I never liked cooking in other ladies' kitchens.

She's asking me where I want to go for the picnic. That we don't need to head to the cemetery; we could drive out to Valley Forge or Fairmount Park or anywhere along the Jersey shore. We could even sit out back of her house—if it suited me—where she's got a little bricked-in yard with a picnic table and potted plants.

I'll have to think about it. It's nice. And we'll get to the grave, I can promise her that.

# More Novels Available From Spinsters Ink

Spinsters Ink was founded in 1978 to produce vital books for diverse women's communities. In 1986 we merged with Aunt Lute Books to become Spinsters/Aunt Lute. In 1990, the Aunt Lute Foundation became an independent nonprofit publishing program. In 1992, Spinsters moved to Minnesota.

Spinsters Ink publishes novels and nonfiction works that deal with significant issues in women's lives from a feminist perspective: books that not only name these crucial issues, but—more importantly—encourage change and growth. We are committed to publishing works by women writing from the periphery: fat women, Jewish women, lesbians, old women, poor women, rural women, women examining classism, women of color, women with disabilities, women who are writing books that help make the best in our lives more possible.

Spinsters titles are available at your local booksellers or by mail order through Spinsters Ink. A free catalog is available upon request. Please include $2.00 for the first title ordered and 50¢ for every title thereafter. Visa and Mastercard accepted.

Spinsters Ink
32 E. First St., #330
Duluth, MN 55802-2002
USA
218-727-3222 (phone)                    (fax) 218-727-3119
(e-mail) spinster@spinsters-ink.com
(website) http://www.spinsters-ink.com

Helen Campbell lives in Germany with her husband and two children and lectures for the University of Maryland European Division. She was awarded a Fiction Fellowhip from the Pennsylvania Council on the Arts in 1997. *Turnip Blues* is her first novel.